ONLY ONE BED

Volume 1

LUCY EDEN   REBEL CARTER   RENEE DAHLIA

LAUREN CONNOLLY   SARAH E. LILY

A.Z. LOUISE   TORRANCE SENÉ   ALI WILLIAMS

Violet Gaze Press

Editor: Ali Williams

Book Cover Design: Under Cover Designs

Proofreading: Jack Holloway

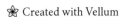 Created with Vellum

CONTENTS

About One Bed of a Pick Up Truck   1

ONE BED OF A PICK UP TRUCK   2
Lucy Eden

About The Author   33
Lucy Eden

About Only One Flower Bed   34

ONLY ONE FLOWER BED   35
Rebel Carter

About The Author   65
Rebel Carter

About The Bed Hierarchy   66

THE BED HIERARCHY   67
Lauren Connolly

About Lauren Connolly   109
About Lauren Connolly

About Uplift   110

UPLIFT   112
Renee Dahlia

About The Author   151
Renée Dahlia

About In The Cards   152

IN THE CARDS   153
Sarah E. Lily

About The Author   183
Sarah E. Lily

About Romantic Intent   184

ROMANTIC INTENT   185
A.Z. Louise

About The Author   213
A.Z. Louise

About What You Need   214

WHAT YOU NEED   215
Torrance Sené

About The Author   245
Torrance Sené

About Holding On   246

HOLDING ON   247
Ali Williams

About The Author   277
Ali Williams

About Violet Gaze Press   279

ABOUT ONE BED OF A PICK UP TRUCK

Julian Harris-- yes, that Julian Harris-- is a world-famous photographer who wins awards and travels the globe photographing celebrities, history-making events and, things I could only dream about. He's also my older brother's best friend and the boy, excuse me, man I've had a crush on my entire life.

A series of unfortunate events leave us stranded on the side of a mountain road in Upstate New York and something about the way he looks at me makes me wonder if Jules see me as something more than the awkward teenage girl he used to call Dee Dee.

One Bed of a Pick-Up Truck is a funny, dramatic & steamy short story filled with an older brother's best friend, friends to lovers goodness and is safe with no cheating.

ONE BED OF A PICK UP TRUCK

LUCY EDEN

One

"Hey big head, pass me my phone." Julian slid his hand across the console, his large palm was outstretched, the backs of his fingertips grazing my thigh, making my breath catch in my throat.

I held the phone out of his reach. "No. You shouldn't be using your phone while you're driving and don't call me 'big head.'" He didn't grab for it, but his hand lingered on my thigh for a second before pulling away. I was glad I was wearing shorts and very glad that I shaved above the knee for a change.

"My deepest apologies, Dee Dee," he said, not sounding very sorry at all.

I rolled my eyes and pursed my lips. No one called me Dee Dee anymore except family. Julian was my brother's oldest friend and we all grew up together, sort of. They were three years older than me, but it might as well have been a decade separating us. We'd only been in high school for one year together. I'd been a freshman while they were seniors. Julian and Marcus were popular athletes and I was the nerdy little sister.

I don't mean to make it sound rude. Marcus is a great big brother and Julian was always nice to me, but we always had different interests.

We grew up in the same small town in the mountains of upstate New York. By some chance we both ended up based in New York City. He was a "kind of a big deal" photographer and I was a grad student at NYU. My brother suggested we ride together to his wedding this weekend. I was planning to take the bus so this was a much better plan.

"Hey, what are you over there daydreaming about?" Julian's voice pulled me out of my thoughts. "If you're not going to let me use my phone, you at least have to talk to me."

I looked over to see him grinning at me with two rows of perfect teeth, glittering brown eyes and dimples carved into his perfect deep brown complexion.

I cleared my throat when I'd just realized I was staring at him and dragged my eyes away from him to stare at his phone in my lap.

"Were you really gonna scroll through Twitter while we're on the highway?"

"No, I was going to change the music, Dee Dee. Do

you think I would endanger my life like that?" He shot me a sarcastic grin.

"Nice, Jules." I shook my head at him. "And would it kill you to call me Nadirah."

"No, it wouldn't kill me, but it would be weird as hell." He glanced at me again and huffed out a chuckle. "Is that what your friends call you in graduate school?" He put a weird emphasis on the word "graduate" pronouncing every syllable.

"Well, it is my name." I shrugged and narrowed my eyes at him playfully. Honestly, I didn't mind him calling me by my childhood nickname but I also liked teasing him.

"So, you ready for this wedding?" he asked. My brother was marrying his college sweetheart, Wendy. She was a Spelman grad and they waited for her to finish law school to set a date. Between Wendy, her mother and my mother, this was shaping up to be the wedding from hell and it wasn't even mine.

"I've been ready for this wedding for months." I shook my head and chuckled. My soon to be sister in law was beautiful, funny, intelligent and usually one of my favorite people in the world. However, studying for the NYS bar exam while trying to plan a wedding might have pushed her over the edge.

"Wendy's been driving you up the wall too?" He chuckled.

I snapped my head to look at him.

"Yes! Has she been torturing the groomsmen too?"

"Oh yes. You can't tell anybody this, but your brother

and Wendy have been fighting about Rob's dreads." Rob was one of Marcus' fraternity brothers from Morehouse.

"Rob's dreads? Why?" I furrowed my brow.

"She wants him to cut them for the ceremony. She wants everyone to look the same in the pictures." He shrugged and shook his head.

Wendy has been a bit of a bridezilla but I didn't know it was that bad. Although, she did make one of her cousins cry at our last dress fitting.

"So what did Rob say?"

"Rob didn't say nothing. He doesn't know. You know Marc is not going ask one of his brothers to cut his locs. He's been growing them for five years."

"Wow, that is a lot. All we have to worry about is Wendy's diet."

"Diet?"

"Yes, she expects everyone to do this new keto style diet before the wedding. She signed us all up for an app where we have to log all of our meals and workouts and she checks it daily."

"So, those Krispy Kreme donuts you had at the last rest stop...Did you log those?" Julian turned to me with a smirk.

I pursed my lips and cut my eyes at him.

"Wendy is out of her damn mind. She'll be fine when the wedding is over, I hope. But I'm too busy with school to pay her and her drama-filled wedding planning any mind."

"So how is school going?"

"It's good. I'm really lucky to have gotten accepted into

the program but it's so much work. How did you get through grad school." I didn't know much about Julian's grad school experience, except for the tidbits I could get from my brother without drawing suspicion. But I knew it involved a lot studying abroad and photographing things I would probably only read about. I, on the other hand, lived in the research library, not remotely interesting.

"Well, I think my grad school experience was a little different than yours."

"Yeah, I guess studying photography is a lot more glamorous than getting an MBA."

"It's not always glamorous."

"But it must be so cool, traveling the world and photographing amazing locations."

"Yeah." He nodded then he glanced at me. "You been checking up on me?" He hit me with a sly smile that made my cheeks heat.

"No," I stammered. "Well, yeah, a little." More heat flooded my neck and cheeks. "Marcus talks about you all the time and I might have Googled you once or twice."

"Wow." He grinned and nodded. "My very own stalker."

"I wasn't stalking you." I whispered and looked out of the window. I wasn't sure why I was suddenly so embarrassed. It could have been because I was stalking Julian. For as long as I could remember I'd had a crush on him. I didn't see him often—he and my brother didn't hang out in the same circles as I did. Then he moved to Brooklyn right after graduation, but, when we were younger, I grabbed any excuse to see him and get close enough to smell the axe body spray he used to douse himself in. He was always really kind to me and asked me about school and things I was interested in, like he actually cared. I'd spent years convincing myself that he was just being nice to his friend's little sister… until the night of my senior prom.

"Hey, Dee D— Nadirah," Julian covered the space just above my knee with the large warm hand that wasn't holding the steering wheel. "I was just kidding."

I took a deep breath and forced myself to look at him.

"If we're being honest, I've done my share of digital sleuthing, checking up on you from time to time," he said with a little smile. It's possible that I imagined it but I could've sworn I'd seen Julian wearing his own look of embarrassment, but it was fleeting. He pulled his hand off my thigh and said, "But, hey, doesn't everyone do that?"

"Yeah, I guess." I forced a smile. "So, tell me about the unglamorous world of photojournalism."

"There's not much to tell. I have an agency that tells me where to go and point the camera. I have a few clients I do side gigs for." He shrugged. He was being modest, but his glittering eyes and smirk gave him away. Julian was an amazing photographer. He had a camera with him almost every time I saw him growing up. No one was surprised when he got accepted to The Pratt Institute to study photography. My mom, who was friends with his mom, and Marcus never neglected to mention Julian's many awards and achievements. It was always "Did you know Julian flew to Camp David to photograph Barack and Michelle?" or "Julian won a Lucie award this year." I Googled Lucie awards to discover they were a *big deal* in the photography world.

He didn't seem to be affected by his fame. Though I hadn't seen him in almost two years, he still seemed like the same Julian I knew.

"I think you're leaving a lot out but I'm not gonna press you. I know you're busy jet setting all around the world photographing snow leopards and taking selfies with the Dalai Lama." I smiled at him and he snorted a laugh.

"Not as busy as you, college girl." His voice got a little lower and he looked away with a small smile that didn't reach his eyes.

"What's that supposed to mean?" I turned to look at him. He fixed his eyes on the road refusing to meet my gaze and it made me a little nervous.

Was I missing something?

He paused for a moment before he said, "You never called me." He took his eyes off the road for a second to glance at me and my face must have reflected the confusion I was feeling because he continued, "When we ran into each other at MoMA? We exchanged numbers and said we'd meet for lunch. I knew how nerve-wracking grad school is, so I asked to you call me…" He trailed off.

I remembered that day like it was yesterday. It was an exhibit for a photographer I heard Julian talk about. I couldn't get any of my friends to go with me, so I went by myself. I wasn't expecting to see him there— okay, maybe I was hoping… a little. The main reason I went was because a small part of me wanted to go, to feel close to him: to see what he saw in this artist and feel what he felt when he looked at an amazing photo. I stood in a gallery on the second floor examining a black and white photo of a child holding an orange when I felt eyes on me, smelled the intoxicating scent of a man's cologne mixed with soap and heard a familiar deep voice.

"This is one of my favorites," he whispered in my ear causing a wave of full body shivers that settled between my thighs. I inhaled another breath full of his delicious scent and exhaled slowly. "Benito spent the whole day shooting in this small South American village. Just before he was about to leave, this little girl comes up to him with a thank you gift."

"The orange," I whispered back.

"Mmhmm. It was one of her few possessions and she wanted to share it." He nodded and rested his chin on my shoulder. He'd never done it before. It was such a welcome and intimate gesture. It flooded my body with warmth and feelings that I thought were long buried, but they were back and all grown up.

"She was only four or five and already full of such kindness and generosity. People like that are rare. You can go your whole life without meeting someone like that. So, when one comes along you have to do whatever you can to hold on to them." He paused for a moment, causing an unexplained belly flutter, before continuing.

"Benito only had his camera. He snapped one quick photo of her, packed up and left. A year later, he won a Pulitzer...for this photo." He straightened, ushering a cool breeze on my shoulder and I'd turned to face him.

He was still handsome with an athletic build, an easy laugh and deep brown eyes with long lashes that should be illegal. We spent the next two hours wandering around the museum catching up on old times. I talked about papers I was working on and internships I was hoping to land. He talked about some of his cooler assignments and living in Brooklyn. We definitely exchanged numbers but I wasn't sure if Julian really wanted to hang out again or if he was doing that thing that people do when they haven't seen each other in a while: vague invitations with no real plans to meet. When weeks went by without him calling me, I thought I had my answer. But apparently, he'd been waiting for me to call and almost two years went by.

"Hey," he called to me with a laugh. "It's not a big thing. Shit happens. People get busy."

I felt my face heat again and my heart was pounding. I was replaying every moment of the day in the museum.

How many times had I caught Julian looking at me? How many times had he casually brushed my arm or went out of his way to touch me? Was he flirting with me and I was too oblivious to see it?

"Hey, Dee Dee. You okay?" Julian was looking at me with a concerned expression. I was still trying to make sense of this new information. My eyes drifted up towards the windshield. I saw a baby deer standing in the middle of the small mountain road we'd turned onto after we'd left the highway.

I screamed Julian's name. He looked up just in time to avoid the fawn but too late to avoid running off the road and down a small embankment.

Two

. . .

"Fuck. Fuck." Julian smashed the steering wheel with his fist. "Dee Dee, are you okay?"

"Yeah," I panted. I was a little shocked from the accident but otherwise I was fine. "I'm okay. Are you okay?"

"Yeah. I'm good. You sure you're okay?" he asked again and I nodded.

"Did we hit the deer?" I bit my bottom lip and raised my eyebrows. Julian hit me with a quizzical expression before he burst out laughing.

"Are you for real?" he asked between chuckles. I narrowed my eyes, pursed my lips and nodded. We ran off the road and practically into a ditch; it would be nice to know we didn't do it for nothing. Plus, I didn't want a Bambi body count on my hands. "Nah, we didn't hit the deer."

"Can you drive out of here?"

"Let's see." Julian shifted into drive and hit the gas. The truck lurched but it didn't move and we could hear the wheels spinning. He tried the same thing in reverse. No luck.

"I'm gonna go check it out." He unbuckled his seatbelt and opened his door before turning around to look at me again. "You good, Dee?"

I nodded and gave him a little smile. He returned my smile with a wink and closed the door.

I started drawing in deep calming breaths. My hands were shaking in my lap and my heart was pounding. I wasn't sure if I was reacting to the accident or to our conversation about our day at the museum. In the following weeks I'd thought about him non-stop. I reflexively kept one hand on my phone at all times hoping to feel it buzz with a call or a text from Julian. But as the weeks and months passed, the butterflies died one by one and the excitement I'd felt was replaced by the same foolish feeling I felt as a teenager, pining for a cute older boy who was just being nice to his friend's kid sister.

Is it possible that I misread his signals back then? If I did, what am I supposed to do with that information? What if I bring it up and I'm wrong? I'd be stuck in this truck until we get to the wedding and then stuck at a mountain resort with our families for the entire weekend. My brain was still whirring when Julian tapped on my window.

"Jesus Christ!" I jumped in my seat and clutched my heart. After rolling down the window, I screamed, "You scared the shit out of me."

"Sorry." He rested his elbows on the open window and leaned in, grazing my upper arm with his fingertips. "I didn't mean to scare you."

"I'm fine." I wasn't, but it had nothing to do with the accident. "What's going on back there?"

"Well, the ground is really soft and we have two flat tires. I'm gonna call triple A and see how soon they can get us out, but I have to walk around because the reception is spotty around here. So sit tight and I'll be right back." He tapped the door of the car and started backing away.

"Wait. You're leaving me here alone?"

"I won't go far. Just enough to get a signal."

"No. We're in the mountains of Upstate New York. I'm not comfortable with you wandering around these woods by yourself. I'm coming with you." Our town was small and diverse, but not without issues. There were an unspoken set of rules my parents expected Marcus and me to follow, and I know Julian's family was the same way. One very important rule was strength in numbers. I unbuckled my seatbelt and reached for the door handle. The door was open an inch when Julian pushed it closed and leaned in the window.

"I love that you're so worried about me," he began, and my heart thudded at the word love, "but my number one priority is keeping you safe. Number two is getting us to that wedding. If I fail at either one of those things there won't be anything left for Wendy to strangle after our mothers are done." He grinned at me. I rolled my eyes, let out a chuckle and nodded. "Sit tight...Nadirah." He gave me a lingering look that melted me before he turned and walked in the direction of the road.

Apparently, I'd been holding my breath because as soon as I lost sight of Julian I let out a huge sigh. I thought about turning on the car to play some music, but I didn't want to risk draining the battery. I scrolled through my phone for a few minutes, but I couldn't do much without a signal and I didn't want my phone to die in case we were stuck out here for longer than we expected. Staring into the woods where Julian disappeared was too stressful, so I started looking around the truck for something to read. I knew that Julian loved books and I was surprised that I couldn't find one.

The glove compartment opened with a pop because I'd officially reached owner's manual levels of desperation. After one final glance into the woods with no sign of Jules, I dug through the glove compartment. I pulled out a stack of papers and I was careful not to read any of them when a photograph slipped from them. My breath caught in my throat when I saw the image. It was Julian and me on the night of my senior prom.

That morning, the boy who'd asked me to be his date decided that he wanted to go with someone else. I was devastated, embarrassed and planned to spend the night in my room crying when Julian showed up.

Apparently, my mom called my brother in Atlanta, who called his best friend in New York. Julian found a suit and drove all the way from Brooklyn to be my date. He set up his camera on a tripod in our living room and he took about a million pictures of us using a tiny remote control.

My parents have a framed photo of us posing side by side and staring at the camera with big smiles, but I'd never seen this shot before. In the photo I was holding in my lap, Julian and I were facing each other. He must have said something funny because we were laughing as I adjusted his tie. In the split second that photo taken, our eyes locked. It was a completely unplanned candid moment and it was the most beautiful picture I'd ever seen. It reminded me of Benito's little girl with the orange. It was a perfect moment full of power and emotion captured in a split second.

The driver's side door clicked and creaked as Julian pulled it open.

"Okay. I managed to get a signal." He climbed into the driver's seat. "Triple A says it's gonna take at least three hours to get someone up here, so that means at least—hey what's up?"

I wasn't aware until Julian said something but I'd been staring at the photo in my lap with tears in my eyes.

"Why do you have this?" I whispered as I handed him the picture. He took it from my hands, gently brushing my fingertips in the process.

With the photo in his lap, he exhaled a deep breath and whispered. "It's my favorite photo in the world. The best one I'd ever taken."

"Julian…" my voice trailed off because I wasn't sure what to say or how I wanted to process this new information.

"When Marc called me and told me what Tyler did, I was pissed. I was relieved when he asked me to take you as a favor, because I was gonna do it anyway—"

"Why?" I asked.

"Because." He exhaled. "I've known you almost our whole lives. I cared about you. And if we're keeping it a hundred, I wanted to whoop Tyler's ass for canceling on you, the day of prom. Who does that shit? Especially to someone like you."

"Someone like me?" My ability to form sentences and use words escaped me as I listened to Jules speak.

"C'mon, Dee Dee. You're smart, funny, kind and I didn't realize it until you came down those stairs but you're the most beautiful woman I'd ever seen."

"Wow. I never knew you felt that way."

"I didn't either until I got home and saw the pictures. Do you remember that night?"

I'd never forget that night. My mom came into my room and sat on my bed. She rubbed my back and told me that my prom date was here and it wasn't Tyler. She helped me get dressed and put my make up on.

I was almost a hundred percent sure I was going to walk down that stairs to find my dad or, by some miracle of airline miles, Marcus in a suit.

But it was Julian.

He was grinning at me, holding a corsage to match my dress. We posed for pictures. My mom cried and my dad joked about using his shotgun if Julian kept me out late. We went to prom and stayed long enough to make Tyler jealous. We were crowned prom king and queen, but I'm sure it had more to do with Julian's lingering popularity at our high school and everyone knowing what Tyler did to me. He took me out for pizza and we sat in the parking lot and talked until it was time to take me home.

"Yes," I whispered. "Of course I remember. That was one of the best nights of my life."

"Me too. I started thinking about you in a way I never had before." He sighed. "And I haven't stopped."

"Why didn't you tell me that night?"

"I wanted to but…" he trailed off.

"But what?"

"You were seventeen."

"So, you were twenty."

"And…you were seventeen." He looked at me and raised an eyebrow.

"Well, I wasn't seventeen at MoMA."

"No, you definitely weren't." He bit his bottom lip with a wistful expression. "When I saw the subject of my favorite photo in the world standing in front of my second favorite photo in the world, it just…it felt like fate." He turned his body to face me. "You were even more beautiful than I remembered. And different somehow. I can't explain it but walking around that museum, talking to you and learning about all the amazing things you were doing and seeing. I felt like I wanted to do and see those things with you. I wanted to experience the world through your eyes. I wanted to share my world with you. When you had to go to class, it felt like someone was squeezing my chest. For weeks I was afraid to travel anywhere without cell reception, because I was afraid of missing your call, but you never called."

He was searching my face for something.

I was searching for something to say.

Everything Jules was saying was everything I wanted to hear but I wasn't sure how I should respond. This intense and heavy moment felt like I was being offered a delicate priceless treasure, but terrified to accept it for fear of breaking it.

"I was...waiting for you to call." I'm not sure why those are the words I chose, but that's what I said.

"Shit," he whispered. "No cap?"

I shook my head.

"Damn." He reached up and scratched his head. "What would you have said if I did call?"

"Hi." I tucked my lips between my teeth to stifle a laugh. Julian laughed in response and the tension in the truck shattered like a pane of glass. "I guess we would've gone to lunch and taken it from there..." I shrugged.

"Wow." Julian reached up and scratched his head again. "I need a minute." He opened his door.

"Wait. Where are you going?"

"Look, I know where my head's at. It's been there for years and I'm a little tight that it's took me this long to tell you, but things will be complicated with us from jump. Your brother is my best friend. Our families are close." He reached for my hand and squeezed it. "Honestly, I don't care about that. I'm ready to risk it all for you, but I want to make sure you feel the same way before we cross a line."

"So why are you leaving?"

"Because, you need time to process this and I really wanna kiss you but if I start kissing you I'm not gonna wanna stop."

My eyes went wide with shock. I opened my mouth to speak but no words came out. So, I closed it again. Julian smiled.

"Nadirah, you don't have to say anything. Even if I just made a complete fool of myself, it felt good to get it out. I'll respect whatever you decide."

He released my hand and left the truck, closing the door softly behind him. A minute later, I heard the click of the tailgate opening and felt the truck bounce slowly as he climbed into the bed.

THREE

Wow.

Just, wow.

Jules had feelings for me. Real feelings.

He felt the way I felt about him all these years and he

never acted on it. This wasn't a hard decision. No other person I've dated, woman or man, has ever come close to making me feel the way Julian had in the last half hour.

I slowly opened my door, jumped out of the truck and walked around to the back where I found Julian sitting on the tailgate staring at the photo. My sneakers crunched over leaves and twigs. The noise made him turn.

"Hey." I called to him.

"Hey." He jumped down and lifted me by the waist to sit before hopping up beside me.

"What are you thinking?" he asked.

I sucked in a deep breath and let it out slowly.

"Well, I'm not sure exactly," I said in a chuckle. "It's a lot of information to take in." I put my hand on his thigh and he covered it with his own.

"Yeah." He nodded. I reached for the photo in his other hand and held it up.

"Why this picture?" I asked. "You must have taken dozens of photos that night. Why is this one your favorite?"

"When your brother told me what happened, I borrowed a suit from my roommate and hopped in my truck. I had zero expectations and I was fully prepared for you to shoot me down. My intentions were pure. I couldn't bear the thought of someone I cared about being let down when there was something I could do to help. But when you came down those stairs…" He sighed. "You were all light and beauty and optimism. No one would have blamed you if you were angry but you weren't. Not only that, you cared about me."

"What do you mean?"

"The moment this was taken," He pointed at the photo, "I had just apologized for not being able to tie my tie correctly—My dad has been trying to teach me for years and I still don't know how. You laughed and said, 'That's why you have me. I've got your back.' And you retied my tie. I'm pretty sure that was the moment I saw you—really saw you as something else. The shutter remote was in my hand and I just pressed it. I wanted to find a way to hold on to that moment forever."

"Julian," I whispered with tears in my eyes. "Why didn't you tell me?"

"Because, Dee, you were—"

"Seventeen," I said in a watery chuckle.

"Seventeen," he repeated with a smile and leaned closer.

"Well, I'm twenty-five now." I placed Julian's hand on my thigh and leaned closer.

"Oh, I know." He closed the distance between us and our lips met. I tilted my head to the side and brought our faces closer.

Julian wrapped his arms around my waist and pulled me into his lap. His tongue slipped into my open mouth and I sighed as our bodies melted together. This kiss was eight years in the making and I wanted to feel every ounce of sensation. He reclined on his back on the bed of the truck and I broke our kiss to reposition myself and straddle him. My eyes went wide at the giant bulge in his jeans.

"Whoa," I whispered to myself as I ran my fingertips over the ridge in his jeans.

"Careful," Julian whispered after a soft hiss, "he's sensitive."

"Julian?" I scooted my body forward so the juncture of my thighs was positioned over his hips.

"Yeah?"

"How long until the tow truck comes?" I glanced around the surrounding woods. It was completely deserted. Julian looked at his watch before he answered.

"At least two hours." He grinned up at me causing a fluttering in my belly and tingling between my thighs. "Why?" he asked but I suspected he knew exactly what I was thinking.

"How much kissing can we get done in two hours?" I leaned forward and brushed my lips over his. Julian skated his fingertips over my bare skin under my t-shirt, causing me to shiver in the mild summer heat.

"I think we can get a lot of things done in two hours." He kissed me again. "What did you have in mind?"

I grinned and covered his mouth with mine. We made out like teenagers in the bed of Julian's truck, clawing and pawing at each other through our clothes. Julian rolled me onto my back and looked down at me, grinning.

"Damn girl." He broke our kiss. "Listen, I should tell you something before we go any further..." His face was serious.

"Okay..." My stomach knotted wondering what Julian was about to tell me. This moment felt too perfect.

"I'm attracted to men and women." He looked nervous as his eyes raked my face for a reaction.

"So, you're bi?" I asked. I had no idea. Of course, my

brother and I would have no reason to discuss Julian's dating life. No reason that made sense.

"Yeah, I am. Would you have any issues with that?"

"No, of course not." I smiled up at him. His face split into a wide grin and he kissed me again. "Would you have any issues with me being bi?" I raised an eyebrow.

"You are?" he asked and I nodded. "Well, that's not gonna work for me." His expression was serious for a second, making my heart stop, before his face split into another grin. I narrowed my eyes at him and slapped him in the chest.

"Ha ha," I deadpanned. "But there is one thing..." I tucked my bottom lip between my teeth.

"Anything," he whispered and I hoped he meant it.

"I'm monogamous and I expect anyone I date to be monogamous too. I mean, no shade if you aren't—it's definitely not for everybody— but it's really important to me." I tucked my bottom lip between my teeth and waited for his response.

"Do I get to be monogamous with you?" He smiled down at me and brushed a curl away from my forehead.

"Do you want to be monogamous with me?" I asked.

"Have you been listening to me for the last hour?" He laughed and tickled me. "Yes, Nadirah Marie Westin, I want to be monogamous with you for as long as you'll let me."

"Damn, my whole name, huh?" I giggled. "So, Julian Michael Harris Jr., I guess we're doing this." I reached up and dragged my fingernails through his fade.

"I guess so." He lowered his body to mine and kissed me again before sitting up and opening the truck box nestled under the rear window. He pulled out some blankets and pillows.

"Someone's prepared." I propped myself up on my elbows and narrowed my eyes at him with a smirk.

"Get your mind out the gutter. Sometimes I sleep in my truck when I'm on assignments." He chuckled and arranged the blankets and pillows.

"Do you have condoms in there?"

"Condoms?" He whipped his head around to face me with his eyebrows raised. I smiled and nodded. He grabbed a duffle bag from the corner of the truck bed, unzipped it and retrieved a strip of Trojans.

"Well then, get over here. We don't have much time."

He walked over to me on his knees and wrapped his arms around my waist.

"You're gorgeous, Nadirah." He pulled my t-shirt over my head and planted light kisses on my collar bone and chest. "So fucking gorgeous."

He laid me down on the blanket and painted my upper body with his tongue and lips.

I wrapped my palms around his waist and smoothed my fingertips over the muscles of his abs and pulled his t-shirt over his head. My God, this was a beautiful man. He had a slim build but every muscle was toned and taut. Sweat began to glisten on his rippling shoulder muscles as I watched him move over my body tasting and tantalizing. I slid my arms out of the straps of my bra to give him more access to my bare chest.

"Did you know you have a cute little mole under your left breast?" He asked between licks and kisses.

"No, but I do now." I sighed in between moans.

"I want to learn every inch of you." He swirled his tongue around my navel, making me squirm in anticipation, before dragging it further south. I reached for the button of my shorts before Julian stopped me. "No, baby. Let me. You just relax."

I leaned back and my head sank into the pillow while I gazed up into the clear blue summer sky, visible through the tall trees. Julian pulled my shorts and panties over my hips. I felt my belly clench and my heart race with every gentle graze of his fingertips on my skin. My body was fully aware and accepting of this welcome but unexpected turn of events, but my brain was having trouble processing the fact that Julian Harris' lips were actually kissing my belly. Julian Harris' fingers were actually gripping the soft flesh behind my knees to pull my leg out of my shorts. Julian Harris had just called me his baby and he wanted me just as badly as I wanted him for all these years.

"Damn," he whispered right before I felt him press the first kiss on my inner thigh. Before I could fully process what was happening, Julian had tossed my leg over his shoulder and was devouring me like I was his last meal. His lips and tongue were everywhere between my thighs, making me whimper and shudder. I rocked my hips back and forth as the pressure built. Julian used his fingers to push me over the edge. My eyes squeezed shut and I grunted in ecstasy and surprise. "Fuck, Dee Fuck that's so good," he said in a low growl after he made me come the first time. He soothed my sensitive clit with feather light passes of his tongue and gentle kisses.

When my spasming subsided, he crawled off of the

bed of the truck, took off his pants and boxers before crawling back onto the bed and laying beside me.

"Hey," I whispered.

"You good?" he replied and I nodded, pulling our faces together so I could taste my pleasure on his lips. Our lips separated with a faint pop and I grinned at him.

"What now?"

"Sit on my face," he whispered.

"Sit on your face? But you just—"

Julian stopped me with a look that said *do you really wanna argue about this*? I straddled his face and leaned forward so I was in the perfect position to return the favor. I used one hand to balance my weight as Jules' tongue threatened to send me to another oblivion and used the other hand to wrap around his shaft. Julian's dick was as gorgeous as the rest of him. It was long, thick and the same shade of smooth dark brown as the rest of his body. His pubic hair was short and neatly groomed. After licking my lips, I leaned forward and placed a gentle kiss on his tip. Julian's tongue froze mid-stroke.

"Fuck, Dee," he hissed. Encouraged, I slid the entire tip in my mouth and sucked. "Shit," he said in a heavy sigh. I took more of him into my mouth.

Julian squeezed my thighs with his large hands and groaned as I rocked back and forth taking more of him between my lips with each return. Soon, I found a rhythm. My fist, slick with my saliva, pumped and twisted the base of his cock while I sucked and slurped at the head and the part of his shaft I could fit into my mouth without choking. Julian moaned and twisted under my attention.

He'd mostly forgotten what he was doing between my

legs, occasionally rewarding me with a lick here and a kiss there. But that's exactly what I wanted. I wanted him distracted and out of his mind. He needed to know how good I could be for him, how good we could be together.

"I'm gonna come, baby. I'm gonna come," he grunted in a frenzied moan.

"Good," I whispered before I started to suck again. I moved one of my hands to gently fondle his balls. I lightly dragged my fingernails over the puckered sack and that was all it took. He exploded into my mouth and his fingers dug into the flesh of my thighs. I swallowed the two thick ropes of cum Jules shot into my mouth. I climbed off of him and he pulled me into his arms. I snuggled into him and draped a leg over his body. Julian kissed the top of my head and covered us with another blanket.

"Yo, is this real?" He chuckled and kissed the side of my head again. "Like, did this really happen?"

"I hope so." I smoothed my palm over his pecs.

"Hey Jules…"

"Yeah?"

"Do you think we have time to use one of those condoms before the tow truck comes?"

"Definitely, beautiful." He squeezed me into him and kissed me. "But I'm gonna need like ten minutes."

Four

WE SPENT THE NEXT HOUR AND A HALF USING THREE condoms in three different positions before we collapsed naked, sweaty and exhausted, tangled in the blankets and gasping for breath.

"Wow," I said.

"Wow," he agreed.

"You know how some couples," I propped my head up on my elbow to face him, "have great emotional chemistry, but the sex is trash or they have amazing sex but they have nothing to talk about?"

"I've heard of such couples, yes." He leaned forward and planted a kiss on my nose. "Why?"

"I don't think that will be us."

"I know it won't." He grinned and smoothed a palm over my ass. "You're perfect."

"No, I'm not."

"You're perfect for me."

"I think you're perfect for me, too."

His grip on my waist tightened and we kissed for a long time.

"I just had sex with thee, Nadirah Westin, outside, in the back of my truck."

"Well, I just had sex with thee, Julian Harris, outside, in the back of your truck." I hooked my leg around his waist and used it to pull him closer. He closed a hand around one of my breasts and kissed me again.

"We should get dressed, beautiful. The tow truck should be here soon."

"Ugh. Do we have to?" I groaned. "Can we just live in this truck and become forest people?"

Julian let out a deep belly laugh. "Listen, if we miss this wedding, we wouldn't have a choice. Going off the grid might be our only chance of staying alive."

"You're probably right."

He retrieved a box of baby wipes from the truck box and we cleaned each other before getting dressed. It felt so natural. We were caring for each other, like we always have and I hoped we always would.

Julian and I stretched out on the blanket and in each other's arms watching the clouds float across the sky as we waited for the tow truck. I was originally supposed to be at the resort by noon for a bridal party luncheon, but hopefully we could make in time for the rehearsal dinner at seven with a couple of hours to spare.

"So what do you want to do about the wedding?" Julian asked when we were about a half hour away from the resort. The tow truck was able to pull Julian's pick up out of the mud. A nearby repair shop replaced the two tires and we were on our way. We could hear Wendy fussing in the background when we called Marcus to tell him about our unplanned delay.

"Well, I was hoping we could skip the wedding and spend all weekend in your room?"

"That sounds like a plan." Julian smiled and reached for my hand. "But I meant, do you want to tell our families right away or keep this to ourselves for a while?"

"I don't know. I haven't thought about it. How do you think our families will react?" I slid my palm over his and interlocked our fingers.

"Baby, we're grown. I don't care what our families

want. I just want you. But I also want you to be comfortable. So, I'm good with whatever you decide."

"I don't wanna hide our...whatever this is. What is this?"

"I was hoping for a relationship? Best friends, lovers, partners, a team?" He raised his eyebrows.

"I'd like that." I grinned at him and I felt my eyes sting with tears. "I don't want to hide either, but maybe we should wait until after the wedding?"

He nodded and pulled our hands to his lips and kissed my fingers.

The gravel crunched under our tires as we came to a stop in the parking lot of the resort. We unbuckled our seat belts and turned to face each other.

"How do I look?"

"Like you spent two hours getting fucked within an inch of your life in the back of a pick up truck," he said and I burst out laughing. "What about me?"

"Well, you're definitely wearing a lot more lipstick than you had on when you picked me up." I reached out and brushed the pad of my thumb over his bottom lip. His lips puckered at my touch.

"Listen." He reached out and brushed his palm across my cheek before wrapping his fingers around my neck. "I know this might feel like it came out of nowhere and we're going from zero to sixty but for me it feels like making up for lost time. I'm ten toes down. I'm all the way in with you." He used his thumb to brush away a tear that rolled down my cheek.

"Me too," I whispered. "So what happens when we get back to New York?"

"I don't know but I'm guessing a lot of that." He jerked his head at the back window, indicating the bed of the truck. I laughed and bit my lip. "Whatever you want. You can stay in your student housing or you can move in with me in DUMBO. We can travel. We can stay home and read books or watch Netflix. As long as we're together, I don't care."

"That sounds amazing." I reached out, wrapped my arms around his neck, and pulled him close.

"I'm pretty sure I'm in love with you, Nadirah."

"I'm pretty sure I'm in love with you too, Julian."

He closed the distance between our lips.

"What the fuck?!"

I wasn't sure how long we were kissing before we heard Wendy's screech, but we looked up to see her and Marcus standing next to our parents. Julian's parents and brother were there as well. We had an entire welcome party waiting at the entrance of the resort.

"So much for waiting." I shrugged. Jules smiled at me before hopping out of the truck and jogging over to my side to help me get down. We clasped hands and walked towards our families.

"So, how long has this been going on?" Marcus asked Julian. His expression was unreadable.

"It's kinda new," Julian responded, with the same blank expression. They looked each other up and down before Marc's face spread with a giant grin and he wrapped Julian in a hug. "It's about fucking time."

"Well, don't even think about doing any dumb shit like getting engaged at our reception." Wendy crossed her arms and pursed her lips. "But yeah, it was pretty obvious that you two were going to get together at some point. I'm happy for you." She wrapped her arms around my shoulders and air kissed me because she'd already had her make up done for the rehearsal dinner.

Our parents were equally enthusiastic and my dad joked about still having his shotgun. Julian hugged his brother before he grabbed our bags from the truck.

"So that went better than I expected."

"It did." He switched both bags to one arm and reached for my hand. "What do you want to do now?"

"Well, we have to get ready for the rehearsal dinner, but I'm available if you need help tying your tie." I shot him a sly smile and he squeezed my hand.

"Definitely."

ABOUT THE AUTHOR

LUCY EDEN

Lucy Eden is the nom de plume of a romance-obsessed author who writes the kind of romance she loves to read. She's a sucker for alphas with a soft gooey center, over the top romantic gestures, strong & smart MCs, humor, love at first sight (or pretty damn close), happily ever afters & of course, dirty & steamy love scenes.

When Lucy isn't writing, she's busy reading--or listening to--every book she can get her hands on-- romance or otherwise.

She lives & loves in New York with her husband, two children, a turtle & a Yorkshire Terrier.

More Books by Lucy Eden
Blind Date With A Book Boyfriend
Everything's Better With Lisa

ABOUT ONLY ONE FLOWER BED

Seven years ago Grant Sinclair left his small town of Plenty, Georgia, to chase his dreams of achieving a degree, traveling, and of owning a business. But when Grant left home to chase after all that good, he left behind more than good.

He left behind the first man he ever loved.

Remi Wilson.

Now he's back and Grant won't give up on Remi even if the other man is bent on being as bitter as unsweet tea.

Only One Flower Bed is an angsty second chance M/M romance that's a little hotter than not, but definitely not lacking in the sweet.

ONLY ONE FLOWER BED

REBEL CARTER

Grant Sinclair squatted down and squinted at the leafy vines growing happily in their loamy home. He reached out and pulled back a few leaves to examine the new fruit. It had been over a month now since he'd tilled this patch of land and seeded it with cantaloupes. The fruit was well suited to the Georgia climate, the warm weather and soil ensured it would thrive. It was far tamer than some of the plants, trees, and fruits Grant had taken to growing lately for his small but upscale clientele.

Plenty, Georgia, was a small town, with deep roots; founded in the mid-eighteenth century, Plenty's citizens were a proud, stubborn but welcoming group that liked to stay put. When you came to Plenty you were accepted wholly and that meant few were of a mind to leave. Many of the current families went generations deep, Grant's family was one such example of deep roots and little movement.

At least until Grant.

Although his leaving hadn't been for long. He'd graduated along with his friends and spent a year or two living and working, thinking a little on the future and realized he wanted something slightly different than what Plenty had to offer. Or rather he wanted what it offered but just more and different.

If Grant had stayed in Plenty, he would have probably been working on the nearby docks helping maintain the boats his family owned for their shrimping business, hell, he might have even become a cop, a familiar face to those he'd grown up alongside of.

But Grant hadn't wanted that. He looked down at the green leaves under his fingers and twisted one curling it back before he buried his other in the dark soil. He scooped a handful of it in his palm and squeezed it tightly making a fist, a sigh escaping the big man with a shudder.

Grant had wanted this. Plants in front of him and dirt in his hands. He wanted to know what made green things thrive and he wanted to give that to people, but it was a skill and a knowledge he'd had to leave home for. He'd gone to school in Athens for four years, got his bachelors in horticulture, and then set off taking jobs wherever he could, saving and learning as he went until he would be able to do the thing he wanted most--open his own business.

He glanced behind his back at the greenhouse, the large structure imposing and standing in sharp relief to the green woods that seemed to be pushing forward, ever reaching into the land he had cleared for his business.

Sinclair & Co. Horticulture. He was the 'Sinclair', his family the '& Co.'

They hadn't been thrilled in his choice to leave but

damned if they hadn't tried to support him at every turn. The land he was building on had once been his grandaddy's, deeded to him at the start of last year so that he could "Get rollin' already," as his grandaddy had explained in his will. Sitting in rumpled clothing from the red-eye he'd caught from Los Angeles, Grant had hardly been able to stop the laugh in the lawyer's office, Mr. Oliveres, a family friend and a man that had known Grant since he could crawl. His grandaddy had chosen the man for a reason, he wouldn't have wanted a stranger with his family. Not after he was gone and Grant was thankful for it. They could hear the old man in the lawyer's dictation and they shared a smile of knowing.

"Guess you'll have to come home," Mr. Oliveres had observed looking at Grant over the rim of his reading glasses.

"Guess I will," Grant conceded leaning back in the leather chair with a sigh and a nod. "Guess so."

City life didn't agree with him, never had, but it'd been a means to an end---that end being a life and business in Plenty. The move home had been relatively easy. Grant had been welcomed back with open arms and slaps on the back and more than one too many invitations for a cold one at the pool hall. It had been like he'd never left and to be honest, he'd been ready for the move back and most folks had been excited to see him.

The rumble of thunder overhead reminded him that it was due to rain today and he stood from his crouch, wiping his hands on his worn jeans. He had a good deal more to do today before the rain came and taking a journey down memory lane wasn't one of them. The thunder grew louder and he stopped looking up at the sky to see that it remained the same overcast gray it had been all morning and afternoon. Still the sound grew louder and Grant turned, searching the sky for the source of the noise. He sighed, hands going to his hips and stared off into the horizon. The storm shouldn't be here until the evening so what was that deafening---

A beat-up blue truck came into sight and Grant went still. He knew that truck, the familiar chrome of the hubcaps, the curve of the hood Grant knew was sturdier than it looked, the almost sky blue paint job that should have been repainted years ago.

And then there was the driver.

The dark-haired, most likely scowling sonofabitch at the wheel that was none other than Remington Wilson.

Hands still at his hips, Grant's fingers squeezed his sides almost painfully when he was offered a clearer view of Remi's face. He was indeed scowling, and he was just as handsome as ever.

If the move back home had been easy and everyone being glad to see him had made Grant think his decision to return to Plenty fated, then the sight of Remi seemed single-handedly determined to send Grant running. There was nothing easy about Remi. Never had been, but that didn't mean Grant hadn't tried.

Didn't still try.

It was why he had thought of none other than Wilsons' to fulfill his monthly supplies. Remi's family ran the hard-ware store and keeping business local was key to Plenty's ability to thrive and survive with big box stores and the damned internet slashing prices meant to drive small businesses into the dirt. Everyone in town had done their part to keep Wilsons' going, just like they did for all the locally owned businesses. Plenty wasn't about to let their small town vanish under the heel of new development. Grant had made sure every dollar spent had gone right into local pockets and Wilsons' had been the only choice that made sense for his business---except that somehow that came attached with twice a month visits of scowling Remi Wilson bent on making the encounter as uncomfortable and prickly as it ever had a need to be.

He sighed, watching the truck bounce up the dirt road before it came to a skidding stop in front of the greenhouse. "Fucker," Grant muttered under his breath and raised a hand in a terse wave. Remi didn't wave back, just threw open the truck door and leapt from it with a scowl on his face.

He didn't want to be here. Couldn't be making it more clear that he didn't want to be here, but Grant ignored it and ambled forward, working to keep his posture loose. They'd been friends once, or at least sort of--- Grant found it hard to remember with the way that life in Plenty was tangled together until the threads of separate lives tangled and knotted, creating a mess you couldn't even begin to sort. He swallowed hard and took in the sight of Remi's familiar body, the man's broad shoulders and muscled arms drawing his attention for a beat before he forced his eyes back to his face.

He'd give anything for their once upon a time sort of friendship, the kind born of playing on the same sports teams, sitting in the same church pews and running around the same streets. Anything was better than what they had now which was open hostility. It'd been that way ever since Grant had announced he was leaving. It should have been an exciting night; they'd been out for Grant's 22nd birthday and it had been somewhere between the third shot of tequila and the beer he'd just been handed, that he realized what he had to do.

He had to leave town otherwise this would be all he knew. It wouldn't be a bad life. Just not the one he craved. It would be the one he fell into, not created and that would not stand. He'd already applied to UGA, received the acceptance letter and had just been sitting on the news, but there in the dim pool hall with his friends Grant had shared the good news with them all. Everyone had been stunned into silence but they'd recovered quick enough with congratulations and shouts for another round for "the college boy!"

All of them except for Remi.

He hadn't missed the dark look that had passed over his face, or the way his normally warm gray gaze had gone hard all over in front of Grant's very eyes. It was like looking at an enemy, or worse a stranger. He'd tried to head it off, catch up with the other man when they'd both stepped out for some air---Remi to smoke and Grant, to well, talk because the two of them had struck up something that year. Something Grant had always felt inside but never really acted on, but it had felt so good and natural with Remi that he hadn't questioned it. Not when they'd first kissed, on a night much like this, hands and mouths exploring the other tentatively in the dark and then again with more confidence the longer the minutes stretched on.

The men hadn't labeled what they had. It was easy that way. The days and night shared between them in town. A few of their friends knew and no one was really surprised by it, which made Grant wonder what they'd known before even he had, though he felt like it would only ever be like this with Remi. It had only taken a handful of years away from home to know he'd been right.

No one had set him on fire like Remi. And no one had ever frozen him out in quite the same way either. Both capable of stopping his heart and breath so quickly he'd wondered if it had ever happened.

And God, they had been something, hadn't they? His skin flushed remembering how Remi's fingers had felt in his hair. The gasp of the other man as he thrust into Grant, their bodies close until muscle and skin were flush to the other in a way that had him forgetting where he began and Remi ended. It was nothing but a tangle of limbs with Remi's cock in him, the way he stared at Grant, his gray eyes all fire and need until it was the only thing Grant could focus on. Remi had been his world in those moments, minutes marked by the sting of Remi pulling on his hair until his scalp ached, seconds kept by the slap of skin on skin, breaths and heartbeats in unison until he couldn't remember if it had been an hour or an eternity since Remi had taken him, claimed his body as his own until the pair of them spiraled up and over the edge of pleasure they had been building together.

He'd loved every second of it. Could still hear Remi's gasp and shout when he orgasmed, body curling in close to Grant's as he did. He'd never been far behind, the sight of his lover finding release enough to urge Grant to his own end.

They'd been like that right until the night he'd announced his decision to leave town.

Remi hadn't wanted to talk that night. He hadn't wanted to talk any other night either leading up to when Grant had left for school. And when he'd come home Remi had only deigned to speak to him to let him know just how unwelcome Grant was in Plenty.

His skin burned at the memory of Remi's hands on him, the phantom pang once again reminding Grant that he wished to hell he'd told Remi first and not blurted it out as he had. But things were always easier in hindsight, weren't they?

After that night Remi hadn't wanted a damn thing to do with him. He suspected today wouldn't be much different but Grant fixed an easy smile on his face as he rounded the truck and made his way to the back where Remi was already climbing into the bed of the truck, eyes focused on the goods Grant had ordered.

"Afternoon," Grant offered, coming to stand at the end of the truck bed. Remi nodded, and offered a grunt in greeting.

"Ah, looks like it'll rain," he went on, clearing his throat when Remi turned towards him with a sack of fertilizer over one shoulder. The other man's eyes lifted to the sky for a second before he shrugged and nodded.

"Suppose so." Remi tossed the bag onto the ground beside Grant and moved to grab another. "Got your fertilizer. Tower lights too. Be done in a few if you tell me where to put it."

Grant swallowed at the words. It was Remi's way of telling him to give him space, to not talk to him, and Grant sighed playing along for the sake of keeping the peace.

"Sure thing. You can bring it in back. Near the orchids."

"Sounds good." Remi nodded, his shoulder-length brown hair falling forward into his face when he bent to grab another bag. He tossed that onto the ground beside the first and continued about his work. Even if the other man didn't want to talk, he hadn't told him to leave and so Grant watched him work in relative peace, the way he usually did when Remi came round.

The air around them was hot and humid sticking to their skin and if it hadn't been from the breeze the impending storm was kicking up, it might have been unpleasant, but it wasn't---certainly wasn't with the view Grant was afforded by a working Remi, shirt sleeves rolled up and hair free from the knot the man usually wore it in. Remi's features were sharp and severe, his countenance stern but that wasn't surprising, not when it came to Grant or anything to do with him. Not as far as Remi was concerned.

Grant sighed and cleared his throat cautioning another glance at the silent man as he worked. Another bag of fertilizer landed beside him and he stepped back and said, "it's hot out yet. Want a water?" His question was completely innocuous, innocent at best, it was humid and hot, the air holding the heavy feeling that told of an upcoming summer storm. From the feel of it, this one was going to be more than a passing shower. He glanced up at the sky and pretended to be interested in anything else but Remi.

When in doubt, and confronted with a man that made your heart stop, focus on...the weather? He would have scoffed at himself if it wasn't the only thing he could speak on intelligibly. He much suspected this was why the weather was a favored topic of small talk in the South.

God, he'd give anything to run his hands through that hair again. He knew it was softer than it looked, just like the man it belonged to. He glanced at Remi when he wasn't even given the normal grunt in response. He'd stopped working and was looking at Grant with a look he couldn't quite figure out. Not annoyed or angry, but curious? Except that it was gone in a flash and once more the familiar hard look slipped over Remi's face like a mask.

He pursed his lips. "M'fine."

"I know but--"

"Don't need nothing from you. Never have. Never will. Let me work, dammit."

Grant held up his hands and was unable to stop the startled laugh that puffed free from his lips. "Well, all right then," he said and shook his head taking a step back and then another, "was tryin' to be friendly is all."

"Should know by now I don't want it."

"See that now. Make no mistake." Grant dropped his hands and turned on his heel. He didn't need this. If Remi was bent on holding a grudge from near back seven years then the man was welcome to it. He had a business to run, and if peace wasn't on the table then it would just have to be one of those things in life.

Worse things had happened to better people. Not

having Remi Wilson would be marked as one of the lesser things to happen in history. Even in a place like Plenty. But even as he thought it Grant bit his lip because from the cold and hollow feel their exchange had left him with, he wasn't so sure.

The work passed quickly enough, or at least he thought so. Remi was silent as ever as he unloaded the new goods, taking them where they were to go, and Grant did his best to avoid him. If Remi was coming he was going or busying himself in the endless rows of greenery that needed tending to. It should have been relatively simple to give him space but even so the two of them kept meeting eyes, looking up at the wrong times or nearly brushing shoulders as Grant exited to check on the hedges he'd just had delivered, but not had the time to bring in.

They were like two magnets. It was agony.

Always had been.

More so when Remi fixed him with the smoldering gray gaze that Grant knew intimately, though he much preferred when it was directed at him in a more kindly manner. He blew out a deep sigh, watching Remi from the corner of his eye, where he was finishing up the last of his order. The other man was scribbling out an invoice, minutes from leaving, and though he knew he should be happy that the tense time would be over when Remi left, Grant was more morose than anything.

They'd been something; he didn't know what to call it, but it had been something better than now.

"Remi...hey, listen," Grant began putting down the shears he held and starting forward. "I don't know how things got to where they are now but, ah, I just wanted to say that I'm real sorry."

Remi's hands stopped where they were, the pen no longer moving. "What?" he asked, his voice low and hardly carrying over the now constant rumbling of thunder and moan of the wind that was picking up in earnest.

"I said I'm sorry."

"You're sorry?" Remi looked up at him, eyes stony and cold. He tucked the clipboard close to his body with a snap and barked out a laugh. "Why am I not surprised you're apologizin' now."

Grant blinked in surprise and rocked back on his heels. "What are you--"

"You would be the one to bring it up, even if you were fine leavin' it."

"Woah, woah," he held up his hands and came forward. "Remi, look, I want to talk to you about that. I miss--"

"Here's your damn invoice. Be back in two weeks with whatever you need." Remi ripped the invoice free and held it out with a jerk of his hand. It was like a shield between them, or maybe a knife? Grant figured it was meant to be a knife, not a shield, not with the way it was stabbing him and reminding him of the distance between the two of them now. His eyes narrowed, his displeasure showing plainly on his face.

"You know what?" Grant said, voice low. He could feel the thunder now, it was rumbling deep in the earth, the vibrations humming through the dirt and up his feet. He locked eyes with Remi and took another step closer. "I'm sick and tired of this bullshit, Remi. Grow up."

Remi jerked back as if he had been slapped and drew himself up to his full height; an impressive sight, as the man was well over 6'3. He crossed his arms, biceps straining the material of his work shirt as he did so. Grant clenched his fist and focused on the thunder's presence. Now was not the time to get distracted by a well placed flex.

"Grow up?" Remi cocked his head to the side and scoffed, gray eyes narrowing. "You're the one forcin' me to keep coming up to this damn place week after week, month after month. Drive me half crazy with it!"

"Ah, hell, Remi. No one's ever made you do a damn thing you didn't have a mind to do and you know it."

"Shut up, Grant. Pay the damn invoice and--"

"And what? You'll be back in two weeks?" Grant crossed his arm and lowered his chin challenging the other man with a pointed glare.

Remi's mouth snapped shut, his jaw clenched. Grant could tell from the way his lips pursed that the other man's teeth were probably grinding painfully against each other. Good, he thought, he was glad for the discomfort Remi was in, he hoped the next time the man clenched his damn jaw that his teeth cracked and fell out of his head. He was tired of being the only one to try and fix what had happened. He'd tried to talk to Remi all those years ago, had tried it again the first time he'd seen his familiar face. It had been impossible not to---the sight of him had brought back all the times they'd shared, the kisses, hungry hands and the feel of skin on skin that had left him feeling drunk when not a drop had passed his lips.

Grant hadn't wanted liquor. He'd wanted Remi, all of

him, morning, day and night, and for a time he'd had him. It hadn't been fair that his play at a bigger future had cost him what they'd found in the other, what he hadn't been close to finding in anyone else since.

So now, as they stood off against the other, Grant was glad Remi was uncomfortable. That his jaw was probably aching. That there was nothing left for them to say. He'd said his piece, shut the other man up and that was enough for him, so he jabbed a thumb at the door behind Remi and said, "See yourself out. I'll be along. Storm's coming."

Remi said nothing for a second and that moment stretched into two before he sighed the breath coming out of him in a long sigh. He slapped the invoice onto the work table next to him and shook his head. "Pay up by Monday." He turned on his heel and stalked out of the greenhouse.

"Mississippi one…." Grant crossed his arms and sighed before uttering, "Mississippi two…" He wasn't in much of a mood for running into the other man when he'd just let loose on him. "Mississippi three…." He sagged against the table by the door and felt his heart lurch when Remi's truck roared to life. He stayed put counting to the time of fifteen before he let himself move. He closed the door with a slam and locked it though he didn't much know why. No one came out here but him, and everyone knew it was his land. Things didn't go missing in Plenty, not like in the city, but he did it anyhow. He stopped at the door of his truck and looked off in the direction Remi had gone. There was no sign of him. If his heart wasn't still slamming in his chest, he'd have never known he was even there.

Grant didn't like that. But it was what it was, and at the landing of a fat raindrop he pulled his door open and swung up into the cab of his truck, determined to put the whole thing out of his mind. It was hardly 5 o'clock, if he let Remi take over his thoughts now, he wouldn't get a wink of sleep.

His hands clenched on the steering wheel. That was a laugh. Remi Wilson had occupied more than his fair share of Grant's thoughts, and even if he tried to put it out of his mind, he'd stew over what had happened today for the rest of the evening. He sighed and leaned forward, looking out the window as the rain began to fall in earnest. A crack of lightning brightened the sky as sure as a camera flash and Grant jumped, despite having grown up with such storms. He'd loved storms when he was a child but it didn't rain quite like this in Los Angeles; there the storms rolled in, water on pavement, the heat and bustle of the city devouring the wild of a thunderstorm.

But here?

In Plenty storms were allowed to be. Their power and force unfettered as it settled on the land and people. There was a beauty to it, a certain solitude that could happen when everything was a flurry of water and light, the outside disappearing from thought with each passing second. The drum of rain on a roof, the way it tapped against window panes, it was all a melody he knew by heart, except that now Grant hated it.

Hated it for the fact that it reflected the anger and confusion at seeing Remi as he had. His emotions felt as tumultuous as the rain and lightning, and he didn't much care for it. He didn't want a storm. Not now. What he wanted was to go home and change out of his work clothes. He wanted to pull on a pair of sweats, reheat whatever leftovers he had, and watch whatever sports he could find. He'd watch ice curling, competitive chess, or bobsledding if it just meant he could shut off his brain for a solid half hour.

Remi always did have a way of making him feel like he was coming apart at the seams. Grant's grip tightened once more on the wheel and he leaned forward squinting out the windshield against the raging storm. He was just turning the corner, his truck climbing a long hill that had the engine straining and wheels spinning against the now muddy road. Grant blew out a sigh as he crested the hill and vowed to have the road regraveled. The last time he could remember it being done was when he was in high school, and from the way his truck was working overtime it was sorely needed.

Grant squinted against the falling rain and turned carefully, easing around the corner to see the sight of another vehicle very nearly sideways across the road.

"What the hell? Who is that?" He reached out, speeding up the windshield wipers to get a better look at who had managed to get themselves stuck this far out from town. It was only when he drove forward another hundred feet that he recognized the familiar flash of teal blue.

It was Remi.

"Sonofabitch," Grant huffed out a laugh. Remi was standing with hands on his hips, hair and clothes plastered to his body and face. He swallowed hard and was grateful for the small flair of pleasure he got at seeing Remi stuck in the mud after their little run in. He laughed then, even threw his head back and let the sound of it fill his truck. Maybe he wouldn't be trying to clear his mind tonight, not with the image of a stranded Remi to keep him entertained. He was still laughing when he slowed, or at least he meant to slow as he came down the hill--- instead his wheels spun and locked and before he knew it the truck was sliding forward.

"Shit!" Grant turned the wheel guiding the truck away from Remi and onto the shoulder. He swore as the truck came to a sliding stop. He sighed and refused to look out the window where he knew Remi was. Where the other man was probably, as in, definitely staring at him. He threw the truck in reverse and hit the gas but to his chagrin, the truck only rocked back an inch before the wheels began to spin.

Out of the corner of his eye he could see Remi's figure approaching and he grit his teeth and tried once more to back right out of this bad dream. "I shoulda never laughed at his ass. I knew it." His foot pressed on the gas again, he pressed on the pedal until the damn thing nearly went through the floor but again the truck didn't move and still Remi came closer.

"This is exactly what I get. Fucking karma and--"

The rap of knuckles against the glass of driver door made his jaw tighten and he would have bit right through his tongue if he had caught the thing just then. He took in a deep breath and this time it was his jaw that ached when he threw the car in park and turned his head to look at Remi.

Grant's breath shuddered at the sight of one rain-soaked Remi. His shirt was nearly transparent and Grant felt his gut clench at the white material that could have been poured, not fitted, to Remi's body. Every muscle ridge, dip, and godforsaken plane of flesh was on display for an audience of one. If Grant had entertained any thought that he'd be thinking of anything else but Remi that night, it was over and done. His jeans were slung low on his hips, waterlogged and weighed down until it exposed a strip of tan and muscled skin to him. Grant licked his lips and when Remi threw out his hands gesturing at him in a move that could only be classified as "What the fuck?" he sighed and rolled down the window.

"Yeah?" he said.

"What the fuck?" Remi threw his hands up.

Grant rolled his eyes. "What?"

"Were you tryin' run my ass over or were you not paying attention on your own damn road?"

"You're one to talk! You're the one in the middle of the fucking road, Remi! I went off the road trying to miss you." Grant jabbed a finger at Remi. He scoffed and raised a hand shoving his hair back out of his eyes and glared at Grant.

"Because when was the last time you had this road graveled huh? It washed out! A goddamn cup of water woulda washed this thing out!"

Grant bit his lip and said nothing. He had him there.

"It's on my list!"

"Sure it is!"

Grant opened his mouth to shout at Remi but then shut it with a snap and inhaled deeply. Why the hell was he screaming at Remi in the middle of a thunderstorm?

"Look," he said, after he had taken a beat to calm himself, "let's get out of here. Does your truck start?" he asked.

"No. Engine got flooded. I'm stuck until I get a tow."

Grant hooked a thumb at his cab. "Get in then. We'll come back for it after the rain."

Remi gave a quick nod and strode around the truck. A second later he was climbing into the cab and he shut the door with a slam. Neither of them said anything, both men sitting in the stillness with the rain thrumming overhead. Grant took in another deep calming breath and glanced out towards Remi's truck. It was at a low point of the road, the water high there, and he shook his head at the sight of it.

"You're right. I should have been concentrating more on maintaining this road. This is on me."

Remi snorted but said nothing and leaned back in his seat. Grant took it as an acknowledgment of his apology and he once more made to reverse onto the road, except that once more the truck failed to move.

He cleared his throat and turned the wheel choosing to try again and made no progress. Remi turned towards him then arched an eyebrow and had what Grant knew to be a smug look on his handsome face.

"You're stuck," he said matter-of-factly.

Grant shook his head and cranked the engine again trying to drive forward, but his wheels spun uselessly kicking up mud in vain.

"Grant, you aren't going anywhere."

"Yes, I am."

"You're dead in the water."

"Like hell." Grant floored it, and this time the truck

lurched but it wasn't forward. Instead, it was to sink down into the soft red Georgia mud and he growled in frustration. "Fuck." He slammed a hand on the wheel and glared with unseeing eyes ahead of him. He was still glaring ahead of them, eyes focused on the rain-splattered windshield when the sound of Remi's low chuckle began. Grant's fingers flexed on the wheel. "Something you'd like to say?" he asked.

Remi scoffed and shook his head. "Come on, let's get a move on." He threw open the door and exited the truck, all the while still laughing. Grant didn't want to follow suit, but he knew it was the only way they were going to get out of this. Reception was horrible and even if it wasn't there was no way they would be able to call a tow while the storm continued to rage. No one was going to come get them, not this far out of town and not on this beat up and washed out road. He sighed and followed Remi out of the truck. They were walking all right but when he turned in the direction of town he saw that he was the only one.

"Where ya going?" Remi called out to him and he spun around to see the other man walking in the direction of the greenhouse.

"To town!" Grant yelled. He threw his hands out in frustration when Remi showed no sign of slowing down. "Where the hell are you going, Remi? Come back here!"

Remi kept walking, not even sparing a glance at Grant which meant he was going to have to go after the man. "Fucking hell," he muttered, stomping after Remi. He swore when he nearly went sprawling in the mud. Perhaps stomping was a bit ambitious, given the mud he was trying to navigate. He righted himself and took in a deep breath, willing himself to be calmer, but it was no use; the confusion and anxiety he had suffered at Remi's treatment had been transformed into anger and it was with the burning hot edges of it itching at his skin, that Grant continued on after Remi.

He only slowed when he caught up with him at the base of the hill his truck had struggled to traverse only minutes before. "Why are we going this way?" he grit out between clenched teeth.

Remi lifted a hand and pushed the hair out his face squinting at Grant in the rain. "Because town's too far. We make it back to your greenhouse, wait this thing out, then we can call from that phone you had put in."

Grant stiffened. The phone, that was right. He'd had the line put in and it had been a big to do in Plenty as no utilities had been put in this far out of town. He'd forgotten all about it, that's how damn mad he'd been at Remi.

"Good idea," he admitted, jaw still clenched. "Let's move it," he said, brushed past Remi, and continued on down the road. How had he forgotten about the telephone back at the greenhouse? He slowed though, when he wondered on how Remi had remembered it at all. When he was dropping off supplies to Grant, he couldn't get done and gone fast enough...but somehow he had remembered a phone that hung on a hook beside the back door before Grant had even thought of it.

Maybe the other man noticed more than he let on.

Grant tilted his head, catching sight of Remi out of the corner of his eye...or as much as he was able through the downpour. He was walking along, matching Grant step for step, even though the man was doing his best to leave him behind. Remi's brown hair had come loose and was plastered to his neck, the ends of it reaching his collarbones and making Grant think of what it had been like to kiss the surprisingly soft skin there. Grant's lips pressed into a frown and he forced himself to look ahead. They had about a mile left of walking before the greenhouse would be in front of them and he didn't much like the thought of torturing himself with a walk down memory lane for the whole of it.

Thankfully his focus and strength of will, plus the ever-growing need to get out of the battering storm which only seemed to increase in intensity, gales of wind, and nearly sideways blowing rain gave the right motivation for getting indoors. He sighed in relief as the greenhouse came into sight and before long he was pushing open the door and shaking himself off as he stepped inside. His skin was practically singing in relief after enduring the storm and he shivered, shaking his arms out and yanked his shirt off. The last thing he wanted was anything touching his body, it was almost too much after the rain.

"What the hell, Grant?" Remi slammed the door shut behind them and scowled at him.

"What?"

"Put your shirt back on."

Grant scoffed. "No."

"What are you trying to do, huh? Put your clothes back on," Remi ordered, spitting the words out at him. He stepped close then, his body crowding Grant against the worktable behind him. He backed up in surprise, his back hitting it and he blinked in surprise at the anger he saw in Remi's gray eyes. They stared at one another in silence then, chest rising and falling in rapid succession, until they were nearly touching. If Grant leaned forward he could press his mouth to the very spot he'd thought about earlier, that dip in Remi's body right before his broad chest began. It would make him gasp, he knew that sound well, and then he'd put a hand to the other man's cheek, fingers seeking and moving until he was cradling his head, until his fingers were twisting in his brown hair, giving the locks a tug until Remi's head was tipping back and offering the expanse of his throat to Grant's mouth.

He knew all of this and yet he did not move. He was still too angry over the way Remi had been acting since he'd set foot in Plenty, too angry over his behavior even today. He'd tried to fix it over and over again only to have it thrown back in his face. He wouldn't touch him.

Not yet.

"I said no," Grant growled. He leaned in then, eyes locked with Remi's for a beat before he dropped his gaze to his mouth. That mouth was beautiful as anything carved from stone had a right to be. Pillow lips soft and inviting, or they could be, had been once. Now they were twisted in anger at him.

He wouldn't touch him. Not until Remi begged.

Remi looked surprised at his answer. A look of uncertainty passing his face at Grant's answer. He backed up a step but Grant came with him, pushing away from the table, eating up the space between them with sure steps.

"Whatever," Remi said but his voice was weaker now, a

tremble could be heard in it and Grant had never heard anything sweeter. This was more like it. This was the man he had once known.

"Whatever?" He tilted his head to the side and for a moment he felt like a predator stalking his prey. He almost stopped then, but he had had quite enough of Remi Wilson's shit. He rolled his shoulders, aware the movement brought attention to the muscles he'd grown through the honest work of lugging fertilizer, hours of digging holes and laying new ground.

"Why're you actin' shy now, sweetheart?" he asked and Remi's head snapped back as if he had been slapped. Grant had always been the gentle one out of the pair of them, pet names and sweet nothings plentiful on his tongue when it came to talking to Remi. Sweetheart had been his favorite because of course it had been Remi's favorite. Anything Remi had wanted, Grant had given him willingly...everything of course, except for staying in Plenty.

The thought had Grant in motion once more. He'd loved this man with everything in him and Remi had ended it, shut the door on them before they'd had a chance and he was damn mad about it, and it was time Remi found out.

"Don't call me that."

"Stop it."

"Stop what?"

"Fightin' me. Fightin' us." Grant made a line in the air with a hand, the gesture sharp and quick, just like the hurt he'd felt every time Remi turned his back on him. "I'm sick and tired of the bullshit."

Remi began to shake his head but Grant continued on cutting him off and this time it was Remi back pedaling until his back hit the glass of the greenhouse wall. "I don-_"

"Stop it, sweetheart." Grant leaned in, voice rugged and rough. "You know what I mean. You hurt me. *You hurt us.* Why? Why do you keep doing it?"

Remi blinked, his normally cold eyes suddenly going soft before he was blinking back tears and moving to look away from Grant, but he was done with Remi Wilson not looking at him.

"Look at me," he ordered. Remi's eyes snapped back to his face in an instant. "I'm mad as hell, Remi."

The other man's handsome features twisted in pain and he sucked in a ragged breath. "I know."

"I still love your sorry ass," Grant told him.

"I know."

"Tell me what else you know?"

"I know that I still love you too."

Grant leaned back then truly surprised at the confession, but the anger that had been awakened in him showed no signs of abating and he crossed his arms over his bare chest and leveled a look at Remi that said that those words weren't enough. Not by a mile.

"I'm sorry," Remi continued on, voice catching and Grant raised an eyebrow at him.

"Show me, sweetheart. Show me how fucking sorry you are because I'm real," he rubbed his bottom lip with a thumb and made sure to do it nice and slow remembering how Remi had liked his mouth. "Real damn mad."

Remi swallowed hard, eyes tracking the movement,

and then he was moving, sinking to his knees in the soft dirt beneath them. The area was a clear space in the business of Grant's greenhouse. It was normally used for outgoing orders but he hadn't quite gotten around to that this week and he'd never been more glad for the open space.

Remi looked up at him then and Grant swore. "Say it again," he managed while Remi reached for his belt buckle.

"I'm sorry," Remi breathed out yanking his belt free and working on his jeans with eager fingers. "I love you. I'm so fucking sorry. You left, and it killed me. I've been so angry, and I just-just need your hands on me so much that I can't stand it--"

Grant bent low, catching the man's mouth with his own and stealing his words. He kissed Remi with the kind of need that only the seasoning of years apart and aching could give. Their mouths moved together, lips and teeth clashing as they relearned how to breathe as one, how to move together, but Grant had always been a quick study and it appeared Remi was as well. They were just that way together and a shared moan passed between the once lovers, their kiss transforming until it was the only thing Grant cared about.

The world could fall down around them and he wouldn't care. Not if he could keep Remi Wilson with him, kissing him like this and touching him as he was. God it was perfect. They separated with a shuddering gasp, both men's breath coming short as they did so and there were no words, not right now.

They broke apart, Grant standing as Remi pulled

Grant's jeans and pants down, the garments catching at Grant's knees but there wasn't time to step out of them, not when he needed the other man as he did. He gasped when Remi's hands found his balls, fingers fondling them gently as he began to stroke his dick with ever increasing strokes.

"Fucking hell," Grant breathed, his head lolling back and he reached out, putting a hand on the wall behind Remi. He opened his eyes then, when Remi moved close, his tongue circling the head of Grant's cock before he took the head of it into his mouth with an eager moan.

"That's it, sweetheart," Grant encouraged him. It hadn't been like this with anyone, not since he'd left Plenty and now with his cock in Remi's mouth it was like coming home. His hips moved then thrusting forward into Remi's mouth as his free hand caught in his hair. He wrapped the length of it in his fist urging the other man forward and the only way to describe the sound from Remi at that was *licentious*.

He was loving it. Always had loved making Grant weak-kneed, still did.

He gasped as Remi began to suck and bob his head in earnest, his mouth hot and welcoming as he brought Grant closer to the edge. He swore and tried to focus on the rain still falling outside but the truth was that he wasn't going to last much longer. Not when the man he loved was on his knees working him over, not when it had been a long dry spell for Grant. With anyone else he could manage it, but Remi? Remi was pure magic and he felt the familiar tightening of his balls signaling that he was about to crash right over the edge and lose it entirely.

"I'm gonna cum, sweetheart," he bit out, breath short now and he leaned forward, his hand balling into a fist on the cool glass in front of him. "You gotta stop--" his voice cut off when Remi began to suck him off with even more energy. He looked down, and saw Remi looking up at him with a gleam in his eye. He knew exactly what he was doing, wanted to do in fact if the messy sounds he was making were any indication; the wet sound of his mouth on Grant's dick, the way he was practically smirking around said dick with his long pretty hair wet and stuck to his face, and god, his free hand cradling Grant's ass, fingers sliding between the cleft of his ass and a seeking finger pressing against him in the way he knew drove Grant crazy, all of that---well that was when he came undone.

"Remi!" Grant came with a shout head, falling back, back bowing as he shot his release into Remi's eager mouth. And that mouth swallowed every last drop of it, and if he could have passed out he might have, except that now he had Remi back and that kept him standing and as lucid as he could manage.

He opened his eyes and Remi had only just pulled off his dick when he dropped to his knees in the dirt with Remi. Who gave a shit about mud and dirt in places it might not be the best to have? He'd willingly scrub dirt from every inch of himself so long as he could keep looking at Remi, keep touching him, keep telling him how he loved him.

"I still love you," Grant breathed again, hands cradling Remi's face and he kissed him again but this time it was gentle. Remi wrapped his arms around Grant and kissed him back, his hands were trembling as the touched Grant and he could feel the reverence in his touch. It broke Grant's heart and filled it all at once.

"God, I love you. Never stopped," Remi breathed, pulling back to look at him, and the look the men shared was one of wonder and awe. They laughed then, quiet in the roar of the storm still going on outside of glass walls of the greenhouse. Whatever happened out there was the world's, and in here?

In here they had forever.

They had each other. Their arms went tight around the other and they kissed again, their kiss, this kiss the first of so many to come, was kind and loving, slow in its promise that he'd never forgotten the shape of Remi's mouth or what it had been like for them, careful in its promise of tomorrow and that he never would let him go again.

ABOUT THE AUTHOR

REBEL CARTER

Rebel Carter loves love. So much in fact that she decided to write the love stories she desperately wanted to read. A book by Rebel means diverse characters, sexy banter, a real big helping of steamy scenes, and, of course, a whole lotta heart.

Rebel lives in Colorado, makes a mean espresso, and is hell-bent on filling your bookcase with as many romance stories as humanly possible!

More Books by Rebel Carter

Heart and Hand: Gold Sky Historical Series Book 1

New Girl in Town: Older Woman Younger Man Romance

Love and Gravity

ABOUT THE BED HIERARCHY

One innocent night can change the course of a life. Theo discovered this first hand when Olive Buchanan came into his world for less than twenty four hours. Six years later, he still can't get over the memory of her. That's the only reason he's agreed to attend the Buchanan family's annual vacation; to prove that his best friend's little sister is not the perfect woman his mind has made her out to be.

HE HAS ONE WEEK TO PUT ASIDE THIS SECRET OBSESSION and move on. A task that is suddenly difficult when he finds himself getting closer to her every night...

THE BED HIERARCHY

LAUREN CONNOLLY

MONDAY

This will be the final page in a chapter of my life.

Her chapter.

It was rude of her, to only make one appearance in the beginning. But things will tie off to a nice end when I see her this time. This infatuation will cease, and my life will move on.

I pull into the driveway of a house painted an odd shade of purple. The lilac fits in though, one in a line of colorful houses stretching along the beachfront.

Thick, salty air coats my skin as I step out of my car. Living in Raleigh, North Carolina, humidity is nothing new. But here on the coast, the ocean waves season the wind.

"Theo is here!"

Glancing up at the shout, I spot Melony Buchanan on the second-floor deck, a phone to her ear, hand over the receiver. There's one more floor above her, this house towering high over the dunes. The woman waves down at me, and a second later a familiar head peaks over the top railing.

"You made it! Just in time for crabs." Tim Buchanan, a man I share too many embarrassing college memories with, grins down at me. The siblings' faces are strikingly similar from this angle. Round cheeks, sharp noses, wide mouths made for smiling.

Just like their sister.

"Crabs sound great!" I shout up at him, heading for the stairs.

The heat of the day has begun to fade along with the setting sun, which takes away the excuse for my sweaty palms.

You've built her up in your memory. She's just an ordinary girl.

The pep talk doesn't help as I climb up to the first deck, where I give Melony a wave, and then the second deck, where I give Tim a hug.

"Thanks for inviting me. You sure I'm not crashing?"

"No way!" He pats my back before letting me go and heading for the sliding glass doors. "The Buchanan family vacation is open to friends. Has been since we were teenagers and mom and dad got tired of entertaining us. Come on, let me grab you a beer. How was the drive?"

A shiver runs through me as I step from ocean humidity into cool AC. With a reverse floor plan, the house boasts an open kitchen/living room combo that covers almost the entire top floor. On the far wall is another set of doors, plus a string of windows that reveal the Atlantic Ocean.

"Not bad," I murmur, my eyes trailing over the shadowy heads on the other side of the glass.

An icy bottle presses into my hand, and I glance down to see Tim handed me a wheat beer. "Thanks, man."

He points to the ocean-side doors. "Go say hi. Just need to finish up with this."

Clearly, my friend is in charge of dinner for the night. He grabs an oven mitt and proceeds to pull a tray of cornbread from the oven.

The first summer after I met Tim, our freshman year at UNC, I heard about the annual Buchanan family vacation. Every August, Mrs. and Mr. Buchanan find an interesting spot somewhere in the United States and rent a house large enough for them and their kids. They covered the cost, but their offspring got kitchen duty for the week to pay their way. I wonder if I'll get assigned a dinner. Hopefully everyone likes grilled cheeses.

After a bracing breath, I step out onto the deck and into a gathering.

Immediately, my attention strays to the woman on the porch swing.

Olive Buchanan.

She sways her seat and licks salt off the rim of her mixed drink. Mocha brown eyes meet mine, crinkling at the corners with her wide grin.

"Theo Phillips," she greets me. "You've finally jumped into our pool of sharks."

"We are not sharks!" Mrs. Buchanan announces, standing from her lounge chair and approaching me with arms wide for a hug. "Don't listen to Olive. We are a pod of friendly dolphins."

I chuckle, enjoying the tight way the woman squeezes me, like I'm a child of hers returned to the fold. She and her husband have stayed at my place in Raleigh a handful of times. Tim's dad shakes my hand, not bothering to lower his beer from his lips as he does.

I've been warned the Buchanan parents take their vacation drinking seriously, and that I should expect a week full of tipsiness.

The next few minutes involve greeting Tim's fiancée Caroline, and meeting Melony's wife Diana, and three-year-old son Mason. Tim's lab, Cooper, approaches me with a wagging tail and lolling tongue. After introductions, I end up leaning on the railing, sipping my beer, and listening to the family discuss the merits of beach versus mountains. Apparently, last year the vacation house was in Wyoming.

"Olive, why don't you show Theo his room? So he can get settled before dinner."

"You mean so he knows where to stumble to after you ply him with your skinny-dipping sangria?" The young woman responds, smirking when her mother only shrugs with an innocent smile.

Skinny-dipping sangria?

I don't have time to ponder what that drink might entail, because the next moment, Olive's warm, strong hand has hold of my wrist, and I'm being led inside.

"Where are you going? Dinner's almost ready!" Tim yells after us as his little sister pulls me toward a set of stairs.

"Keep your pants on. Just showing Theo our room."

Our room?

Down one level, we come to a closed door. "This has to stay shut at all times. Jezebel and Cooper don't mix."

"Jezebel?"

Instead of answering, Olive opens the door and pushes me through, revealing another flight of stairs. The ground level of the house lacks the open flow of the top floor. We walk down a short hallway, passing a bathroom, before entering a room with two beds.

"Welcome to the bottom of the bed hierarchy." Olive gestures with her half empty glass to the small space.

"The what?"

There's an open suitcase full of women's clothes on the floor and rumpled covers on the larger of the two beds.

This can't be happening.

What's the big deal? You're ending her chapter, remember? A mocking voice in my head throws the words back at me.

"The bed hierarchy," Olive explains, oblivious to my inner panic. "If you're going to attend Buchanan family vacations, you better memorize it." She sits with a bounce on the big mattress, the movement dislodging a few strands of hair from her messy bun. The dark curls brush her cheeks, framing intelligent eyes that watch me as I stand in the middle of the room. "It's undeniable that every rental has better bedrooms than others. That's why you want to reach as close as you can to the top of the hierarchy." Olive holds a hand high above her head. "Number one, Mom and Dad, a.k.a., the wallet. They're paying, they get first choice."

I sit across from her, trying not to stare at her toned, tanned legs.

Her hand drops an inch lower. "Tier two, infant. You have a newborn; you get a good room. Tier three, pregnant. Big belly, big bed." Olive pats her flat stomach and takes an over-exaggerated swallow of her alcoholic beverage.

"What comes next?" I ask, fascinated despite my apprehension.

"Next is couple with young kids. So that's where Melony, Diana, and Mason fall. Then you have couples, Tim and Caroline. Next is single with a pet." Olive tilts a thumb at herself. "Last is single. Or, at least, didn't bring a partner with them." She points to me.

"I'm single." The words are out before I consider why I felt the need to share my relationship status. "What about guests?" My last hope I'll find my way into a room without this woman sleeping feet away from me.

She snorts. "That's not a category. You fall where you fall. And you, Theo Philips, are under me."

If only.

I shake my head at the thought then flinch at a strange yowling noise.

"What was that?"

"That's Jezebel." Olive tilts her head, and I follow her gaze.

Framed in the doorway is a grey-striped cat with a snaggletooth.

"Is she winking at me?"

"Nah. She's only got one eye. She came like that, so it's not my fault." The Buchanan tilts the rest of her drink back, smacks her lips, and climbs from the bed. "Dinner time. Let's go before Tim starts whining."

I follow, giving the slightly demonic-looking cat a wide berth. Another threatening yowl follows us up the stairs.

The rest of the evening is full of delicious food, loving bickering, a borderline violent bout of charades, and bottomless cocktails that take all the adults past midnight.

And, all throughout, my attention returns to Olive.

My eyes track her movements. My ears seek out her voice. When she laughs, I find myself smiling along with her.

When everyone heads to bed, I trail behind her. After finishing in the bathroom, I return to our room to discover Olive propped in her bed, lamp lit, book perched on her folded knees.

Attempting to keep my eyes to myself, I focus on the twin bed left to me. Only, there's something sprawled across it. Or someone.

Jezebel has apparently decided she is above me on the bed hierarchy. When I reach a hand out to shoo her off, the entire room fills with her menacing growl.

Hands up, I turn to Olive. "Mind removing your cat?"

The woman uses her finger as a bookmark, then glances between the animal and me, grimacing all the while.

"Sorry. *I'm* not even brave enough to mess with her once she's claimed a sleeping spot."

"Are you serious?"

"Well, there's her claws. And fangs. And admirable commitment to lifelong vendettas. I like you, Theo. But I'm not sure you're worth it." Olive opens her book back up. "Maybe try the couch?"

I'm torn between annoyance and laughter. Be careful what you wish for and all that.

Problem is, when I climb the stairs again, pillow under my arm, I discover Mr. Buchanan passed out on the only couch long enough to accommodate me. His snores rattle the entire top floor.

"How is it that the guy on the top of the hierarchy is sleeping on the couch?" I demand of Olive when I walk back into our shared room.

Tossing her book aside, she chuckles. "Oh yeah. I forgot the bottom most tier. Snoring. Puts you below singles."

"Guess I'm taking the floor then." I eye the hardwood unenthusiastically.

A sigh draws my attention back to Olive. She scoots over, pulling back the covers.

"Come on, Mr. Bottom of the Rung. This bed is plenty big enough to share." Her hand pats the mattress.

This is ... not good.

Or is it exactly what I need?

Sleep next to Olive Buchanan. I'll wake up in the morning beside a grouchy, sleep-mussed version of her.

And then my six-year-long crush will be gone.

Right?

"Quit hovering. I'm tired. And I don't mind. I mean, it's not like it's the first time we've slept together, right?"

TUESDAY

WAKING UP WITH A HARD-ON IS NORMAL. HAVING IT pressed against something warm is not.

Blinking the sleep from my eyes, I glance down and realize that while I stayed on my designated side of the bed, Olive shifted during the night. Not only that, my bed mate has slung a leg over my hips. A bare calf brushes my erection.

Fuck.

Other than her sleepy attempt to straddle me, Olive has kept the rest of her body to herself. She has her pillow in a bear hug, clutching the thing to her chest as if scared it might decide to leave her once she's unconscious.

Any hope I had that a sleep-mussed version of this woman would dampen my obsession is obliterated.

Olive is adorable. And sexy.

Her tank top is gifting me with a decent amount of side boob.

Or, more accurately, torturing me.

This isn't a cure from her. This is just showing me more of what I've missed all these years.

And the chapter continues.

Most people would think I'm mad from the way my mind has fixated on her. But when she came into my life it was like a comet crashing to Earth. She forever altered my topography.

Six years have passed, but the memories never faded.

First week of the semester, junior year, Tim informed me his sister was coming to visit. Her summer break extended a few days longer than ours, and she was looking for a final rager before returning to her rigorous nursing program in Delaware.

When the young woman appeared, she was all tan skin, silky black hair, and mischievous smiles. I didn't know whether to curse at Tim for not inviting her sooner, or growl at him for not warning me to brace myself. The idiot probably didn't even realize how attractive she was.

But my friend definitely knew how fun she was. We spent the day exploring and eating barbecue. Then we spent the night finding the best parties. Tim's girlfriend at the time showed up and stole his attention, leaving me on Olive duty. Not that I minded. At one point, the two of us were on a ten game winning streak, our duo dominating the beer pong table.

We probably would've gone longer if the cops hadn't showed up.

With Tim missing in action, I snuck Olive out of the house using a tiny bathroom window my shoulders could barely wedge through. We sprinted down side streets, navigating back to my apartment where we collapsed in the entryway, gasping and laughing.

Olive spent the night at my place after getting a text from her brother that he was safe and she should stay put. We watched reruns of *The Office* on my laptop and talked until 3 AM. Maybe it was the feeling of us being partners in crime, or the remaining buzz from cheap beers, or something as simple as Olive's disarming smile.

But that night I told her things I hadn't even told Tim. Like how I wasn't the one to choose biology for my major, that my dad did because he wanted me to go on to medical school. I admitted how that future terrified me, but I couldn't see a way out of it. Our conversation echoes in my mind as I watch her sleeping face.

"How often do you talk to your dad?"

"Maybe every other week."

"How long do you talk for?"

"Half hour or so."

"An hour a month," she murmured. Then nodded her head. *"Twelve hours a year."* Olive met my eyes then, her gaze no longer fogged by alcohol. *"Give him that. Hell, be generous and give him a few full days of visits. But the rest of the days? The three hundred some a year you live without him around? Claim them. Do what you want with them. Because those are yours, Theo. Your hours. Your days. Your life. Not his."*

Soon after speaking those profound words, Olive dozed off, and I followed. I woke up the next morning to an empty bed and a note.

Thank you for sharing some of your hours with me. -O

She was gone.

Already driving back to Delaware. Back to her real life. No doubt completely unaware of how she had changed mine.

I switched my majors, took on different classes, had the worst fight with my dad I've ever experienced, over the phone. He cut me off, refused to pay for classes to earn what he referred to as a ridiculous and useless major. So I took on two jobs, giving up my free time to earn enough money to finish with a degree I actually wanted.

And sure, I might not make as much money as a video editor as I would have as a surgeon, but I also don't live in a continuous depressive state because I hate my job.

Surprisingly, my choice actually brought Tim and I closer together. A lot of the people who called themselves my friends drifted away when I couldn't go to their keggers or bar crawls. But Tim made sure to eat regularly at the restaurant where I waited tables. He'd join me for late night study sessions at the library. When money was tight, he'd swipe me into the dining hall.

Tim showed me what true friendship was. Which made the fact that I secretly fantasized about his sister awkward. For me at least. I never told him how her visit was the catalyst for the upset in my life. How I wanted to thank her for it. How I wish I had gotten the chance to wake up with her the next morning.

Would her leg have rested across my stomach like it does now?

In the way her limb had laid claim to me during the night, my hand also decided to settle on her calf. Unconsciously holding her in place.

Olive Buchanan clearly still holds sway over me. Coming here was a mistake.

Trying not to wake her, I slide out of the bed, feeling a combination of triumph and disappointment when I'm able to complete the maneuver without my hardness brushing her again.

Instead of using my time in the bathroom to give my dick what it wants, I turn on the shower, twisting only the cold nozzle. Touching myself to thoughts of Olive would be giving my brain permission to keep fantasizing about her.

I need an Olive exorcism.

The best I can do is a freezing shock to my system, then a long run along the beach.

The sun shades the morning sky with vivid oranges and pinks, and I try to focus on those colors rather than the black of a certain woman's hair, and the cinnamon tint of her skin.

"Sleep well?" Tim asks from his spot beside the coffee maker when I get back to the house.

"Yeah." *Too well*.

The Buchanans don't have any kind of formal breakfast, everyone wandering out of their bedrooms at different times to scrounge through the kitchen. Even three-year-old Mason grabs himself an apple juice from the fridge while his mom pours the two of them bowls of cereal.

After scrambling myself some eggs and successfully not burning my toast, I settle at a table in the corner with my laptop.

I'm immersed in editing a client's video interview for their documentary, when there's a subtle shift in the air of the room. Without moving my head, I glance to the side and spot a shapely figure clad only in a bathing suit, reaching for a bowl on the top shelf of a cabinet.

Olive is awake.

I can't avert my eyes fast enough. The swimwear isn't even that provocative. The practical cut looks like something a lifeguard might wear. But it reveals more of her body than I ever expected to see.

Less than my inappropriate fantasies hoped for, though.

Silently cursing at myself, I force my focus back to the half-edited video. But my concentration is broken a minute later when the Olive settles across the table from me.

For a few minutes, she loudly eats her cereal, staring at me while I try to ignore her.

I'm being rude in the pursuit of self-preservation. But if I thought my silence would bore her and send her away, I was naive.

With a clatter, she sets her empty bowl down on the table.

"What are you doing, Theodore Phillips?"

The use of my full name is strange enough to have me sliding off my headphones and meeting her eyes. Bad idea. Her noir gaze is easy to get lost in.

"Editing a video."

"You're working?"

I nod.

Olive sighs dramatically, leaning toward me across the table. The move puts her cleavage on distracting display. "Do I need to define the word *vacation* for you?"

I bite the inside of my cheek, but it's not enough to fight off my smile.

Olive grins back at me. "Okay. Here's the deal. I'm going down to the beach. You have a half hour to finish up whatever you're working on and join me."

"What happens if I take longer?"

The woman stands and circles the table, coming to a stop beside me. Suddenly, I realize we're alone, the other Buchanans having wandered off.

The tangle of fingers in my hair focuses my entire attention back on Olive. She tugs on the strands, tilting my head back until we're staring at each other.

"Thirty minutes, Theo. Or else I'm coming up here, dripping wet"—

I'm glad my lap is hidden by the table so she doesn't see how rock hard I am.

—"and I will drench your laptop in salt water."

"That's cruel." My voice rasps, and I'm not sure if I'm talking about her threat against my computer, or the erotic way she's delivering said threat.

"I take self-care seriously. See you in a bit." Then, so quick I almost doubt it happened, she presses her soft lips against my forehead.

In the next moment she's across the room, rinsing her bowl in the sink, while I'm a maelstrom of lust and need.

Olive doesn't linger, grabbing a beach towel and sun glasses before disappearing down the stairs. Just as she moves out of sight, I hear her final warning.

"Countdown begins now!"

WEDNESDAY

BEFORE THE BUCHANAN FAMILY VACATION, I'VE NEVER understood the appeal of a sex dungeon.

Who wants to get tortured in the name of sexual pleasure?

But that's basically what these past couple days have been. Only, without release at the end.

Yesterday, I made it to the beach before Olive fulfilled her threat. When I dropped my folding chair next to Tim's, I glanced at the ocean just in time to watch his sister walking out of the water.

Every inch of her skin glistened. Wet hair stuck to the curves of her neck and top of her chest.

Pure, visual, torment.

As she crossed the sand toward me, or more accurately toward her family, I couldn't help staring. And I wondered how I ever deluded myself into thinking spending more time with her would cure me of this wanting.

The rest of the day involved me making regular trips into the waves to cool down the response below my waist. The frequency was a consequence not only of Olive's almost bare body, but also the sound of her laughter, and the eager way she related stories of her work in an ER in Chicago. Olive's intelligence turned me on just as much as her generous ass did.

As the sun sank below the horizon, Melony cooked burgers on a grill in the driveway as the rest of us played cornhole and drank Mrs. Buchanan's different cocktail experiments. Eventually, my worries faded to the back of my mind. I existed in a hazy cloud of booze-induced happiness.

Until bedtime. Jezebel once again staked her claim, and Olive made the same offer with a smirk and a pat of her mattress. I gave in even easier than the first night.

That morning I woke, finding myself in painful arousal and my years-long crush half straddling me in her unconsciousness.

And just like the previous morning, I slunk out for an icy shower and muscle-exhausting run.

Not sure how much longer I'd be able to hide my dick's reaction to her teasing and playful threats, I made sure not to pull out my laptop. Instead, I walked down to the beach with Tim and Caroline before Olive even made it upstairs.

She joined us an hour later, and the delicious torture of her presence recommenced.

Eventually, I had to escape, worried I'd do something stupid like confess my obsession in front of her entire family. While she went for a quick dive in the waves, I returned to the house and borrowed a bike. As I rode for miles, cicadas sang a constant song, while the sun beat down on my shoulders, the heat of it almost unbearable.

And as I pedal back up the driveway, I realize that all the excursion did was fill me with regret.

The hours I spent avoiding Olive are ones I'll never get back.

At the end of the week, we'll go our separate ways. Another six years might pass before I get to see her again. Maybe even longer.

My chest tightens, and I find myself jogging up the outer stairs, hoping that the setting sun means she'll be back at the house.

I'm in luck. Pulling open the sliding glass door, I spot her in the dining area with Tim's fiancée.

"What do you think?" Olive asks.

"I don't know. Can't you use any table?" Caroline responds.

Olive's finger taps against her lip as she ponders whatever the two women are discussing. Her eyes land on me, and she gives a little wave. "Come here, Theodore. I need your opinion."

No one calls me Theodore other than Olive. She doesn't even use it consistently, but I think I'm picking up on her pattern. The youngest Buchanan likes to be overly formal when she's poking fun at someone. Which is why the moment she calls her brother 'Timothy' we can all expect a round of verbal sparring.

Whatever joke I'm about to be the butt of, I don't even try to avoid. She beckons me, I come. Running away didn't work. Maybe I should stop fighting so hard and just let myself absorb the happiness of being around her.

It's worth a try.

"Yes, Oliviadore?" I respond, reaching her side.

She chokes on the next word she was about to speak, clearly thrown off by the nickname. Then I'm hit with a grin so joyful I have to stifle a groan.

This is what I get for playing along with her. More fuel for my pining.

Recovering from her surprise, the tempting woman mutes her smile and speaks in an even more formal tone. "I was just hoping to get your opinion on this table, Theodorenessa."

Gauntlet thrown.

I pick it up.

"What about the table, Oliviadorella?"

Melony comes in from the porch with her son, joining Caroline where she stands, watching our back-and-forth with wide eyes.

Teeth pinch Olive's bottom lip as she clears her throat. Then, "I was hoping to put the championship team back together and have a beer pong tournament tonight. Do you think the dining room table will serve, Theodorenessavain?"

Good one.

Making as if I'm examining the surface, I lean down, eye level with the table top, fighting as hard as I can against laughing. "I'm not sure it'll count as an official tournament, with these dimensions so far out of regulation. But it'll have to do ..." I let my sentence trail off.

Just as she begins to raise her fist in victory, I finish.

"Oliviadorellamare."

"Oh no," Melony whispers, her voice low with mock horror as she clutches her young son against her chest. "Tim! Come quick! Olive broke your friend!"

"What did she do?" Tim asks as he climbs the stairs into the room, Cooper on his heels.

Even with his appearance, I can't wipe away my goofy grin.

"Nothing!" Olive declares. "My partner and I were just strategizing our beer pong reunion. That is, if any of you have the balls to go against us." She bumps her shoulder against mine and wags her eyebrows. "The ping pong balls, that is."

"I've got the biggest ping pong balls y'all've ever seen!" Mrs. Buchanan announces, strolling into the kitchen from her bedroom and toasting the room with her half-empty glass of sangria. The Buchanan parents are the only ones with a bedroom on the top floor.

The literal top of the hierarchy.

"Maybe you don't want to brag about that, dear." Mr. Buchanan adds, following close behind his wife.

The entire room dissolves into laughter.

That evening, Diana takes charge of dinner, making tacos for the lot of us. After food, once Mason is tucked into bed, the tournament begins.

Six years may have passed, but neither Olive nor I have lost our skills. A big motivator for me is the enthusiastic hug I receive as a reward for every cup made. At 1 AM, Melony and Diana have been knocked out and have retired to bed. Mrs. Buchanan has nodded off on the couch while Mr. Buchanan watches the final round. Olive and I have two cups remaining, but a single red solo stands in front of Tim and Caroline.

"You got this babe," Tim whispers to his fiancée as she aims. An arc of her arm and the ball lands pretty in our front cup. My friend lets out a whoop, sets himself up, aims, then throws a rim shot.

Curses pour from his mouth as his sister cackles evilly beside me.

"Let's put them out of their misery." Olive steps up to the edge of the table. Everyone still awake watches with rapt attention as she lets her ball fly. There's the perfect plop of plastic against beer. She made it.

But we can't celebrate yet.

"Okay, Theo. You got this," her whispers of encouragement tickle over my spine.

What will she do if I make this cup?

Only one way to find out.

Line it up. Let it fly. Watch my best friend's face fall as he realizes he lost to his obnoxious sister.

"You beautiful man!" Olive flings her arms around my neck, pressing a smacking kiss to my cheek. I take advantage of her affection, gripping her waist and holding her against me for one brief, glorious moment.

Then I let her slide away.

Tim and Olive throw good natured barbs at each other

as they clean up the cups. Mr. Buchanan scoops up his wife, carrying her to bed. Caroline and I head down the stairs, she turning off at the second floor, and me continuing on to the first.

The victory, small as it was, has adrenaline trickling through my veins.

Will Olive still be riding the high of it when she comes to bed?

Could the excitement lead somewhere when we're lying next to each other?

All fantasies are side-railed when I reach the bedroom. Jezebel is there.

But she's not in her bed.

The obstinate cat has chosen to curl up on the windowsill, leaving the twin bed free and clear for the guy on the bottom of the hierarchy.

Damn it. I can't lose this.

I glance over my shoulder to make sure I'm alone.

"Here, kitty. Come on. Look at this cozy bed." My hand pats the soft blanket as I plead with the cat.

The only acknowledgement I get is a slow blink.

Olive will be down here any second. Desperation bleeds into my whisper. "Work with me, Jezebel. Don't you want an entire bed to yourself? Doesn't that sound better than a stupid windowsill?"

Not even a muscle twitch.

Footsteps sound on the staircase, and I see my chance to feel Olive's skin against mine slipping away.

And that's how I find myself picking up a demon animal, tossing it onto the bed and shoving my hands into my pockets a second before Olive strolls into the room. A delayed yowl of affront rumbles from the one-eyed cat as she glares at me.

"Did you try to move her again?" Olive asks while rummaging around in her suitcase.

I keep my expression innocent. "That's her bed. I know when I'm beat."

THURSDAY

IN THE DREAM WE TOUCH EACH OTHER.

The scene my mind creates is more than I've ever had with Olive, but still not enough. Everything is a hazy mixture of hands and lips and tongues. There's an edge of pleasure, a precipice I balance on. And just when I'm sure I'm about to dive off the cliff—

I wake up.

Clenched teeth cage the curses I want to mutter at finding myself in the same position as the last two nights.

Hard with a perfect, oblivious woman's leg slung over my hips.

And so, the torture continues.

I'm about to make the same retreat I have every morning when I catch sight of the alarm clock on the bedside table.

3:34 a.m.

Shit.

Too early to be a reasonable time to get up and start the day. Somehow, I have to find a way to fall back asleep. And so I lie still, trying to relax my mind.

In the darkness, my body is intensely aware of the woman sprawled next to me.

My hand rests on her leg, having found the position while I slept. There's a slight prickle against my palm, as if she's gone a day or so without shaving. The texture is somehow more erotic than smooth skin.

She's real.

Yet still unreachable.

Olive's pillow must not be too far from my shoulder because an occasional puff of her warm breath teases me. There's also a slight pressure against my upper arm. Her hand must have found its way to my side of the bed while she slept.

Maybe I should have claimed my bed when the cat abandoned it. Is this almost-intimacy worth the painful knowledge that it isn't real?

A soft touch on my arm has my spine going rigid. My focus hones in upon that one inch of skin, waiting to see if I imagined the sensation.

Then, a second later, it comes again. A light stroke. A small tease of a finger trailing down my bicep.

Is she awake?

Worried I'm deluding myself in the pursuit of my secret longing, I perform my own test. Where my thumb rests on her calf, I draw a simple, yet purposeful circle.

The response is another path drawn with her finger, then a full palm cupping my shoulder.

Olive is awake.

And she's touching me.

I don't know what this means. Logically, the best thing

to do is ask. But I'm suddenly terrified that if I speak a word, whatever spell we're under will break.

This is some kind of chance, and I don't want to lose it.

So I let my hands speak for me. My grip drags up her calf, pausing to massage the soft skin behind her knee.

Was that a gasp?

The breaths teasing over my skin seem to grow faster.

Then the body at my side shifts. Not away, as I feared. But closer.

A heavy, toned thigh comes to rest on my hips, brushing the top of my erection. Now I'm the one gasping.

Heat builds where our bodies press together, and I can imagine the edges of her sleep shorts riding up. If the lights were on, I might see the rounded curve of her ass. Maybe the material would shift enough for me to glimpse whatever scrap of cotton covers the center of her.

Without sight, all that's left to me is touch.

Taking her move toward me as further invitation, my hand ventures the rest of the way up her leg. Just as I discover where skin and fabric meet, there's a distinct rock of hips. A demand.

Could she want this as much as I do?

Probably not as much, but I'll take what she's willing to give.

Pushing until I find elastic, I use my index finger to follow the path leading in between her legs. The material there is damp. When I press against it, I'm rewarded with another rocking of her hips.

I take my time, stroking the fabric, giving her every

opportunity to push my hand away. Then, suddenly, she moves, and I feel soft mounds press into my shoulder as hands wrap around my unoccupied arm. Demanding nails dig into my skin.

This could be so many things. A beginning to something serious, or a quick fling at the beach with the closest warm body. Either way, it's still Olive, and I can't imagine giving up this chance to explore the secret parts of her.

Hooking my finger, I tug her panties to the side. Slick, wet heat tears a low groan from my throat. The first definitive sound in our quiet bedroom.

That is until I stroke the tight bundle of nerves at the top of her slit.

"Theo," she moans my name against my neck, where she's tucked her head.

Hell.

How long have I fantasized about that? About this?

In the darkness, I stroke Olive Buchanan, savoring every gasp and whimper, cataloging the shape of her body where it presses against mine, memorizing the smell of sweat and arousal.

There's movement, a tugging at the waistband of my shorts, and the next moment I'm on the verge of spending because her firm hand grasps the hard length I've tried to ignore this whole trip.

So much denied pleasure has my balls tightening.

Needing to feel this woman come apart before I lose my mind to passion, I sink one, and then two fingers into her pussy.

There's a cry followed by a wet swipe of a tongue on my neck.

With a thumb on her clit, I curl the fingers buried inside her, stroking her soft inner walls.

Before, Olive's body rocked against mine in an invitation. Under my ministrations she writhes in an uncontrolled demand. All the while her skilled hand works up and down my cock, using the drops of my precum to lubricate the motion.

"Close," she whispers before scraping her teeth along the taught muscle in my neck. The delicious pain has my hips jerking, my spine bowing off the bed.

Knowing I'm seconds away, I slip a third finger into her. She cries out, and I feel the orgasm pulse through her, the muscles inside her squeezing my hand.

The sensation is so erotic, it does me in.

"Olive," I groan her name, the longing in my voice turning the word into a confession delivered in the darkness. Pleasure spikes from the base of my spine, coursing up my dick. Wetness spurts from the tip of me, as her hand slides away.

We both lay panting, our breaths filling the small bedroom. At some point, hers slow and grow even. I sense she's fallen back to sleep, our escapade pairing with the early hour to bring on exhaustion.

Feeling my own lids grow heavy, I take a moment to pull her underwear back into place and shuck off my shirt where most of my cum landed.

Our actions and the darkness making me bold. I pull Olive against my chest.

~

WHEN I WAKE UP, I'M ALONE.

Memories return immediately, and my dick responds.

But my mind shuts the reaction down because there's no delicious warm body next to me.

Did she regret it?

Did she have fun, but only want to do it once?

A glance at the clock helps ease some nerves. I slept in. It's an hour later than I normally get up. Olive probably just woke up before me and wanted to start the day.

This is what I tell myself in the shower and as I walk up the stairs. But any hope I have of getting answers is dashed when I find the entire Buchanan clan gathered in the kitchen and dining area.

"Morning, man." Tim slaps me on the back as he walks by. The friendly gesture sends a spike of guilt through me. He has no idea what I was doing with his sister just a few hours ago. "Grab some eggs off the stove. I made too many."

"Thanks," I mumble.

After scooping a helping of scrambled eggs onto a plate, I slip into a seat across the table from Olive. She smiles at me over her cereal bowl.

I want to take that as a good sign. Problem is, her expression looks completely normal. It's the same sweet and saucy smile she gives me every morning.

What is she thinking?

"Well, it's been fun!" Diana announces, dropping her plate in the sink before wandering around the room to hug everyone.

"You're leaving?" I ask, surprised.

The rental goes until Saturday morning. At least, that's what I remember Tim saying.

Is today the last day? Was that my last night with Olive?

"Yeah. We've got a longer drive, and I have to be in the office tomorrow for a meeting," Melony explains, gathering up toys that Mason has scattered around the living area.

Relief filters through my chest, but it's smothered almost immediately.

"Bet you're both looking forward to having your own rooms for the last couple of nights." Mrs. Buchanan smiles as me over her mimosa, as if she didn't just punch my stomach with her words.

"Huh?" Is all I can manage.

"Olive moves up the hierarchy," Caroline explains while stirring sugar into her coffee.

I glance across the table at the youngest Buchanan, trying to keep all emotion off my face.

"My stuff is already in the basement room," Olive states before spooning cereal into her mouth.

The tightness in my chest eases a fraction.

"Don't be lazy, baby girl." Mr. Buchanan scolds his daughter. "Probably wouldn't take more than fifteen minutes to shift everything. I'm sure Theo would appreciate moving to a bigger bed."

My head ducks before the room can see how much blood pools in my cheeks. If anyone does glimpse the color change, maybe I can blame it on a sunburn. None of them know I've spent every night in the bigger bed already.

The urge to insist Olive doesn't have to move rises in my throat, but I shove it down.

Who in their right mind would opt for a twin bed in a shared room when they could have space all to themselves? No doubt what we did early this morning would be written across my face if I tried arguing.

Out of the corner of my eye, I catch Olive's head tilt. Still trying not to telegraph to the Buchanan family that I know what their baby girl sounds like when she comes, I keep my gaze on my breakfast.

"Sure. Guess I should claim the honor while I can," Olive murmurs.

There's no distinct emotion in her voice that I can discern. Not disappointment. Not relief.

She sounds … neutral.

The next forkful of eggs I swallow is as tasteless as rubber.

A BED WITHOUT OLIVE IS USELESS.

Three nights was all it took to turn me into an addict, and now I can't sleep without the weight of her limbs on me. I want her to press me into the bed with her body.

Without her, I'm unmoored, shifting constantly. Unable to find comfort.

I came here with the hope of freeing myself, only to discover I'm even more lost than before.

"Damn it," I mutter, throwing my blankets off. Standing from the bed, I pace to the door, wondering if a midnight run on the beach might help me clear my mind. If not, maybe it'll exhaust me enough to go to sleep.

Problem is, when I step out into the hallway, I find my way blocked.

In the glow of a nightlight plugged into the wall, she stands a foot away, hair tangled over her shoulders, clothes wrinkled, eyes wide at my appearance.

"Olive? What are you doing here?"

For a moment her gaze traces over me, and I realize I'm shirtless for the first night since arriving. When we shared a room, I thought it might make her uncomfortable. But from the way she devours me with her eyes, I'm wishing I'd tried this earlier.

Instead of answering my question, Olive asks her own.

"Do you want your own room?"

"Hell no," I mutter before thinking it through.

But her wide grin keeps me from regretting my answer.

"Me neither," she admits.

Then her hand raises, displaying a small item pinched between her fingers.

A condom.

The curve of her brow is a silent question.

"Hell yes," I growl, grabbing her up with arms around her waist.

We fall onto the bed together, bouncing as our weight hits the springs. Once we settle, her stare connects with mine. We stay still like that, no words exchanged.

I know the sounds she makes when she comes. I've felt her inner walls grip my fingers.

But I've never kissed Olive Buchanan.

Six years, and I've never known how she tastes.

I dip my chin, finding her lips with mine. She doesn't need coaxing. In fact, I maintain control for a second at most. Then I'm on my back, her hot thighs bracketing my hips, her hands pressing my shoulders into the bed.

Olive dominates me. Her frenzied attack makes me hard.

She came here to fuck me, and I'm ready to get fucked.

Does this encounter mean anything more than two bodies joining together?

Maybe if she didn't sit up to pull off her top, exposing her bare breasts, I might have asked for a pause so we could talk.

But the time for conversations is done when her softness presses against my chest. This time when our mouths meet, our tongues stroke together. The taste of her is heady, and I suck on her lower lip eagerly.

She smells like sweat and sunscreen. Our bodies writhe until the last scraps of clothes get kicked off.

Every bit of my skin begs to be touched by her, but no area more than the hard length jutting from my hips. I stroke my hand over her ass, finding her core, groaning at the way my fingers slip in her arousal.

Olive breaks away and leans back. That's when I realize she's still holding the condom. Moving with hurried grace, she rips the package open and rolls the protection on me. No hesitation.

"We should've been doing this since night one," she murmurs.

We should've been doing this for years, I'm about to

respond. Only, she chooses that moment to sink down onto my cock, slowly taking each inch of me.

My head turns to the side, teeth sinking into a pillow, all to stifle the guttural moan she elicits with her tight sheath. Thank god we have our own floor.

"Look at me, Theo."

When I do, it's hard not to immediately spill.

Olive is a queen, mounting me like the throne she deserves. Her posture is straight, her tits jutting out proudly, nipples tight with the command to be worshiped.

Muttering curses, I drag my hands up her body, cupping her breasts as I let my thumbs explore the mouth-watering buds. Soon, I'll suck on them. But for the moment, I'm just looking for something to hold onto, to keep me grounded, as she begins to ride me.

The woman I've fantasied about for years gazes down at me, panting breaths tensing her chest as she uses me for her pleasure.

You're using each other, I tell myself.

This is something I wanted, too. To get her out of my head. To move on with my life.

A quick fuck could do that. Get rid of the mystery.

But when Olive tugs on my shoulder, silently asking for me to take the top spot, another shift happens between us.

Now I stare down at her, listening to her whimpers, watching pleasure weighing on her eyelids, all as my hips thrust. Over and over I retreat, then fill her. But I don't feel my obsession fading.

Each moment she watches me claim her, my need only grows.

In a desperate effort to distract Olive from what she'll surely see in my eyes, I snake my hand between us, finding her clit.

"Oh!" She gasps, her legs falling wider, somehow allowing me to go deeper. Then it comes, that amazing clenching of her around me and the satisfied groan from her throat.

I'm on the edge, feeling too much, but confident I've hidden it.

Then her touch trails down my chest, and I meet her eyes as she lets out another gasping word.

"Theo."

A heavy moan, one that speaks of my surrender, accompanies my finish.

Once, twice, a third time I pump into her, trying to focus only on the bite of her nails, and the press of her body to mine.

Not on the pressure in my chest.

If I look at that too closely, let her know what she's done to me, I'm terrified the pleasure will turn to pain.

FRIDAY

THERE'S MORE THAN JUST A LEG DRAPED OVER MY WAIST this morning. As the sun from the cracked curtains spills into the bedroom and pulls me from sleep, I realize there's an entire Olive wrapped around my torso.

We've kicked off the sheets at some point, the heat of our bodies pressed together all that was needed during the summer night.

A delirious haze of happiness just begins to soak my brain when the clomp of heavy footsteps sounds outside the bedroom.

"Wake your lazy ass up, Theo! I need help carrying the kayaks down to the beach."

Fighting off the aroused fog I woke up in, dread sweeps over me as I watch the next few seconds unfold as if they play out in slow motion.

The knob turns, the salt-rusted hinges creak, and as the door shoves open, my best friend steps into the room.

My limbs won't work, shock freezing them in place. Which means I lay sprawled, nude, in the bed, using his naked little sister as a blanket.

Tim's face slides to confusion then sudden, horrified realization.

The sound he makes is some strange combination of a yell and a scream, the volume of it shocking Olive awake. She rolls off of me and straight onto the floor, leaving my half-hard dick on full display. Not to mention, Tim now gets to see his sister's bare front in addition to her ass.

"My eyes!" He yells, slapping his hands over his face and swinging around toward the exit. Only, he misjudges the distance and runs straight into the doorjamb. As he moans in pain, Caroline appears in the doorway.

"Babe? I heard you scream! What—" Her question cuts off when she sees me. Face scorching red, her gaze jumps away, only to find a nude Olive struggling to sit up. "Oh god!"

"What's going on?" A new voice asks.

You've got to be fucking kidding me.

"Let me out of this hell!" Tim yells, still trying to find

the exit with his eyes closed, but his way is blocked by Mrs. Buchanan.

I've just gathered enough of my wits to throw the bed sheet over Olive when a loud bark sounds from the hallway.

"Mom!" Olive shouts. "Did you let Cooper downstairs?"

The answer comes in the form of black bundle of fur weaving through legs, aiming straight for the twin bed Jezebel lounges on. With a shriek, the feline seeks an escape almost as desperately as Tim.

Not finding a clear route out, Jezebel goes up.

Up Tim that is.

Letting out terrified wails as it goes, the one-eyed cat scales the man, using every claw it has to latch onto his scalp.

Mayhem commences.

The next fifteen minutes consist of Olive chasing after her brother, trying to dislodge her pet, all while wearing nothing but a bed sheet. With only a beach towel wrapped around my waist, I follow the family upstairs, feeling useless as the drama continues.

Tim curses, Caroline fights to shove Cooper outside, Olive uses one hand to hold up her toga dress and the other to peel the cat off, and Mrs. Buchanan pours herself and her husband some OJ before adding a liberal amount of vodka to both glasses. The patriarch of the family raised an eyebrow when the parade of insanity reached the top floor, but he's been kind enough to sip his mimosa and not comment on what clearly went on between his daughter and me last night.

"There!" Olive sets Jezebel on the ground, and the cat streaks back downstairs. "Now stop flailing and sit. I need to clean your cuts." She uses a calm commanding voice that probably serves her well in the ER.

"She tried to flay me alive!" Tim wails, flopping down onto the couch.

Olive rolls her eyes at me before hitching her sheet higher and moving to the kitchen sink. As her daughter fills a bowl with soapy water, Mrs. Buchanan sidles up to me, her face slightly flushed. I wonder if the color is from the drama or her morning booze.

"We're all pretty relaxed here, but maybe you want to go put some shorts on?" The woman pats my shoulder with a kind smile.

"Uh. Yeah. Okay."

Fuck. This is not how I planned to do this.

But, to be fair, I had no plan. When Olive showed up at my door, I shut my brain off. No thoughts of consequences or the future.

I just wanted her.

After pulling on some shorts and a T-Shirt, I grab the pajama set I stripped off Olive last night and carry it up the two flights of stairs.

"Here, hold these to the cuts and keep pressure on them. The bleeding should stop in a second." Olive is instructing Caroline when I approach. She gives me a grateful smile when I offer the clothes, taking them from my grasp and heading into the bathroom.

Which leaves me alone with her family.

Suddenly, I feel like all four sets of eyes are boring into me.

Maybe if Olive and I had talked, had figured out exactly what was going on between us, I would be able to meet their stares confidently. I could stand here and say "I'm crazy about her. I want to be with her. What you saw wasn't some fling."

But we didn't talk.

We just fucked.

And if I announce how I feel to her family, only for Olive to come out of the bathroom and brush off the experience, I'm not sure I could pretend to be okay.

So, like a coward, I run.

Literally.

"Going for a jog," I mutter, and sprint down the stairs.

THE MILES THAT DISAPPEAR UNDER MY FEET DON'T HELP. AT one point I wonder if I can run all the way back to Raleigh. That thought doesn't last long.

Even if what comes next hurts, I can't give up any more moments with Olive.

When I get back to the house, most everyone seems to have made themselves scarce. Except for Tim, who lays on the couch with a washcloth over his eyes.

"Your eyes didn't actually burn," I feel the need to point out.

"It soothes me." Tim can be such a drama king when he wants. "You're not my only friend, you know?"

I flinch at his words.

Is he cutting me off?

Tim isn't my only friend either, but he is my closest.

The first I call to talk about big life changes. The one I've stayed connected with no matter how many miles fell between us.

But maybe I should've seen this coming.

"I know," I say, struggling to keep the hurt from my voice.

"But you're the only one she asks about."

For a moment, I wonder if I misheard him.

Is he saying...

"We video chat," he continues when I don't respond. "Pretty much every other week. Just to catch up. She tells me all those gruesome ER stories. I tell her about my job and what Caroline is up to." Tim sighs, sitting up and pulling the washcloth off his eyes to meet mine. Then his gaze flicks toward the ocean view, and I notice a familiar shape out on the deck. "Inevitably, in every single conversation, she'll ask *the* question."

"What question?"

My friend, which I'm pretty sure he still is, smirks. "I don't know if she thinks I'm oblivious or what. I mean, come on. Six years? But she always throws it in like it's an afterthought. Like I won't notice she's asking *again*."

"What question, Tim?" I remind myself it's not good to strangle my friends, even when I really want to.

The guy affects an overly feminine voice and mimes flipping hair over his shoulder. "And how is that buddy of yours, Theo, doing?"

Does North Carolina get earthquakes? Because I think the ground beneath my feet just shifted.

"And you, big idiot that you are, always get this super stupid doe eyed look on your face whenever I mention her. But it still took you *six years* to come on vacation with us? I practically had to arrange our trip in your backyard. Matchmaking is exhausting! Can you just go make an honest woman out of my hellion sister?" He collapses back on the couch, replacing his washcloth. "And learn to lock a fucking door!"

A grin breaks across my face, and I don't hesitate.

The glass door gives a muted swish when I push it open.

And there she is.

Olive Buchanan, woman of my dreams, rocks herself on the porch swing and flips to the next page in her novel, seemingly unaware of my return.

She asked about me. I thought I'd be lucky if she spared me a thought every so often after our one and only meeting.

Turns out, I'm not the only one who couldn't forget that night.

"What would you say," her head pops up as I start to speak, "if I told you I'm planning on buying a plane ticket to Chicago?"

That secretive, enticing smile sneaks across her lips, and I remember the feel of them against my neck.

"Are you going to come visit me, Theodorenessavain?"

"I think I have to, Oliviadorellamare."

She sets aside her book and rises from the swing, sauntering toward me until only an inch separates us. A single finger trails down the front of my sweat-damp shirt, and despite the humid heat of the day, I shiver.

"Well then I guess I'd have to tell you my apartment is

kinda small. And I only have one bed. So you better be ready to share."

Capturing her hand, I bring it to my mouth for a kiss.

"We can make that work."

ONE YEAR LATER

"COME ON, MOM. *TWO* PETS HAS TO BUMP US UP ABOVE *ONE* kid." Olive presses her fists on the heavy wooden table, looming over Mrs Buchanan. The older woman seems more interested in her margarita than her daughter's argument.

"You know the rules."

"Rules change! And might I add, Scoundrel only has the three legs." She waves at the pit bull lounging in a patch of sunlight by the back door. He's found one of the best spots, having a beautiful view of the expansive mountain lake this year's rental butts up against.

I crouch down to scratch behind the ears of the sweet beast Olive and I adopted together two months ago. Jezebel saunters toward us, hisses at Scoundrel, then struts away.

Their friendship is a work in progress.

"Stop whining. I'm on vacation. Theo, come distract my daughter before I make her sleep on the dock."

My fight against a chuckle fails, and I give in to the laughter as I wrap my arms around Olive's waist.

"Theo is my ally, not yours, Mom," she grumps, leaning back into my chest.

Without a conscious thought, my hand sneaks down

to find hers, fingering the sapphire she let me put on her left ring finger the day before we went to the animal shelter.

My little claim. My final acceptance into the Buchanan family.

An announcement to the world that after seven years of pining, Olive Buchanan chose me.

"Top of the hierarchy, or bottom tier," I whisper in her ear. "As long as you're in the bed, I've got the best one in the house."

ABOUT LAUREN CONNOLLY

ABOUT LAUREN CONNOLLY

Lauren Connolly crafts love stories set in the contemporary world. Some are grounded in reality, while others play with the mystical and magical. She works as a librarian in southern Colorado, and she has a furry family that consists of a cocker spaniel who thinks he's a cave dwelling troll and two cats with a mission to raise hell and destroy all curtains. Follow her on social media to receive book updates and cute pet pics.

More Books by Lauren Connolly
   You Only Need One
   Rescue Me (Forget The Past Book 1)
   Remembering A Witch

ABOUT UPLIFT

One TV show, One bed, One moment to treasure...

Anvita Khatri thought she knew everything about manipulating emotions. As a TV producer, her career succeeded based on knowing how to make an audience laugh and cry. But her divorce left her wondering if she knew anything at all. She's determined to take charge of her personal life and stop doubting everything. Homage, her food show, has been wildly successful and her pitch for a new show won over the executives, and it's time to shoot the first episode. Uplift will take struggling small business owners, match them with a mentor, and teach them the skills they need.

Shazza Barnett didn't expect to be widowed at twenty-three. Her husband Shane fell off a ladder while doing roofing. The insurance payout allowed her to buy a small apartment for her and her two small kids. Their roofing business has been floundering since Shane's death. She's had to learn his trade, but it's been hard doing it all herself. When she sees an ad for a new TV show, she figures she may as well have a go, to grow the business. The show is a chance to honour him and get her kids out of poverty. When she meets Anvita, the show's producer, she's overwhelmed with feelings. Feelings she hasn't felt for a long time.

This story is set in the Manjimup region of the south-west corner of Western Australia. We visited here over the summer of 2013/14, and it is a truly beautiful part of the world. The local people of this area are the Nyungar and Murrum people of the Nyoongar nation, and I pay my respects to the Elders past and present. I also acknowledge the Wangal people of the Eora nation, the traditional owners of the land where this story was written.

UPLIFT

RENEE DAHLIA

"You can't be serious?" Anvita clenched her teeth together, held back a curse, and imagined sacking her PA. They'd messed up one time too many. She eased a tight long breath out between pinched lips. Logan tried so hard, and was incredibly diligent, but so often they missed the point of what she wanted them to do.

"I'm terribly sorry. We have only one room booked under your name."

"One room. For myself, my crew, and the contestant we are filming?" Anvita couldn't believe Logan could get this so wrong. Usually their screw ups involved booking flights in the morning instead of the afternoon—am vs pm was tricky—or booking a hotel too far from where she needed to work.

Tomorrow the crew would shoot the first episode of Uplift at the luxury estate owned by the show's celebrity host, Aston Lee. He'd built his business from nothing, and now was going to host Uplift, where he advised small business owners on how to grow and improve their businesses. It was the type of heart-warming show Anvita had always wanted to produce, a way to help people help themselves move upwards. Aston was already at his house in rural Western Australia in the pretty Margaret River region, but he didn't have room for the crew or the contestants. Didn't have room, or didn't want to play host? Either way, the outcome was the same. He'd recommended this hotel. Surely, she'd specified more rooms when she sent Logan the email. She opened her phone.

Logan,
I need a hotel booked for next weekend. We are shooting the
opening scenes for Uplift.
Anvita

Okay...

This was her fault. Logan had been her PA for nearly six months now. She knew they needed details if they were going to do what she wanted, and she'd sent them a rushed email and expected Logan would be able to work out what she meant. Damned silly mistake, and not Logan's fault.

"I'll be needing at least one more room." Anvita had to make it right. She knew why she'd avoided putting her time into this.

Shazza.

The overly bogan name of her first contestant for Uplift had been part of the appeal when she'd read her application because the concept of Uplift was to help small business owners become successful. A bogan name equalled potentially great television. But she hadn't been prepared for meeting her.

Shazza should've been everything that was mediocre; medium height, light brown hair, slightly sun-kissed white skin, and amber brown eyes with tired shadows under them. To complete the picture of Shazza the tradie, her jeans had dirty hand smears across her ass. But Shazza had the perfect shape of a plump woman, with a fat round ass, thick thighs, and large breasts that strained against her work shirt. Anvita shouldn't want to bury her face between those tits until she couldn't breathe. She really shouldn't.

But it was Shazza's smile that really did Anvita in.

Shazza had sauntered into the studio for her interview and grinned at the camera with such joy and hope and a little bit of underlying nervous stress that Anvita had needed to clear her throat before speaking. And so, she'd fobbed the organisation of tonight onto Logan and was now paying the price for her inability to manage their need for clear information. Fuck she missed Molly. Her previous PA had been a law student who'd been brilliant at anticipating what Anvita had needed. The problem with Molly was that she was aspirational and had left as soon as a better opportunity came about. This job was the perfect one for Logan's level of capability. Anvita just had to get better at working with them.

"Sorry, we are fully booked. It's the cherry festival this weekend."

Just her luck. Besides, none of her introspection was going to solve this problem.

"Give me a moment, will you?" Anvita walked out of

the hotel to breath in some fresh air. The hot dry wind blowing from inland dried her eyes and she blinked. A grubby ute turned into the driveway, and parked. Shazza leapt out.

"Anvita. How's it?"

"Yeah, not great."

Shazza frowned. "Oh. Can I help?"

"The hotel is full, and my PA only booked one room."

Shazza shrugged one shoulder. "It's cool. We'll top and tail."

A shiver of desire raced down Anvita's spine. "Um." She coughed. "It's slightly more complicated than that. There's only one room for everyone. The camera crew too."

Shazza screwed up her nose. "Hmm. I suppose the crew could have the room and we'll sleep in the back of my ute. It's not going to rain, and I have a couple of jackets in the back we could use as bedding."

Yeah, that was not going to happen.

"I'll talk to the hotel."

"Be brave. It'll be an adventure." Shazza's optimism rubbed Anvita the wrong way. But after a couple of breaths, a night in a ute under the stars compared to hanging out with the leery glances of her cameraman, Brooklyn, sounded bloody good. She'd better go and sort out their dinner tab and make sure they knew how to get to Aston's house for the morning's shoot. Brooklyn might be a bit of a creep, but he was magic behind the lens.

Shazza stared at Anvita's back as she strode back inside the reception of the hotel. Hotel—huh, it was really overstating the quality of the typical small-town motor-inn to call itself a hotel. Who'd have thought a shitty little town hotel like this would be booked out. It was odd to see Anvita so dishevelled, like she'd been running her hands through her usually perfect hair. Shazza had only met Anvita once, when she interviewed for this tv show, and couldn't help but be impressed at the contained focused elegance. She wore strong colours, bold and sassy, and there could be zero doubt that Anvita knew exactly what she wanted. That's why this was so weird. Okay, offering the back of her ute as a solution was probably not going to dispel any idea about Shazza being a poor tradie. But shit—she was a poor tradie. None of that fancy fucking shit for her.

Plus, Anvita was missing the best part. With the ute, they didn't have to stay here in shitsville hotel carpark. They could park anywhere. Find somewhere with a cracking view, cook some snags over the little gas bbq she kept in the back of her ute. Yeah, that might be weird. She only ever used that to boil water for coffee, and occasionally to toast marshmallows with her kids. It was much safer than a real fire, and fuck, half the time, the place was under fire bans anyway, so she was hardly going to make a proper campfire.

Anvita turned around, her face resigned, although her brown eyes sparkled. "Fine. The crew can have the room. It's twin share plus a couch, so it fits them all. We'll take the…" Anvita shuddered. "Ute."

Shazza couldn't contain the grin. "Sweet. This is going to be such fun."

Anvita blinked once and stared at her as if she'd lost the plot. "Yes, right. Fun?"

"We just need some supplies. How about I sort that out, while you do whatever you need to do with your crew?" Shazza had no idea how television worked, but if crew were like staff, they couldn't just be left to fend for themselves with no instructions. Only yesterday, she'd spent the day apologising to a client because one of her apprentices borrowed a ladder from the client, and then thoughtlessly loaded it onto his ute and drove off. She'd returned the ladder with flowers, and an apology, but it was going to fuck with her online reviews.

Anvita closed her eyes for a long moment. "I'll be ready in an hour."

RIGHT ON THE HOUR, SHAZZA TRIED NOT TO CRINGE AS Anvita sauntered out of the reception room. She'd gone a little overboard at the shops, buying a couple of blankets, some yoga mats, and way too much food for the two of them. A bottle of wine, some cheese, marshmallows, salad, fancy bread, and lamb cutlets for her little bbq. Shit. She should've asked Anvita if there was anything she couldn't eat. She'd probably fucked-up by buying something she was allergic to or couldn't eat for religious reasons. Not that she was assuming Anvita's religion or anything, but she should've asked. Better to ask than assume, especially when it came to allergies. When she was nervous she tended to bluster through a situation, and now she was convinced she was going to hurt Anvita.

"Hey there. Ready for the adventure of a lifetime?" Fuck, Shazza, tone it down a bit. She was used to making things more exciting for her kids. Nah, that was an excuse too. She blew out a long unsteady breath.

"Of a lifetime? Sure." Anvita's tone backed up Shazza's cringe-worthy thoughts and she knew she'd overstepped.

She lifted her chin and breathed in. "May as well make the best of a bad situation." That's what life had taught her, and she was done trying to fit in with other people's expectations.

"I like that philosophy."

"Wait, what?"

"It's a good idea. This isn't ideal, obviously, but the crew are happy to stay in the same room."

Shazza nodded. "Good. Jump in." She hauled herself up into the driver's seat and waited for Anvita to sit in the passenger seat. Her ute was usually a shambolic mess, and she'd spent some time cleaning out all the kid's rubbish before she'd done her shopping.

It still smelled like cookie crumbs and rotten apple cores, overlaid with sweat and sawdust.

"Where are we going?" Anvita clicked her seatbelt in and glanced over at her.

This was the closest Shazza had been to her, and she could see the lighter brown flecks in her dark brown eyes. A fresh perfume of light florals and mint filled the air, a welcome scent against her ute. Suddenly, a rush of warmth in her torso came with understanding. She didn't just admire Anvita for her elegance and presence of mind, she desired her. She hummed under her breath. That'd be why she'd nervously spent way too much money on making tonight comfortable. It wasn't just about trying to impress the television producer with her practical knowledge.

"You okay?"

Shazza cleared her throat. "Yeah. You?"

"Let's go adventuring. I've never slept under the stars before."

"Really?" Shazza turned the key and the growly diesel engine kicked into gear. "Not in your backyard as a kid? Or camping?"

"No." Anvita's tone didn't invite further discussion. Shazza twisted to look over her shoulder as she reversed out of her carpark and tried to ignore the heat from Anvita. It'd been years since she'd felt this desire for a woman.

No, that wasn't quite true.

It'd been years since she'd let herself feel this. Being married to her childhood best friend, Shane, had been great, really great, but it had essentially erased this part of her. Or buried it for convenience sake. She straightened up, turned the wheel, and drove out of the hotel carpark towards her destination. They sat in content silence for a few minutes.

"Hey, do you mind if I put the radio on?" Anvita asked.

"Sure. That's cool. It's probably on some kid's thing."

"How old are your kids?" Anvita tone turned formal. Polite, not curious.

"Tess is seven and Joe is five. They are staying with my mother in law while I'm here."

Anvita nodded. "Oh, That's lovely. It's so nice that they've been able to keep their relationship with that side of the family."

Shazza tried not to sigh. "Shane might be dead, but his family are still our family. His mother, Maria, is a wonderful woman."

"I'm sorry I spoke so awkwardly." Anvita's polite cool tone reminded Shazza of her own lack of elegance. She may as well keep her attraction buried because they were so different.

Shazza shook her head. "Nah, It's cool. Being widowed at twenty-three is a fucked-up thing, you know. People say the daftest things. I'm used to it."

"I guess so. I'm still sorry though."

"Thanks. I appreciate that." Shazza wished there were less social missteps involved with talking about death. People were often hurtful in the guise of trying to be helpful, or polite. And fuck, it wasn't like she was perfect at that either. She'd bet that Anvita dealt with racist shit in the same way, but she wasn't going to ask. It wasn't her place. "Shane and I used to joke that at least one of us got a decent mother in law."

Anvita frowned. Shazza could always count the seconds until the meaning dawned on someone.

"I take it your own mother isn't decent."

"She does her best with her lot in life, but yeah, she named me Shazza." She really didn't want to go into the mess that was her birth family. Her mum wasn't really equipped to be a mother, and Shazza had been brought up by her grandma and aunt. It had sucked to see her friend's families; they all managed to be decent people. They were all poor too, but they loved each other and supported each other which made being poor easier to take.

It'd taken her ages to realise it was good to see their

lives work out well. They'd given her motivation to be the type of mother she saw in her friend's parents, and she worked her ass off to give her kids a better childhood than the one she'd had. She wanted them to feel loved, not fobbed off onto some relative every time it was inconvenient to have a kid around the place. Leaving them with Maria for this weekend twisted her guts with guilt, even though it would hopefully improve their life by growing the business. She'd never been away from them overnight before.

"I thought that was a nickname for Sharon."

"Yeah, nah. Shazza is on my birth certificate."

Anvita chuckled. "I'm sorry. Again. It's not that funny."

It kind of was in a fucked-up way. "It's okay. You won't be the first one."

"I ought to know better than to assume anything of someone."

"If you are assuming my mother is bogan as fuck, you'd be right. And It's not the way she dresses, or the fact that she's poor, because I'm bogan on that scale. It's the selfish way she chases a cheap thrill, how she expects the next man to be the one who will fix all her problems." Shazza shrugged. She'd said more than enough, and she'd spent too much of her life trying to shrug off the cliché that was her mum. "Forget it. It doesn't matter."

They were obviously worlds apart; Anvita was so classy and she was....

She squared her shoulders. Fuck it, she wasn't her childhood. She was a working mother of two who was doing everything she could—even a bloody tv show—to make their life better.

"If it matters to you, then it matters to me."

Shazza nodded but kept her vision on the road. People said shit like that all the time, but they didn't mean it.

Anvita pressed her hands against her stomach as Shazza took items from the back seat and put them in the back of the ute. She was so practical, and it left Anvita with a familiar sense of hopelessness.

"Do you need any help?"

"Nah, I'm good."

"The sunset is beautiful from up here." Anvita filled the silence with inanities. Shazza had driven out of town with such certainty, and then They'd wound their way along a narrow road through the D'entrecasteaux National Park until Shazza had pulled off onto a dry dirt track and parked in a clearing overlooking the ocean. The sunset was worth the half-hour drive. "I can't believe this place. So close to town, and yet, it feels like the middle of nowhere."

Shazza paused for a moment and glanced up. The brilliant orange and pinks streaking over the sky added a red sheen to the duskiness of her hair. "Come and sit here."

Anvita climbed onto the back of the ute and sat down in the spot Shazza indicated. "Here?"

"Yeah. You are right. It is lovely." Shazza sat down beside her and leaned back with her hands supporting her. The position lifted her tits higher, and Anvita quelled the shiver that rushed down her spine. Shazza had kids, she was a widow, she would never...

"This is great. Ouch. Fuck." Anvita slapped her forearm but missed the mosquito that bit her.

Shazza giggled. "I've got some bug spray somewhere."

She rolled sideways and reached into a bag, then pulled out the spray. "Here. Shut your eyes." Spray hit her skin with the taste of harsh chemicals on her tongue.

"Bleurgh."

"I know, it tastes like shit, but it works." Shazza sprayed herself. "Damned bugs."

"Ruining all this good nature with their presence!" Anvita pushed away Shazza's care with a joke. After their discussion over Shazza's name, Anvita needed to apologise again. She'd obviously hurt Shazza with her assumptions, but they didn't have the kind of relationship where she could ask about it. Shazza had already opened up about her husband's death and her obviously unloving mother, and Anvita admired that courage to keep throwing herself at life.

"Thank you for doing this. It's a lot more comfortable than I was imagining." As far as apologies went, it only hinted at what Anvita wanted to say. The awareness she sought felt vague, like a butterfly, flitting away, impossible to catch.

Shazza rolled her head on her shoulders. "I grabbed a couple of yoga mats when I was at the shops. I figured you wouldn't want to try and sleep on the ute deck."

"Do you think I'm a princess or something?"

The corner of Shazza's mouth curled up in a half-smile. "Nah, just a city girl."

"Isn't that the same thing? Too precious for a little discomfort."

Shazza shrugged one shoulder. "I wouldn't wish discomfort on anyone."

"I appreciate that. The idea of sleeping outdoors

doesn't align with my need for creature comforts. As you say, a city girl." Anvita's stomach twisted. She could just push this away and pretend there wasn't a growing sexual awareness between them. Think about family, work, anything that wasn't the way Shazza's fantastic tits strained against her shirt as she leaned back against the ute. "My grandfather came here looking for a better life than back in India when my dad was ten, and we've always been taught to work hard to create comfort and health for ourselves and our family." Anvita didn't usually open up so readily. What was it about Shazza that made her want to chat about herself?

"Is that why you've never been camping?"

"No. That's not it. My parents wanted us to assimilate and do all the Aussie things, but I was so busy at school, and they were working, so we never had the time. If camping is living with bugs, then I don't think I've missed out on too much."

"Nah, yeah. Couple of beers on the back of a ute, That's all you need, mate."

"Are you making fun of me?"

Shazza laughed. "And of me. Look, heaps of what being Aussie is about isn't great. Yeah, camping is fun, and drinking beers with mates is good, but this country was built on the White Australia policy and our history isn't the greatest." Shazza frowned. "And don't look at me like that. I might be poor and white, but I can read."

"Fair enough. Every country has their bad history."

"Yeah, but what are we doing about it? Fucking nothing."

Anvita nodded, also unsure about Australia's weighty history. "But you are thinking about it."

"Sure. Fat lot of good that does anyone."

Anvita reached out and touched Shazza's hand. "Listening to people who are hurt matters more than you think it does. It might not change things on a big scale immediately, but It's not nothing."

Shazza stared down at the way Anvita's hand covered hers. Their hands were so different. Anvita's brown smooth skin was beautifully moisturised, her nails clean and painted with a rich dark red, while her own stubby hands were rough from work, tanned white skin wrinkled with sun damage from working outside, and her fingernails were clipped short. Functional. She wanted to snatch her hand away because they were so different. It would never work. But she couldn't because a gentle soothing warmth travelled up her arm and into her chest and she wanted to hold onto it tight.

"Anvita?" Her voice cracked a little.

"Yes."

"Want a beer?" Shazza pulled her hand away and tugged at her ear lobe. "Or something to eat. I got lamb cutlets for the BBQ, and salad, and stuff."

"Thanks. That all sounds amazing. Do you want me to help?"

Shazza stood up and jumped off the back of the ute. "Nah, It's cool. Just relax and watch."

"I can't let you do all the work."

"Yeah, you can. You have to work tomorrow. Let me look after you." Shazza liked cooking for people. It was the best part of being a mum, feeding her kids and all their friends; no one ever went hungry on her watch. She'd always been plump, and pregnancy hadn't helped, but cooking and feeding people was one of her great pleasures. In another life—one where her family had encouraged her rather than push her away from a career in food —she might've been a chef.

Anvita rolled over onto her stomach, propped her chin on her elbows, bracketing her pretty face with her slender hands and stared over at Shazza. "If you think That's best."

"Like you said, I'm the practical one."

"Hey, I can be practical too. Just not with this outdoorsy stuff!" Anvita's relaxed laugh sent a shiver through her torso and Shazza wanted to make her laugh over and over again. She grabbed a couple of beers from the esky and cracked one for Anvita.

"I hope you like it. It's a local brew." Shazza had spent more than she usually would on this meal, trying to impress Anvita. Hopefully, it wasn't a bad idea. Their fingers touched as she handed over the cold can. A tingle in the tips of her fingers made her want to rub them against her palm to get rid of the sensation. She shouldn't want Anvita this much, except shouldn't had already dictated too many of her twenty-five years and she was tired of listening to it.

"Thank you. Is this how you spend your evenings?"

Shazza snorted. "Fuck no. After I've fed the kids, managed to get them washed, we sit down and read a book together, then I wrestle them into bed."

"Wrestle them?"

"Mum, can we please stay up a few more minutes? Mum, I need a drink of water? Mum, why do I have to sleep anyway? It's boring. That kind of thing. But they're pretty good. Once they are in bed, then I try and answer client emails before I fall asleep too."

"Right. Being a solo mum is a tough gig."

"Yeah. I'm lucky because Marie, Shane's mum, comes over on weekends and watches them while I work." Shane's dad had pissed off years ago, and Marie understood how hard it was to be a solo mum.

"You work every day?"

Shazza sipped her beer. "It's my own business. If I don't work, the staff don't get paid, and we don't eat." She grabbed the little BBQ off the floor of the back seat of her double cab work ute and carried it to a patch of dirt. A table would be better, but this would do. It was flat and the frypan would cook evenly above the single gas burner.

"Of course. It's just that I thought I worked ridiculous hours, but it sounds like you never stop."

"Pretty much." She clicked in the gas canister, checked all the settings, then pulled a box of matches out of the back pocket of her jeans. She turned on the gas, lit a match, and held up her other hand to shelter the small flame from the light breeze. The gas caught with a gentle whoosh. Excellent.

"And here you are. Making dinner and a comfortable bed for both of us."

Shazza shrugged. "It's fine. This is like, restful work, because It's different to my usual work. I'm not really good at sitting still." She glanced up at Anvita whose deep frown marred her gorgeous face. "Look, if you want to do something, how about you tell me something about you?"

The frown disappeared. "Like a story to entertain you?"

"Sure. Whatever." She strode back to the ute to grab the rest of the supplies, then placed the frypan on the gas burner and added a dash of olive oil.

ANVITA'S MIND BLANKED. WHAT STORY COULD SHE TELL that would be entertaining? She always knew what to say, especially at work where her job was all about ensuring stories got told in a way that entertained audiences. They weren't her stories though. Watching Shazza made her brain fuzzy with desire.

"I got divorced last year, about eight months ago. Though That's not exactly an entertaining story." Anvita didn't really want to talk about the specifics of it, but she needed Shazza to know she was single. If ever there was a chance of the desire fizzing between them turning into something real, tonight was their best chance. Alone in the bush with a summer sky of stars above.

"Oh, That's a bit shit."

"Yeah. There were a whole bunch of factors. Anyway, I've been single since then, and…" She let her voice trail off. Shazza nodded but didn't ask anything further. Without a prompt to continue, Anvita realised she could easily talk about work instead. Boring.

"Are you alright?"

"Better than being married to him."

"I'm sorry."

"Yeah, we married quite young. I was a bit stupid. Naïve."

"Can't imagine that. You seem so contained and worldly." Shazza glanced up from her cooking.

Anvita shook her head. "My parents didn't approve. Brian was white, not Indian, but it wasn't all about culture. I think they saw the bigger problems."

"Oh?"

"Yeah. He was basically Scotty from Marketing."

Shazza roared with laughter, her head tipped back. "Holy hell. I cannot imagine you with someone like our ineffective overly fake Christian Prime Minister."

"Like I said, young and naïve. He thought it would be good for his career to marry someone "diverse"." She used air quotes for the word. "I was so thrilled to have his attention at first, hungry for it, but he knew that and used it for his own gain. He'd bring me to work functions, trotted out for the big bosses to demonstrate how globally focused he was. And it worked for him. He raced up the corporate ladder; for a long time, it felt like we had everything." Anvita paused. "My father told me I'd get discarded for a younger, prettier... whiter version once Brian had the job he wanted."

"Is that what happened?" Shazza added cutlets to the frying pan and they sizzled, filling the air with a satisfying scent which made Anvita's mouth water. Her parents were non-veg, and They'd always tried to fit in with Australian customs and food culture, so she'd grown up eating a wide variety of foods from everywhere. Pretty typical Aussie. Lots of Indian cuisine too, comfort foods cooked by her grandparents who'd grown up in northern India.

"No." It had been worse. She hauled in a deep breath. "I met one of his colleagues at a party. Oh my gosh, Nadia was so beautiful, and we had an instant chemical attraction. Like, the total air crackling thing that I thought was just something they wrote in books. It was both amazing and totally awkward at the same time. I realised I'd always been attracted to women as well, and anyway…" Anvita closed her eyes and eased out a long breath. When she flicked her eyes open again, Shazza's face was pink.

"Same, but I married Shane and that was that." Shazza looked back at her cooking and fussed around with the food.

Anvita's lips dried out and she licked them. How could one look make heat pool in her belly like that? "Nadia and I flirted off and on at various functions. I was married, so nothing could come of it, but damn, Nadia was irresistible. It was so hard to stay away from her, like I was just drawn to her, and anyway, it didn't help because I was already regretting my marriage. Brian wanted to start a family; He'd read somewhere that men with children were more likely to become a CEO than men without. But my career was taking off, and I didn't want to sacrifice that yet. It was really the perfect storm; with things so bad at home, it would've been so easy to cheat on Brian." Nadia had the same plump curves as Shazza, her perfect type.

"Did you?"

"Almost. We were at a function, and we brushed past each other in a hallway. I was leaving the toilets and she was going there. She stumbled, and I grabbed her forearm to stop her falling. Brian saw, and assumed we were kissing."

"Shit. Did he get angry?" Shazza's eyes were wide open.

Anvita shook her head. "No. Worse."

"What is worse?" Shazza's puzzled expression brought back all the irritating feelings of that day and Anvita shuddered. She shook her head once to try and get rid of the dreaded prickly sensation.

"Brian proposed a threesome."

Shazza blinked once. "What the fuck? Fucking men."

"And—"

"There's an and?"

Anvita held up her hands and did air quotes again. "It's not cheating because we all want it."

"He said that. What a—"

Anvita sighed. "Yeah, that's what Nadia said. She stood tall, spine rigid, and said she'd never be someone's unicorn." Anvita remembered rushing away to the toilet and searching it up. The concept of a unicorn hunter still brought bile to the back of her throat. Straight men married to bisexual women wanting to find another woman to fuck without technically cheating.

So gross.

"It was the last straw. I realised that Brian said a lot of things that just slid under my radar, things I could excuse as a one-off, except they were regular occurrences." She'd left them both that day; immediately asked Brian for a divorce and had never seen Nadia again. Their flirtation had been the catalyst for the end of her marriage. She was too ashamed to continue.

"Come here." Shazza stood up and held out her arms. Anvita scrambled off the back of the ute, landing with a jar through her ankles. Before she could react to the awkward dismount, Shazza had bundled her into a comforting hug. Her body fitted perfectly against hers, soft and welcoming, and Shazza's hands stroked gently up and down her spine. They stood there, locked together, with Anvita resting her head on Shazza's strong shoulder, just soaking up the care Shazza gifted her.

"Fuck." Shazza's curse broke the connection between them, and Anvita lifted her head. The smell of burnt lamb wafted past. "Sorry, I'll just rescue the dinner."

"And then more hugs?" Anvita wished she didn't sound so desperate, but damn a hug from someone who cared, and who felt like Shazza was exactly what she needed. Until now, she hadn't known that she missed physical comfort. After her divorce she'd kept to herself, needing to be strong for herself, unable to let herself rely on someone else's comfort. But Shazza undid all of that in one hug. She could spend hours nestled up against her soft, yet strong, body.

"Sure. Once we've eaten." Shazza busied herself with the food, and if it wasn't for the way the back of her neck had more colour than usual, Anvita would've assumed Shazza didn't feel anything like she did.

Hugging Anvita filled Shazza's body with so many feelings. Immediately, she felt useful. It was lovely to provide comfort to another human. Slowly as time had eased passed them both, with seconds drawing out into minutes, the hug had turned from basic comfort and help-fulness into the tingles of a growing attraction. She'd been very careful to keep her hug gentle and not push for anything more, but her mouth had watered and she really —really—wanted to kiss Anvita. Her hands stroked up and down Anvita's slim spine in soothing movements and she made sure that was the only motion she did. Just waited until the muscles along Anvita's spine started to soften and relax.

The whole story about her deadbeat shitty ex-husband layered everything with a rage that made her want to punch a pillow. Thump it hard to release some of the pent-up frustration that simmered alongside desire in her veins until her blood felt like it bubbled inside her. She might have crossed that invisible line from friendly and helpful into lust, when the smell of the dinner burning had caused her to leap away. Saved from embarrassment by burnt food. The crisp caramelisation on the lamb wouldn't ruin the dish, but she'd turned off the heat immediately and flipped the lamb over so the burnt side wouldn't keep burning in the heat of the pan. Caramelisation—pah, more like carbonation! But it could be fixed, and she wasn't going to let it become a disaster.

"You okay?"

"I'm great. Can you pass me a couple of plates?" Shazza took them from Anvita's hands, careful not to touch her. "And you? I'm so sorry about your ex."

Anvita shrugged. "That's why he's an ex. Sorry to be such a misery."

"Ah, don't stress about it." She plated up the lamb and added some pre-made salad to each plate. Yah for supermarkets and their easy meals. "There is bread too." She handed Anvita a plate and walked with hers over to the back of the ute. She placed her plate on the tailgate of the ute, grateful that she'd thought to unhook it earlier, so the ute was easier to get into and the tail gate created a little table.

"This is terribly impressive."

Shazza's cheeks heated and she hummed an awkward agreement, unable to figure out how exactly to deal with the way she'd gone way overboard in preparing for tonight. She took the few steps to the cab of the ute to grab the bread.

"Say thank you."

"Excuse me?" Shazza squinted at Anvita's grinning face.

"It's okay to accept a compliment."

Shazza coughed. "Yeah, okay. Thanks. Here's the bread." She placed it on a cheap chopping board that she'd purchased today and cut a couple of slices.

"This all smells incredible."

Shazza blew out a little laugh from the side of her mouth. "Whatever. The lamb is burnt, and everything else was made by someone else. I hardly did anything at all."

"Take a compliment." Anvita leaned over and whispered in her ear. "I'm impressed by the effort." The skitter of her breath across Shazza's skin brought back many feelings from her teen years. Ones she assumed had been a phase, or simply just buried under the reality of marriage, two children, and running a small business.

"Eat. That's all the thanks I need." She cut up her own lamb into strips and laid them onto a slice of bread. Once topped with a bit of salad, and another slice of bread, she had a sandwich for ease of eating.

Every motion helped cover up the fragile beginnings of her feelings for Anvita. She craved the normalcy of simply eating, side by side, together, but not, like together, together. The burnt side of the lamb crunched a little in her mouth. Not enough to ruin the meal, just enough to add texture to the mouth-watering flavours. Just as she couldn't ruin the niceness of right now. She stuffed more food into her mouth to stop her blurting out something awkward.

"This is delicious."

Shazza swallowed, then wiped her mouth with the back of her hand. "Yeah. I must be hungry because it tastes a lot better than I thought it would."

"Or you are a good cook and you should—"

"—take a compliment. Fine. It's lovely." Shazza took another bite and turned her face towards the last of the sunset. Orange streaks had settled into a warm glow as the sunset filtered through the bush. They ate together in silence with only birdsong interrupting their peace. It was so lovely to enjoy a meal where she didn't have to badger anyone into using their manners.

"Oh, look!" Anvita pointed towards the little BBQ. A possum sat in the shadows only a few steps away from the frying pan.

"Shoo." Shazza rushed over to the little creature, waving her arms. "It's still too hot, silly animal. You'll get burnt paws." She picked up the frying pan by the handle and suddenly realised she hadn't planned for after the meal. The washing up would have to be done some other time, not tonight with nothing to clean anything with. She only had enough water for drinking. Stupid mistake.

"What's the matter?"

"I forgot to get cleaning stuff." Shazza paused. "Never mind. Once the pan is cool enough, I'll chuck it in the cab of the ute in a plastic bag and clean it when I get home. All the plates and shit can go in there too."

"Shall we give the leftover food to the possum?"

Shazza shook her head. "The salad is probably fine to chuck into the bush for the animals, but human food isn't great for them. We should lock it inside the ute, so they don't scavenge it."

"That makes sense." Anvita nodded then didn't speak again until she'd finished her meal, having eaten it with a knife and fork. Neatly, unlike Shazza's bush sandwich that she wolfed down using her fingers. The contrast between them reminded her of her place in Anvita's life. Shazza might want a soothing hug to turn into something more, but anything between them would be temporary. Maybe she'd be okay with that. Sex was just sex—it didn't have to mean more.

"Here. Give me those." She held out her hand and took the dirty plate and cutlery from Anvita and dumped them into the frying pan. It was cool enough now to be wrapped up and left in the cab of the ute, away from any animals hunting for an easy meal, and wouldn't add too much of a smell to the already blended scents of her ute. It only took a few minutes to clean everything up and then with nothing else to keep her occupied, Shazza scratched her forehead.

"When you are done, come up here and watch the sky with me." Anvita's proposal would have to do. She'd done as much as she could to pass the time, and now the sun had set. She climbed up onto the ute, and slipped off her boots, leaving them neatly in the corner of the ute. Anvita patted the yoga mat beside her and Shazza sat down.

"If you are hoping I'll be able to tell you about the stars and whatnot, you're out of luck."

"Shazza. You don't have to do everything. I'm fine."

"Really?"

Anvita leaned closer, her shoulder brushing against Shazza's with a crackle in the air. "Really."

"Good." Shazza cleared her throat after the word came out all growly and rough.

"There is one thing, though."

"Yes?"

"Can I kiss you?" Anvita's question sent a rush of heat across Shazza's skin. Before she could second-guess herself and think too hard, she reached over and kissed Anvita first.

Just dove in, so to speak, although the reality was that she moved her head with caution. An emotional dive with a physical slowness. Her lips caressed Anvita's cheek, warm soft moisturised skin with a tang of bug spray to remind her of their outdoor location. Anvita shifted beside her and lifted her hand to meet her shoulder. Slowly they lay down, lips touching each other's in the beginnings of a kiss.

"Shazza." Anvita whispered against her lips, then deepened the kiss. It was a homecoming, an arrival, with all the thrill of seeing someone you hadn't seen in forever, and the joy of being safely home. Shazza stared into Anvita's brown eyes, as the light around them faded and sensation took over.

Every minute movement of lip against lip added heat to Shazza's skin, and she shifted so she could hold Anvita's face with one hand. This was the kiss she'd been needing, been waiting for, ever since she'd first seen Anvita at the interview for Uplift. She traced her finger around the other woman's ear and drank in her moan. Anvita pushed gently on her shoulder, and together they rolled so Anvita lay over her, mouths still joined. Shazza opened her mouth, welcoming Anvita in, and the slash of her tongue across her own jolted like a spark down into her chest.

Fuck yeah.

She slid both hands into Anvita's thick hair, the long strands brushing over her hands.

"Hold on."

"Like this?" Shazza dug her fingertips against Anvita's scalp.

"Yes. Please." Anvita sucked on Shazza's tongue, then with a hard kiss against her gasp, she moved down, trailing kisses down Shazza's throat. She let her head rest back against the yoga mat on the deck of her ute, glad she had something between her head and the hard, metal, grubby surface. With every kiss from Anvita, her fingers softened in Anvita's hair, until they slid down to hold her shoulders.

Anvita glanced up. "Still good?"

"Excellent." Shazza hadn't had sex since Shane died. She'd been too busy with work and the kids and holding everything together, and whenever she had a spare moment, grief stopped her from more than using her own hands. "I'm clean, by the way, I had all the tests done after Shane's death."

Oddly enough, none of that mattered right now. Her earlier nerves that had led to her buying too much food disappeared. She wanted this, wanted to kiss Anvita.

"I understand." Anvita lifted her head, and Shazza missed the sensation of Anvita's mouth on her throat. "I didn't trust Brian and had myself tested after the divorce. Thankfully, I was clean then, and I haven't had time for a hook up since."

It wasn't about trust for her and Shane, she just needed to have some other tests done and the doctor had recommended getting the full range of STI ones at the same time. So, she only nodded, not wanting to compare Shane with Brian, simply because it wasn't fair to remind Anvita of her own healthy relationship, cut short by death, against Anvita's obviously hurtful divorce.

"I think we have time now." Shazza wanted this kiss, this whole evening, to be more than a hook up, but she'd take what she could.

"Yes. We do." Anvita unbuttoned Shazza's work shirt and pulled the two halves wide open. "I've wanted to do this since I first saw you."

"Really?" People stared at her big tits all the time, so that didn't surprise her, but when Anvita nestled her face between them and licked, Shazza squealed. If That's what Anvita meant, then Shazza could get on board with that idea.

"Yes, really." Anvita held Shazza's tits in her hands with a reverence that amazed her.

"I'm sorry my bra isn't prettier. Getting something supportive for this size doesn't equate to sexy stuff." Not without a ridiculous price tag, anyway. Lacy and supportive bras were way outside Shazza's pay grade. She'd rather be…

"It's practical. Just like you. And delightfully perfect." Anvita eased all her concerns. It certainly helped that she was holding Shazza's big tits with her hands, and gently stroking them. Anvita's thumbs slid over her taut nipples, and Shazza had to bite her bottom lip to prevent another squeal of delight. The best part was that Anvita took her time, slowly worshipping her tits with her exploring hands. Shazza squeezed her thighs together, wet and ready for more. Anvita stroked and caressed, and toyed with her until she panted. And when Anvita sucked on one nipple—even through the fabric of her practical bra— she moaned loud enough to silence the chatter of the birds in the trees behind the ute.

"More, please."

Anvita's mouth shifted, like she'd smiled, and she sucked again. Shazza's hips bucked up against Anvita's leg, and she needed to hold on. She wrapped her arms around Anvita, her fingers digging into the back of Anvita's neck, and Shazza lifted her head to kiss the top of Anvita's scalp. One more strong suck from Anvita caused her head to drop back, and her eyes almost rolled in their sockets as pleasure rocketed through her body.

"Oh my God, you are good at this."

"Thank you." Anvita slid one hand down between them, trailing along the skin of Shazza's plump stomach. She held her breath. When people said they loved curves, they meant tits and butts, and they pretended the curves didn't go everywhere. Shazza struggled to like the way her stomach hung over the waistband of her jeans, and since having kids, it was covered in stretch marks too. At least it was dark enough now with the sun almost set so Anvita couldn't see them. "I love your body. It's so full and round and soft. Everything that is beautiful in a woman."

"Truly?" Shazza wasn't so sure.

"Really. I've always had a thing for full figured women. Thick thighs, big tits, a full round stomach and hips. The best."

Shazza tried to push away that awful doubt. It had been around her whole life, one compliment from an elegant person wasn't going to get rid of it completely, but it sure helped when Anvita obviously worshipped her skin with her hands and mouth. "Thank you."

Anvita laughed, and her lips vibrated against Shazza's skin, sending sparkles of passion scattering all over her body. "See. I told you you'd learn how to take a compliment."

"That's me. Learning every fucking day." Shazza wanted to squirm against the uncomfortableness of this discussion, but the little circles Anvita drew on her stomach made it impossible to feel anything but brilliant awareness.

"Hey, stop underestimating yourself. I'd be sleeping on a couch with my crew if you hadn't organised tonight."

Shazza had to stop herself from dismissing her efforts. "There'd be no bugs there."

"And you had an answer for that too, although the taste of bug spray on your face wasn't the greatest." Anvita paused and Shazza started to apologise. "But a little bitter tang is worth it." Anvita lowered her head and licked Shazza's stomach.

"Oh, yes." Shazza couldn't think of a retort. She stretched her arms down as far as they would go, but Anvita kept moving lower, and all she could reach was her hair which lay trailed over her bra and stomach.

Anvita unbuttoned Shazza's jeans and Shazza lifted her hips to help Anvita drag her jeans off. Her underwear went with them—thank fuck for that—no one needed to see the ugly old stretched pair of undies she'd been wearing. But Shazza hardly had time to stress about her lack of sexy clothes, because Anvita placed her mouth at the top of her curls. An electrical buzz flooded her body and her hips bucked up against Anvita's face. She wanted to sit up and hold Anvita's head, but her body was too relaxed to try. Anvita's hands explored her thighs, stroking the skin until Shazza was ready to come. Her thighs relaxed, wide, open and encouraging. And when Anvita—finally— stroked one finger along her soaked labia and dipped inside her, she let out an almighty moan and a shudder.

Anvita's favourite thing was the musky scent of an aroused woman.

She'd fucked everyone and anyone before her marriage. Why she'd ever thought she should marry a man was something she deliberately chalked up to being young and naïve. But the way Shazza cried out as she touched her, and the aroma that filled her nostrils as Anvita stroked and played with her, was better than anything else.

This moment felt like home.

She never would have imagined she'd ever want to be outdoors, on the back of a damned ute in the bush, but being with Shazza, like this, all spread-legged for her, and soaking wet, was exactly where Anvita wanted to be. It was like every moment in her life until now had been a rehearsal for this time. And she was determined to enjoy every second of it.

She flicked her forefinger over the tight bud of nerves at the top of Shazza's wet slit and let the guttural wail of Shazza's moan wash over her skin. It would be so easy— no, necessary—to kiss her clit now, suck on it until Shazza came all over her face, but there was one thing she needed to do first. Anvita dragged her knees under her body, and balanced on one hand, while keeping the other circling Shazza's clit. Once she had her balance, she shifted so she was beside Shazza, able to touch her wetness, and kiss her on the mouth at the same time.

The kiss tasted like Shazza, the slightly burnt lamb she'd lovingly prepared for dinner, with a touch of vinegar from the salad dressing, and underneath it all, the soothing taste of summer peaches. Sweet, succulent, and delicious. Anvita kissed Shazza, stroking her tongue with hers, to match the rhythm of her hand, and kept the pace until Shazza grew more desperate. Shazza grabbed her hand and pushed her fingers inside her.

The neediness hit Anvita like a wave, and together, they stroked Shazza, with Anvita's fingers inside her and Shazza's hand over the top of her own to control the pace. In the shadow of the fading light, Anvita could just make out the blissful expression on Shazza's cheeks. She pressed her thumb against Shazza's clit, her hand all stretched out under Shazza's guiding movements, and kissed her as she came.

"Oh my God. That was amazing." Shazza's hand

relaxed, sliding slightly off Anvita's hand. Her fingers were still buried deep inside Shazza, and she could feel Shazza's body slowly return from the brink of her orgasm and start to relax all over.

"Yes. Amazing." She pumped her fingers twice more, before sliding them out of Shazza's sated body. She kissed her on the lips, a gentle, thank you kiss, before rolling away to lie beside Shazza.

"But you?"

Anvita shrugged. "I don't need anything more." She'd almost come from giving Shazza an orgasm, and she was content with that.

"Maybe not, but I want to give you more. Sex is supposed to be good for both people." Shazza half-sat up and traced her hands down Anvita's sides, over the rounded edges of her tits, along her waist, and over her hips. She bent over her and kissed her on the forehead, on the chin, and then on the belly button. Not quite, because Anvita still had all her clothes on, but the intent of the kiss quickly reawakened the burgeoning orgasm.

"Making you come is good for me." Anvita's voice croaked, almost in protest against Shazza's attentions. She hadn't realised she was so close, she'd been concentrating so hard on Shazza's pleasure, but now, as Shazza fumbled with her clothes and dragged her lips across the skin of her stomach, she trembled.

"So fit and beautiful."

"What? You can't see anything." The sun had fully set, and the birds had stopped chattering in the trees in the surrounding bush. Anvita's whisper seemed to echo further than before in the quiet evening. A few stars were scattered in the sky, peeking between the dark patches of the tree canopy.

"I don't need to. I have a good memory, and excellent touch." To hear Shazza compliment herself, instead of those usual backhanded comments, thrilled Anvita as much as her touch did. Fingertips roughened by work added texture to the way they glided over the bare skin on her belly, and the short nubs of her fingernails grazing as Shazza slid her fingers under the waistline of her skirt. All the way around the edge of her clothes until she found the little zipper against her hip. The zip sounded loud in the clean country air, and Anvita swallowed.

"Tip your hips up." The gentle command sang over her and she obeyed gladly. With a woosh, her skirt was tugged down, and Shazza shifted with a huff and a puff in the dark.

"What are you doing?"

"Just getting comfortable."

"Good." Anvita started to chuckle at the way Shazza wriggled beside her, but it came out as a rough cough when Shazza leaned over her stomach, and her tits pressed against the skin of her belly. Did that mean? She stretched out her hands and ran them over Shazza's body. Yes, it did. Shazza had shifted so her head hovered above Anvita's curls, and her broad hips lay beside Anvita's shoulder.

"I've never done this before, so—"

Anvita swallowed. "You'll be great. Just do what you'd want me to do to you." And Anvita hoped she wouldn't expire from the pleasure about to be unfurled on her.

Anticipation built like champagne in her veins. Effervescent.

"Okay?" Shazza's mouth must be very close, as her breath was all hot on her curls. Anvita wriggled her knees to push her skirt further down, so she could spread her legs more. She jerked a little when Shazza traced her fingers from her knee up the inside of her thigh.

"Yes." Anvita could only whisper her agreement as Shazza's mouth brushed over her curls. The wet heat of Shazza's tongue flicked over her clit and Anvita cried out. In the dark of the evening, she could only make out the shadow of Shazza's head, leaving no visual cues, only feelings. And phew, those were building like a rocket. All fire and explosive tension about to achieve take-off in a great pile of flame and smoke. It was all she could do, but cling onto Shazza's back and round arse as she licked and sucked at her.

"Holy fuck you taste delicious." Shazza's breathy awe added more heat to her core. Every stroke of her tongue had Anvita panting. She bucked her hips, desperate to get more, crying out for more, and her fingers dug deep into Shazza's flesh. Shazza scraped her teeth over Anvita's clit and that was all it took. The most epic orgasm walloped her, her body shuddered and moaned as sensation ruled. The rocket flew out of the atmosphere and Anvita clung on for the ride of her life. She slid her hands between Shazza's legs and slipped into her moist entrance, purely by instinct. She needed to be as close to Shazza as possible as her body unwound from the release of pleasure.

Anvita lost track of time, but eventually she managed to speak. "Thank you so much."

Shazza chuckled, and cool air from her mouth across Anvita's vulva sent a shiver of delight up her spine. "Just imagine how good I'll be with practice."

"Girl, you are going to destroy me for anyone else."

Shazza's laugh filled Anvita's chest with joy. "That's the idea." She shuffled around again and lay with her head touching against Anvita's shoulder. Anvita reached out and held Shazza's cheeks and kissed her gently on the lips. The taste of her own orgasm on Shazza's lips was the last thing she knew before she dozed off, utterly sated.

Shards of pink and orange pierced the sky as Anvita cracked open on eye. She'd slept all night on the back of a ute? Shazza must have covered them both with blankets at some point because she was cosy and warm. After a couple of blinks to clear her eyes, she realised that she was warm thanks to Shazza's body pressed up against her. If they could achieve this level of bliss in the outdoors on the hard back of a ute, imagine being in a real bed with her. Anvita closed her eyes again and hugged Shazza a little tighter. If she could hold onto this moment for a little longer before she had to face reality, she would.

"Good morning." Shazza's voice was husky in the morning. "We'd better get going if we are going to get tidied up for work and have some coffee."

"Oh my god. Coffee. I don't suppose…"

"No, my organisational skills didn't go that far. Besides, I'm sure you want decent coffee, not camping quality."

"Yes. And hey, thank you for last night."

Shazza rolled over and squinted at her. "No worries."

"The sex was excellent. I'd like to do that again sometime. Maybe after filming, you could come back to my place?" Anvita held her breath as Shazza frowned. Had she misread the situation?

"After filming I have to get back to the kids."

Anvita tried to hide her disappointment. "Of course." That was it then, the best sex of her life was just a one-off, thanks purely to a weird situation. She should thank Logan for doing exactly as she'd requested.

"If you don't mind spending time with my kids, you could stay at my place after work," Shazza said. Anvita's pulse sped up.

"There's just one problem."

This conversation was going to be the death of her. Despair then hope and now a problem? "Oh?"

"I only have one bed."

Anvita laughed, partly in relief but mostly with hope. "I think we can make that work. And speaking of work, we really need to get on the road if we are going to get to Mr Lee's house on time to start the day's filming."

ONE YEAR LATER

ANVITA WALKED IN THE FRONT DOOR TO THE HOUSE SHE lived in with Shazza and their two kids. She smiled at their grandmother Marie, who had picked them up from school today. Marie lived in a granny flat in the backyard but was keen to leave for her weekend with friends on

Rottnest Island. It was only one of the reasons Anvita was home early today. All three of them waved as Marie waltzed down the front path to her car.

"Hey kids, want to go camping this weekend?" Anvita was ready to burst with her news. Shazza had agreed to her plans but didn't know all the details because Anvita had wanted to surprise her with the location, although given the date, she'd probably already guessed.

It'd taken several months of Anvita basically just living in Shazza's tiny flat before they made the decision to buy a house in the suburbs. After that first night, she hadn't intended to move in, but one night turned into a week, and then a month, and before she knew it, she hadn't been back to her apartment to sleep for ages. They'd spent hours researching schools who would accept a family with two mums and bought a very suburban house nearby, going halves on the mortgage. Shazza had sold her apartment and the business was growing rapidly thanks to the exposure she'd gotten during Uplift's first season. Anvita kept her apartment but shared the ownership with Shazza, and the rent from that place covered the mortgage she still had on it. In the past couple of months, Anvita had a promotion at work, so now she had acquisition power and could help get stories from diverse writers made into tv shows. Life was pretty damned good.

"Camping? But you hate the outdoors." Joe said.

"It's the bugs." Shazza's daughter, Tess, rolled her eyes. "I don't like bugs either."

"This weekend is a special one for me and your mum, and I thought we could go camping in a special place with all of us."

The front door banged.

"I hope you intend to pack the tent, because I'm not keen to sleep on the back of the ute again. My back was sore for a week after that." Shazza's laugh filled the house with warmth, and Anvita knew her love for Shazza would be forever. This was her family now. Shazza, Tess, Joe, Marie and her.

"Actually, I had Logan book two rooms in the motel for us." Her PA had grown in confidence with more time in the role, and slowly she'd been able to give them more responsibility. She was glad she'd persisted with Logan because over the last year, They'd become a real asset to her in her work.

Shazza's laugh grew bolder. "So not real camping."

"As you say, It's not good for your back to sleep rough. And that motel isn't the flashiest. It's almost like camping." Anvita kissed Shazza on the lips, a welcome home kiss, and grinned. "How was work? I hope you are ready for a weekend of pampering."

"I love you. Let's go back to where it all started."

"I love you too." Shazza had a heart big enough for all of her family, and they worked together to keep Shane's memory alive for the kids too. One night on the back of a ute had given Anvita her best life.

ABOUT THE AUTHOR

RENÉE DAHLIA

Renée Dahlia is an unabashed romance reader who loves feisty women and strong, clever men. Her books reflect this, with a side note of dark humour. Renée has a science degree in physics. When not distracted by the characters fighting for attention in her brain, she works in the horse-racing industry doing data analysis and writing magazine articles. When she isn't reading or writing, Renée spends her time with her partner and four children, volunteers on the local cricket club committee, and is the Secretary of Romance Writers Australia.

More Books by Renee Dahlia

Her Lady's Honor: An Historical Lesbian Romance
Liability (Farrellton Foster Family Book 2)

ABOUT IN THE CARDS

Emme is about to embark on the creative project of her dreams but first she'll need help from Kendall, the local river guide and Emme's long time crush.

What will a day on the river and a night by the fire have in store for these two women?

IN THE CARDS

SARAH E. LILY

Grunting from exertion, whilst trying to spit out tendrils of curly red hair that had invaded her mouth, Emme tossed her well-loved black camera gear bag into the backseat of Kendall's dusty red truck, "I really appreciate this. It means a lot, honestly."

Kendall's mischievous top lip curved in the right corner, "Hey, it's not that big of a deal. It's going to be a beautiful day, might as well be on the river. Plus we haven't hung out since Sierra's engagement barbeque."

Emme's stomach dropped a bit. That damn smirk. That damn swagger. It had been a killer in college, and it appeared it had exactly the same effect on her now, that it had when they were rushing to biology class, drinking cheap beer, or chilling out to perpetually sad indie pop music. Who knew swagger aged well, like whiskey?

Dragging the toe of her neon pink sneaker through the gravel, turning it into a parking lot Zen garden, the photographer collected her secret self. "I know, but you guide people on the river all week...and they actually pay you."

"I told you not to worry about the money. It'll be fun. I haven't actually camped out since my brother's bachelor party, where the highlight was his best friend getting drunk and pissing in the food cooler. This is bound to be better. Although I should have asked, do you have a habit of peeing in coolers?"

Emme half snorted, half giggled, "I can guarantee that nothing of the sort will happen on this excursion. The strongest thing I packed was soda that wasn't diet."

Kendall covered her mouth feigning shock, "Emme, I believe you have gone to the dark side."

Emme wrinkled her nose at Kendall, then turned to finish loading her things into the truck, smiling the whole time and trying to remember the last time she felt nervous excitement.

A memory of their senior formal popped into her head, a kaleidoscope of Polaroids cascading through her mind. She had spent weeks looking for the perfect dress, something that said, "I'm a woman and I'm proud of my body but I don't give a fuck what you think of my body."

Something blue that definitely had nothing to do with the fact that Kendall had once told her that blue made her green eyes glow. Two days before the dance she'd stumbled across a vintage, indigo, sequined creation that molded to her hips as if it was second skin, the bodycon design hinting at the curves that lay beneath. The big night came and when she'd slipped that damn dress on, she felt radiant, excruciating excitement, and for an evening, unstoppable.

She was a goddess in that thing.

It was going to be one of the last nights the class would be together before graduation and the inevitable natural scattering of newly enlightened minds into the world. She knew Kendall would be there with Marina, and Emme had her date Tyson, but if for a few minutes she glowed and Kendall noticed, all the nervous buildup would be worth it.

Everything would be worth it.

Kendall had stared so much that Emme was pretty sure she remembered her stepping on Marina's feet during a slow song. After the dance, Emme and her show-stopping dress went home alone, to the dismay of Tyson, a cutie from her art and theory class. He was nice but it just didn't feel right. Not because he was a guy, because goodness knew she liked guys just as much as she liked girls, but because he wasn't her.

He wasn't Kendall.

And years may have passed, but still no-one was Kendall. Their ride to the boat dock wasn't far, but it was long enough to allow Emme's attention to linger on the way her friend worked the stick shift. *Christ on a cracker. When did changing gears become so hot? What else could those hands do?* Emme thought to herself. *It's been five fucking years since college, and she still does this to me.*

Morning sun cascaded through the window creating a delicate pattern across the river guide's neck. Emme watched the pattern, noticing how the dappling of the light across Kendall's rich brown skin resembled a delicate piece of lace. She focused on the visual, cataloguing it in her mind. Something so beautiful needed to be remembered.

"Em, you okay?

"Yeah of course, why?"

"You're pretty quiet over there."

Just busy salivating over your damn sexy neck.

"Yeah, no, I'm just enjoying the sun."

Kendall glanced over at her passenger with a puzzled expression, "Okay, well we're here and you'll get plenty of sun. I hope you brought sunblock because if I remember right, you go from red to lobster in 60 seconds."

"Yep, still true. The curse of being a redhead."

Emme quickly unbuckled and hopped out before Kendall could notice that she was undeniably the color of a tomato. No, make that a humiliated tomato and it had nothing to do with the sun.

After taking a couple deep breaths, she pulled it together and headed around the bed of the truck to get her next set of instructions from her guide. With all the deep breathing required to be around Kendall, she resigned herself to the odd hyperventilating moment on this trip.

Kendall was already preparing to unload the canoe, loosening red and green striped bungee cords.

"Can I help?"

Please don't let this end with me losing an eye to a bungee cord.

"Yeah, sure. Stand toward the end of the canoe - get ready to grab it when I loosen the last cords."

As explained, Kendall undid that last bungee cord, and Emme grabbed the end of the canoe. Slowly, they walked it over to the dock and lowered it in place. Emme found herself mesmerized by the sight of her partner for the day. She was pure strength and beauty as she grabbed that canoe. Muscle and tendons came to life starting in the tops of her hands, running up her thick toned arms and into shoulders that could have been carved by the Goddess herself.

Gently, Kendall began to lower the canoe to the ground signaling Emme to do the same. As Kendall squatted down, Emme focused on not choking. Had Kendall's calves always been so beautiful? And her thighs, rippling with power...

Those thighs should not be allowed on a someone who is already that gorgeous. It's just not healthy...for me.

There wasn't another person alive that got Emme's water boiling quite like this woman. She'd dated some sexy people, but Kendall was in a league all her own. Part of it was definitely plain old physical chemistry.

Emme's earliest physical memories of Kendal were of her applying bug repellent to her neck and collarbones. Bug repellant changed in Emme's mind forever when she realized the sheen and highlight it brought to Kendall's perfectly crafted collarbones. How could anyone judge a mosquito for wanting to land there and drink of that gorgeous neck? Emme had spent quite a few quiet shadowy nights bringing her body release imagining licking that neck. But there was something else she felt around Kendall. It was as if their spirits reached for each other. Sometimes Emme thought she felt an actual tug. She envisioned a shimmering gold thread running between their hearts.

It brought her comfort imagining she'd be tied to Kendall in that way no matter what.

"Earth to Emme."

"Hmm? Oh, yea sorry."

"Are you okay? You seem to be somewhere else. Everything okay? Is this a bad weekend?

"No, no, this weekend is perfect. I am just really looking forward to the river."

"Dreamy Emme, always dreaming! Girl, can you just try to be in the moment for once? Stay with me!"

Emme smiled remembering how Kendall would always call her out when she seemed to float away. If only Kendall knew that she was what was usually distracting the dreamer.

"I guess I was just thinking about the weekend ahead. Fantasizing about what's to come."

Fantasizing about you.

"Well, no need to fantasize because it's about to be reality. Just gotta put in our gear and then ourselves."

"Speaking of that, I don't actually know how to get into a canoe. They've always seemed a bit wobbly to me."

And I do not need help being wobbly!

Kendall turned making purposeful direct eye contact with Emme, "Don't worry Em, I'll take care of you."

Emme's heart jumped and simultaneously her stomach dropped. Those words, Kendall's voice, and that look... what a trifecta! Heat was spreading up her chest to her face.

Pull it together Emme, it wasn't a promise of everlasting love. She's just saying you won't drown on her watch

"Thanks. Um, what do I do first?"

"I'm going to stabilize the canoe while you get in. Try to stay balanced and low to the canoe."

Kendall leaned over the dock and grasped the sides of the canoe, "Okay, now just step in, but remember, stay low."

Emme was fixated on Kendall's face. Had she ever really noticed the perfect curvature of Kendall's cheekbones? Light danced across them bringing to mind the way music notes seem to dance across skin. They can be felt but not touched.

With those thoughts in mind, Emme took a step into the canoe, at her full height. She'd obviously missed the stay low part. The canoe started to sway and Emme's barely there balance was nowhere to be seen. She could see herself going down and hoped maybe she'd float away without Kendall noticing. Kendall must have recognized the signs of an Emme going down because in a flash she had one strong hand around Emme's wrist and was pulling her back toward the dock. Emme landed knees first with a thud that rattled her teeth.

Of course.

"I said stay low, not do a pirouette," Kendall said while trying to hold in laughter that was threatening to spill out.

Emme looked into the mischievous eyes and laughter began to bubble up like when adding vinegar to baking soda in a science fair volcano. How could a look, a simple look, fill her with such pure joy, even whilst she had two, throbbing, soon to be black and blue, knees? Her spirit was magical, infectious, and healing in a way that Emme almost couldn't bear. What would it feel like to bathe in that spirit? To lap it up like the most decadent cream?

"You hush and help me up. It's not my fault you are unaware of the fine art of canoe ballet!"

"It would be an honor my lady. Perhaps you will teach this art you speak of."

Both women laughed until their stomachs hurt and eventually made it into the canoe and on their way.

A FEW MINUTES OF SHARED SILENCE FLOATED WITH THEM as they both took in the scene around them. The water was clear, moving with purpose and determination. Birds chirped and sang to one another like call-and-response in church. The sun's rays felt like liquid honey, and Emme luxuriated in the sensation. Grasses and flowers fragranced the air, and it reminded her of a delicate perfume she had smelled before but couldn't quite place.

Kendall's paddling appeared ritualistic and meditative. There was a rhythm to it that reminded Emme of drumming's power to take a person to another place, another world. She seemed to come back from her communion of sorts with the river.

"I know we are doing this because you need to take photos for a new project, but you've yet to actually tell me what the project is. Though I completely understand," she added, at the look on Emme's face, "if it's top secret and you can't divulge it without having to kill me!"

Emme bit her lip nervously, "Uh, well I haven't told a ton of people..."

Kendall starred at Emme for perhaps a bit too long,

"I'm just teasing a bit, and you don't have to share if it's private."

Emme felt bad. She did want to share, but she was nervous. She had been outlining, then scrappin' and re-outlining this project for at least a year, and it felt somehow private or, maybe, more the beginning of something special. How could she explain the way tarot helped her discover the power of intuition? How it was a tool for self-reflection as well as divination?

Her biggest fear was that Kendall would think her ridiculous. Would her friend be able to fathom a world where all are connected, and where all have travelled through life together many times before? A world where ancestors, angels animal spirits and other guides can and do watch over them.

Could Emme articulate the sense of coming home she'd felt when she walked into her first metaphysical shop? That sense of belonging so totally to something bigger than herself, but which made space for her, despite its vastness.

Well maybe she'd just start with the basics.

Hi Kendall. How are things? I am a Witch. Anyhow...

"No, I do want to tell you." With a cleansing breath Emme continued, her words running on until her sentences blurred into an outpouring, "I practice tarot and have for a while, it's a big part of my spiritual life and I've created my own deck of nature-based tarot cards, and the idea is that hopefully the photos from this trip will complete the project."

A large breath, and then she waited. She waited for Kendall to roll her eyes, snicker, or say something about

New Age mumbo-jumbo and incense smoke. What she got instead was one of Kendall's most beautiful smiles. The kind that made her chestnut brown eyes seem backlit by amber flames. A wave of something akin to warm cashmere and cream washed over her.

"That's incredible! You are so creative and I think tarot is fascinating. I've always wanted to understand it more."

Emme's stomach flipped in surprise. Kendall was interested, fascinated even. She hadn't realized how scared she was of judgement until there wasn't any. What else could she share with Kendall? Maybe she wasn't giving her enough credit. A voice inside of her whispered, "It's going to be okay." Emme took another deep cleansing breath.

"Really? I had no idea you were interested in this…"

Emme's mind jumped to the tarot card she drew that morning, The Queen of Cups.

Trust my intuition, pay attention, lead with my heart.

Kendall gave a slow lazy grin, "Em, there are a lot of things you don't know about me."

And that quickly, Emme's mind went from the Queen of Cups to a dull heat gathering behind her belly button.

"Like what? Give me an example."

Kendall paused to consider, "I sometimes eat dinner for breakfast."

"You mean breakfast for dinner."

"Nope, I mean pot roast and mashed potatoes at 8 am."

Emme giggled, "That's healthier than most cereals. Give me another one."

"Sometimes, when I can't sleep or wind down, I watch…" she paused and then said, "…videos."

Emme's face began to heat up, "What kind of...*videos?*"

"Tutorials mostly, like how to grout a shower, or refinish a piece of furniture. I'm really into this one on how to build a tiny picnic table that's actually a chicken feeder"

Emme laughed so loud, a bunch of birds fled a bush rather abruptly.

Gods, she has no clue that her soul is like a healing balm for my tired heart.

"Do you have chickens?"

"Well, no. Is that funny?" asked Kendall with a hint of challenge in her eyes.

"Of *course* not," giggled Emme, her amusement giving her away. "I mean, it's just so *industrious.*"

And so sweet, honest, and perfectly you. "One more, something *really* good."

Kendall's lids slowly lowered sweeping long-lashed downward, and then her eyes met Emme's, "I have piercings...ones you can't see."

Emme's throat went dry, "Where?"

"My nipples."

Emme's breasts tightened, and her own nipples hardened at the thought of Kendall's, erect and pierced, glimmering in the light. Instantly, a pulsating sensation began to grow between her legs. It was so noticeable that she found herself clenching her thighs together in an attempt to stop it, or maybe feel it more. Emme's tongue felt extra moist and her mind's eye provided an impeccable image of Kendall's nipple glistening with Emme's saliva and Kendall's arching form.

She blinked her eyes and found the object of her desire

was staring directly into them. Was Kendall breathing faster? Biting the corner of her bottom lip? Clenching her jaw?

Kendall took an obvious deep breath. So deep, it seemed like she was trying to inhale Emme herself. "Your turn. Tell me some things I don't know about you."

I'd like to tear your clothes off and kiss every inch of you right in this boat.

"Well, I sleep with a purple shimmery stuffed mermaid named Violet."

Kendall belly laughed and Emme's own stomach spun as if butterflies were dancing a tarantella. "Okay, what else?"

"I sing power ballads in the shower."

Is she thinking of me naked and wet?

"And?"

"I have a tattoo."

And back to my body we go...

Kendall seemed to sit up a bit straighter.

"Where?"

Emme sheepishly glanced around at the non-existent bystanders, "On my left and right hip."

"You said *a* tattoo. That sounds like two."

A gust of wind brought her mass of red curls over her face just in time to cover her flushing cheeks.

"Well, they are a pair, so I count them as one."

"What are they?"

"The right hip is the sun, and the left hip is the moon."

Kendall was quiet for a moment longer than was comfortable for Emme.

Had she said something wrong? Did Kendall have an aver-

sion to hip tattoos? Why was she gripping the side of the boat? Maybe she wasn't really into tattoos. Well that would just be fucking great.

Kendall was tapping her foot in rhythm with her now drumming fingers.

What in hell is she thinking? Note to self, look into tattoo phobias.

Kendall seemed to snap out of whatever she was feeling, "This is where we go to shore. We can pitch our tents over there to the left, and there is a safe fire pit to the right." Then, in a flash, Kendall was out of the boat and walking the final bit to shore.

Emme took the much-needed respite to roll her neck in an attempt to release the tension that had formed and run her hands through her now even wilder wind-tousled nest of curls. Why was she feeling sad, a sense of loss?

It was as if she had lost something with Kendall that she didn't even have. Her heart thumped harder watching Kendall move farther and farther from her. Nothing had happened. They were just chit-chatting. So why did she feel so off?

Letting her fingertips trail through the water, Emme imagined the coolness running up her fingers into her arms and soothing her neck and back. Once a sense of calm returned, Emme prepared to disembark the little canoe of confusion and prepared to make land with the sexiest river guide imaginable.

The location was perfect, and Emme was so glad she had taken Kendall's recommendation. Originally, Emme thought an area upriver, known for its tall trees, would be the spot, but then Kendall told her about this area that had beautiful trees, and a hill with a fantastic view of the river basin below. She could already see trees that called to her and large slabs of stone that had weathered lifetimes. The forest was teeming with life and this spot seemed livelier than any other she'd experienced. This was going to be perfect.

There was so much to photograph, beetles, trees, berry-bushes, and butterflies. She knew she would be able to complete the entire deck with the images from this trip and maybe start a companion deck. While she worked, Kendall walked with her, pointing out things and explaining their role in the local ecosystem. Emme was amazed at how much Kendall knew and how effortlessly it seemed to come to her. Kendall really seemed to feel the nature in her bones. Maybe she had some witchyness to her too. Wouldn't that be interesting?

Eventually Kendall stopped pointing things out and the conversation slowly transitioned. They talked about silly mundane things, like the college version of who's who and where they were now. Emme updated Kendall on her family, her sister's twins, and her best friend's current, new obsession, custom tambourines. Kendall talked about her plans to turn her garage into a studio where she could work on boats and birdhouses, her raised bed garden, and an ever-growing collection of vintage typewriters. It felt so peaceful and calming to be wandering around the woods together.

Emme wondered what it would be like to have a special person in her life like Kendall...maybe Kendall herself. The heat started to pool in her lower belly again, and she knew she needed to distract herself. She'd had this conversation with herself over and over. Kendall's presence in her life was more important than giving into damn desire.

What if it didn't work out? Would they remain friends? Probably not, it would hurt too much. Would they see each other and cross the street or pretend to be on a call? That was too painful to even contemplate.

Emme forced the negative thoughts away. "Can I photograph you?"

Where did that come from?

"Me?" Kendall seemed genuinely surprised.

"Only if you are comfortable with. It's no big deal. I can't help it. Once a photographer always a photographer."

Kendall seemed to be seriously considering the request, "No, it's cool. What should I do?"

Emme looked around and there, a few feet away, was a beautiful large rock covered in emerald-green moss. "Go over by that rock and just look at me."

Kendall looked a bit sheepish but did as she was instructed. Emme picked up her camera and placed Kendall in the frame. She felt bold when she had a camera in hand. "Okay, just look at me. Don't worry about smiling or anything. Just do what feels natural."

Emme's beautiful subject was looking at the forest floor at first, then slowly lifted her head and looked directly into her photographer's soul. The shutter seemed to be snapping on its own, like it knew Emme was becoming lightheaded from the intensity of the moment.

As quickly as it started, it ended. Emme put down her camera. "Do you want to see?"

"No, who likes looking at themselves? You can show me after you work some editing magic."

I wouldn't alter a single pixel.

"I'm getting hungry. Is there a place you think would be nice to stop and eat?"

Kendall looked around, thinking for a moment, then pointed up and to the left a little, "There's a nice area over there where we can eat."

Within minutes, they were laying out a green-checkered blanket and preparing to indulge in homemade sandwiches, large pickles, and soda.

After taking a few bites Kendall looked at Emme quizzically, "You don't have to answer this, but what happened to Dominic?"

Emme's heart stuttered at the mention of her ex; the last thing she really wanted was to talk about that breakup with Kendall.

"He's running a small engine repair shop I think."

"You know what I mean. What happened between you and him? I heard from Sierra that you were wearing a ring for a while."

Damn Sierra and that mouth of hers.

Emme exhaled and put down her sandwich. She'd known this would come up, and, honestly, she was surprised it had taken this long.

"Nothing happened...ever, and that was the problem. He's a great guy for someone, just not me. We didn't have that thing that causes a person to rush home from work just to see the other person or get butterflies when they text – even if all that text says is 'forgot to get milk.' We were great housemates, cornhole partners, and friends. I know there's more, and I want more. I tried to make it work and yes there was a ring for a little bit, but I gave it back. It was painful, but more for our families than us. In all honesty, I think he was relieved when I finally told him that this wasn't working. I heard he's dating a dental assistant and they have a puppy."

Emme sat back feeling relieved and picked her sandwich back up. She'd done it. She'd spoke the dreaded words and now it was over. For a while, she had viewed it as a failure on her part but was now at peace, mostly. Kendall didn't seem shocked. No one ever was. Everyone else must have known before her. Emme wanted her lunch companion to know the truth and maybe more than that, that she was unattached.

"What about you? I've not heard of anyone steady in your life since Marina."

Kendall sat quietly, then folded her hands behind her head and leaned back against her pack, causing her neck to extend and her chest to become more prominent. "Marina and I had a great time in college, really we did. I mean she was my first real girlfriend, the one who held my hand when I came out to my family, the one who helped me figure out who I was, and who I was only trying to be. But we always knew our time was limited from the beginning. Her heart was in New York - busy restaurants, running the kitchen like the drill-sergeant-queen she was always meant to be. My heart has always been here with the river, slow and steady. I can appreciate bigger and faster, and I visit her a couple of times a year, but my home is here. I've dated here and there, but you know how it is."

Emme's heart was step dancing, "No, how is it?" She was feeling brave.

Kendall's face was a blank mask for a second, but then a slow smile crawled across her features, "Let's go, my little photo-bug. We should head back and set up our tents while we still have good light."

My *little photo-bug...*

Emme wasn't sure what to be more delighted about, the nickname, or the fact that Kendall had said that she was hers...

She quickly helped pack up and then, once again, her breath was matching the rhythm of her camera shutter, and Kendall was humming something that sounded lovely but unfamiliar.

"What are you humming? It's pretty."

"It's my favorite song."

"What's it called?"

"Wherever is Your Heart. It's by Brandi Carlile."

Emme felt like that was significant but wasn't sure why. She'd have to unpack it later.

Time went quickly after that until they found themselves back at the base camp.

"I'll help you put your tent up, and then we can do mine," said Kendall.

She grabbed the greenish-brown pack that Emme had brought and stared at it for a minute.

"This is rather...vintage."

Emme's cheeks flushed with embarrassment, "The tents all belonged to Dominic, and I never bought my own, so I borrowed this one from my grandpa Jake's barn. He said it was fine the last time he used it."

Kendall started laughing, "Your grandpa Jake hasn't camped on the river in at least 10 years."

Emme rolled her eyes playfully. "Oh, shut up. I'm sure it's pristine."

Kendall flashed another one of those million-dollar smiles "Let's check it out and if there is an issue you can share mine."

Share mine.

Emme had a brief thought of throwing her tent in the river or the fire...an accident of course, but then came to her senses. They were friends, here to do a job of sorts, and... Kendall was so hot that if anything did happen, Emme would probably die of heart failure and never get her tarot deck out into the world.

Kendall began to open the 'vintage' bag as Emme started moving some larger stones out of the way. Kendall abruptly started laughing so loud that Emme, startled, fell over a log they were using as a bench.

Looking up at Kendall from her new vantage point, Emme noticed two things. One, Kendall was now crying with laughter, and two, she was holding up a decorative holiday flag, the kind for the yard. This particular flag had a giant purple bunny on it that said *Hoppy Easter.* Emme must have grabbed whatever her grandma Mary stored her seasonal yard flags in.

Emme felt the feeling of giddiness, joy, and peace start at her toes and move into her chest as she began to laugh and laugh until she could barely breathe. Kendall held out a strong and calloused hand that felt warm and gentle when Emme took it. She pulled the red-headed witch to her feet with so much strength that they almost bumped chests.

They stood there, inches apart, staring into each other's eyes. Had Kendall always had gold flakes in her eyes? And those smile-lines around her eyes and mouth were a post-college addition for sure. They added a sense of knowing to her face. It was intriguing. It made Emme want to know what Kendall knew. Kendall took a slow step backward and a very obvious deep breath.

"Well, those are not going to be useful for this trip, so let's put my tent up, and then you can do some night shooting whilst I make dinner. If you'd like to, that is."

Kendall's tent, an actual tent, was very nice and went up easily. It was small, but two people could fit, if they didn't mind touching every now and again.

Emme managed to distract herself from the image of the two of them lying, side by side, in that small tent, by getting lost in her photography, shooting macro images of tiny blue flowers along the riverbed, and then a line of marching ants that mesmerized her.

A water droplet clung to a leaf and reflected light in a way that reminded Emme of a crystal. Thinking of this, she put her camera down and reached for the rose quartz she wore around her neck. It was one of her most comforting stones. She thought of it as the chicken soup of stones, something that just made everything better.

Rubbing the stone, Emme closed her eyes and tried to ground herself. She imagined rays of shimmering light coming from her and into the earth, only to be returned back to her, a meditative ritual that always helped renew her connection with the Earth. A few minutes passed and

Emme felt centered and refreshed, refreshed enough to continue taking photos. Before too long, she heard fire crackling and smelled something delicious. Her belly started to grumble, so she made her way back to Kendall.

"Soup's on."

"It smells divine."

Kendall smiled, "It's my dad's camp chili."

Kendall's father has passed away the summer before. It wasn't a surprise, but it had still been terribly sad, and Kendall had been very close to him. Em lowered her gaze and tried to pick the right words, "Kendall, I know you must miss him."

"Yeah, I really do but I am glad he isn't in pain anymore. I feel close to him when I'm on the river."

She handed Emme a bowl, and they sat on their makeshift log-bench, letting the fire warm their bodies and spirits. It crackled and danced with such ferocity that Emme felt as if the fire spirits were reaching out to their onlookers.

"Campfires feel magical," she said as she stretched her legs to feel more of that warmth.

Kendall turned her face toward Emme. Her eyes seemed softer, "They do with you."

Emme stared, not knowing what to say, but knowing the silence would definitely kill her.

Say something, say anything

"It feels pretty special with you too."

Kendall smiled ever so slightly and gently put her hand on Emme's.

Oh my Gods, oh my Gods, oh my Gods... Emme felt herself flailing internally.

They sat like that for some time, in the quiet, with nothing but the sound of crackling flames and crickets to fill the silence.

"Um, I have a tarot deck with me. Would you like a small reading?"

Kendall smiled knowingly, "Please!"

What does that smile mean?

Emme jumped up to get the deck and warn her body to pull itself together before it literally flew apart.

"Okay, let's do a simple three-card draw. Past, present, and future."

Emme started shuffling the deck, cards flowing like water between her hands. Warmth grew in her hands and ran up her arms. This was her thing, her gift, her normal. Then she handed the deck to Kendall. "Use your left hand to divide the deck into three piles."

Kendall did as she was told.

"Now put them back together into one pile and hand them to me."

Kendall's fingers grazed Emme's as she handed the cards over, and Emme felt the warmth exchange between them. Emme inhaled and exhaled deeply three times, before placing the three chosen cards face down in a row. As she laid each card she spoke Kendall's name in her heart and mind.

Spirit, please share with me the message Kendall's meant to have.

Emme flipped the first card, Two of Wands. She flipped the second card, Strength, and the third card, Ten of Cups. She stared for a moment, allowing the cards' meaning to float to the surface of her mind and then mingle with one another to create a full picture.

"Is it good?" asked Kendall.

"There isn't a good or bad in tarot." Emme touched the Two of Wands, "This is your past, and it says that you have worked hard, had success, and a lot to be proud of, but you are still searching for something. You have steadily been moving forward but to what end?" She then touched the Strength card, "This is your present, and it says that you are strong and courageous but may be fighting your instincts out of fear. Self-control can be a strength, but it can go too far and become a hindrance." Lastly, she touched the Ten of Cups, "This is your future, and it says there will be a loving relationship, happiness, and harmony. If you look at the card you can see that your cups, literally, runneth over with joy."

Emme looked up, watching Kendall's eyes flicker with the fire. Kendall was silent but her eyes were saying something significant. Emme didn't know what to do with the energy flowing between them, so she instinctively picked up her deck and started shuffling them over and over, letting their familiar comforting feel sooth her.

Kendall stood up, opened the tent and turned a small light on before putting out the fire. The color of the now glowing tent reminded Emme of the Himalayan salt-lamp she kept by her bed. That unique orange-yellow glow soothed her through the many nights she spent alone, many of which she'd spent, thinking of a certain river loving beauty. It was too much. She started fiddling with small rocks, turning them over and over in her hands, handling them with as much care as she would living-room furniture.

But when she looked up, she noticed that Kendall had walked over to her, and had put out her hand. Emme paused then placed hers inside of Kendall's. Kendall gave her one of those slow lazy smiles that turned Emme to liquid, "Time for bed, my photo-bug."

Emme felt electricity snapping through her fingertips and her blood flow beginning to pulse between her legs. Kendall let Emme in first then zipped the tent flap behind herself

Was that Kendall's breath on the back of her neck? All the hairs on her body stood at attention. They were both illuminated by the golden light of the camping lamp, the quality of light making Emme feel ethereal, goddess-like even. She was basking in her feminine power. It was an energy building inside, stoking an internal flame that brought a powerful awareness to her senses.

She sensed the presence of the Goddess Spirit within her and she silently said thank you. She knew sexual energy was special and a gift but in this moment, she felt those truths to her core. She'd been aroused before and had had good sexual experiences but never had she felt this level of anticipation, desire, hunger even. It was as if this night had the power to quench a thirst she'd never been free of.

They were both on their knees facing one another. The space between them felt alive and magnetic, pulling their bodies closer and closer. Kendall placed her hands on either side of Emme's face and pulled her near. It was as if there was fire in those hands, yet no pain. Their lips were almost touching, but Kendall paused and instinctively Emme knew that she was being given time to consent. To decide if she wanted this to move forwards or to pause and lie next to each other as friends.

Curls bouncing, she smiled and nodded, urging her river queen on. Her lips were gentle and soft with a plushness to them. It didn't take a witch to know they would be, but she hadn't expected them to feel so delicate. The pink tip of Kendall's tongue darted out and gently licked the outer edge of quivering lips. A gravely moan escaped Emme's throat, and Kendall pressed on with more force and less control.

Emme melted into that kiss, allowing this strong fierce woman to guide her. She felt so owned and adored by just this kiss alone. Nervously at first, but then with more confidence, Emme opened her mouth to Kendall, allowing her to explore. She tasted of sunshine, fire, and salt. Emme felt her sense of self-control breaking down. Her legs were trembling, not from the position, but from such extreme want. Had she ever wanted anyone or anything this much? Her body answered her question as she felt herself clench, her inner core wet and wanting.

Kendall's right hand had traced the lines of Emme's face, down her sweat-beaded neck, along one trembling shoulder, and was now cupping her full pale breast in the most reverent manner. The moment Kendall squeezed that blush pink nipple between her thumb and forefinger, Emme let out a throaty moan that had the temptress smiling against her mouth. Emme started moving her hands down the rippling back of her deepest desire and rested them on strong prominent hips, squeezing a bit, letting her fingertips sink into the toned flesh.

Kendall pulled away from Emme's wanting mouth, "Em, if you keep touching me I'm going to lose it, and I've waited a long time to feel you under me. I want this to be about you tonight."

A long time? How long? Later! Later!

Her words were so heartfelt, and her eyes spoke of such desire that Emme could only nod her acquiescence as her friend, and now her lover, gave her a look of appreciation and gently guided her to lay back and let the soft forest floor beneath the tent take her weight.

A slender brown finger danced up Emme's stomach, pulling her shirt up with it. Kendall's right hand firmly gripped Emme's side and pulled her, tucking the redhead in under as she lay on her left side. Once in place, Emme could feel Kendall's breast on her own. Had she ever felt something so perfect? So right? Could her heart and soul handle such a truly flawless sensation?

This was ecstasy on a spiritual level. Two souls joining.

The nipple ring Kendall had previously described only added to the sensations Emme felt around her own tingling, electrified nipple. Knowing lips and teeth trailed up and down Emme's neck and collarbone, whilst a gentle but firm knee was grinding against Emme's engorged clit.

Emme gave up trying to control her reaction. Passion like this was a divine gift. So she gave into it.

Moaning and rolling her hips, deepening the sensation, Emme blindly grabbed at Kendall's shirt indicating it was time for it to come off.

The message was received, and Kendall deftly

removed both their shirts while keeping a slow steady rhythm against Emme's now completely engorged clit. Kendall's full breasts looked sinful, with shimmering silver rings hanging from large dark nipples. Emme wanted desperately to lick and tug on the rings, but she had agreed to Kendall's request, so she nibbled on her swollen lips instead. Emme felt a bit brave and bit down with a little more force which earned her a deep growl in return. Within seconds, Kendall's mouth was covering Emme's right breast while her hand massaged the other one. She sucked and licked with such force that it stole Emme's breath.

The photographer's eyes were focused on her river guide's face. She'd never seen anything so erotic in her life. Kendall looked confident, fierce, and reverent all at one time. Emme pondered this for a moment, and then Kendall bit down on Emme's nipple and simultaneously pressed the palm of her hand against Emme's clit. Her eyes rolled to the back of her head. Her body was on fire and was being driven mad. Her brain short-circuited, "Kendall, please, I don't know how much more I can take."

Kendall stopped what she was doing and brought her mouth to Emme's ear. "Emme, do you need to come?" Her tone was liquid sex and just managed to drive Emme higher.

Emme fought to get the words out, "Yes, please."

Kendall pressed herself into Emme a bit more, "Okay, Emme, I'll give you what you want. I've been picturing this in my mind for a long time, and the wait is killing me too."

Just the idea of Kendall fantasizing about her for who knows how long almost drove Emme over the edge.

Kendall kissed her one more time, deep and full, before moving down to her breasts. Each nipple got a suckle and nip before she continued heading down. Emme felt a warm wet tongue swirl around her belly button followed by a deliberate puff of breath. In a swift seamless move, Emme's shorts were off, and Kendall was looking down at her panties.

"Open your legs, Emme."

It was definitely less request and more directive.

Emme parted her legs allowing her knees to fall to either side.

Kendall leaned over and pressed her mouth over Emme's panties. The sensation was enough to cause Emme's back to arch up and a keening sound to escape her lips. This must have been some sort of sensual rocket fuel for Kendall, because the groan and vibrations against Emme's clit were heavenly. Without thinking, Emme began to moan Kendall's name while thrusting up toward her face.

With that final act of desire, Kendall pulled Emme's panties to the side and flattened her tongue, slowly pulling it upward from the bottom of Emme's vulva to her clit, where she then sucked delicately.

Emme gasped for breath and clenched her fists in the blankets to either side of her. With one long strong arm, Kendall reached up and pinched Emme's nipple while she drove her tongue deep within Emme's vagina and used the thumb of her free hand to rub Emme's clit in circular motions.

Emme exploded from the inside out. She bucked and gasped and keened while Kendall gently held her in place. Her salty liquid splashed Kendall's tongue, and she lapped it up.

Slowly, she crawled back up Emme's body and rested her face in the crook of Emme's neck. Both women were breathing rapidly for a while. Once they came back down, Emme threaded her hand through Kendall's.

"Em you have no idea how long I have dreamed of doing that! You tasted just like I imagined you would, heavenly."

Emme buried her face in Kendall's neck, not knowing how to respond.

"Thank you" came out in a whisper.

Kendall gently lifted her lover's face so that they were looking into one another's eyes, "Hey, are you okay little photo-bug?"

The use of the newly formed nickname gave Emme the burst of confidence she needed. "That was mind-blowing. I've never experienced something so...amazing. Were you scared?"

Kendall laughed, "Not at all. I knew it was the right time."

"How"

She lifted herself up above Emme's face, "I guess it was in the cards."

ABOUT THE AUTHOR

SARAH E. LILY

Sarah E. Lily is a Queer, romance-writing, tattoo-wearing woman, and is rather proud of it. Since writing her first story in the 4th grade - a funny little piece about an all girls boarding school - she hasn't stopped dreaming and imagining in story form yet. Sarah's hope for her own work is that it shows people there is no need for shame or guilt when it comes to desires. Everyone deserves to see themselves in a happily ever after no matter what that looks like. When she's not bopping around New England with her family, she's most likely reading something with vampires, practicing a bit of Tarot, or trying to perfect her mashed potato recipe.

ABOUT ROMANTIC INTENT

When Mat tries to take time out to think after getting fired from her job, she ends up at a campsite with a trunk full of supplies she doesn't know how to use. A mischievous puppy and a ruined tent end in a grudging partnership with Ryan, an experienced camper who wants nothing more than to lend a hand. But Mat isn't the best at accepting help, and she has enough on her plate without the attraction that begins to build between them. As a storm brews overhead, Mat has to come to terms with much more than temptation.

ROMANTIC INTENT

A.Z. LOUISE

Nature was not my preferred habitat. I've always been an indoor kid, more interested in exploring through a video game or my imagination as my Dungeon Master spun me an epic tale about elves or something, but sometimes a person needs a change of scenery. That was why I found myself pulling into the gravel parking area of a campsite on a Friday evening, my trunk full of gear and my stomach full of butterflies.

I already felt unprepared, and the sight of the parking lot only made things worse. Everyone who was unpacking their cars seemed to have forty times as much stuff as I did. Anxious, I almost started my car again to cut my escape, but I had always been more stubborn than I was scared.

Usually.

The second I got out of my car, I saw a dog, which I took as a good sign. Any day when you see a dog is a good day, especially when it's an excitable border collie who runs right toward you while you're taking stuff out of your trunk.

"Hey, puppy!" The words had barely come out of my mouth before the adorable little bastard lifted his leg and peed on my packed-up tent. "Oh no." I froze, arms hanging limp at my sides as I looked around for the dog's owner and spotted a white man jogging toward me.

"I'm so sorry," he said. "He's been cooped up in the truck and got overexcited about all the people. It's his first camping trip, isn't it, Basil? Here, I'll help you hose it off and set it up. I've got some beers if you –"

"Leave me alone," I said. "I don't need any help." But the pee had soaked right into the fabric, which had claimed to be waterproof. I could already feel the tears starting, and blinked up at the pale blue sky. I was trying to escape real life, and for a second I thought about just putting the tent in the trash and going home, but home was way worse than the pee tent at this point.

When I lowered my gaze, the dog was wagging at me, his owner still standing there staring at me. I scowled back at him, took in his auburn hair and freckles. Being mad made me feel less like I was going to cry.

"Um." He glanced down at my soaked tent. "Do you want to use my tent tonight? Until you can get to a store and get one that's a little more...weatherproof?"

"No. I do not." I turned away from him and grabbed my backpack, sleeping bag and cooler, meaning to leave the pee tent where it was. I had enough on my hands; I could deal with it later. Besides, being a Black woman alone in the wilderness (okay maybe not the wilderness, since town was like fifteen minutes away, but it was close enough), cozying up to some rando white guy was the best way I could think of to get murdered and dumped in a river or something.

"Come, on, it's a really nice one. You'll be cozy."

I rounded on him, no clue what I was going to say but sure it'd be rude. But he looked so earnest, and his little piss-demon was wagging his tail. And now that I thought about it, dead bodies in rivers didn't have to pay bills, so maybe being marginally nice to him wasn't all bad.

"How are you sure I won't just steal it?" I asked.

He shrugged. "I dunno. I'd probably deserve it. Come on, I'll help you set up."

I gritted my teeth over a groan. Just what I wanted, to spend more time with this jerk. But based on his massive, well-used backpack and overall ruggedness level, he looked like he actually knew what he was doing, so I put aside my annoyance (and murder worries) and followed him to his truck, and then to set up his tent.

I dropped all my stuff to help, but he began to set it up without even a glance at me. I hoped he couldn't tell that my Tent Plan had been to wing it, but his aggressive competence made me pretty sure he already knew. It also made me a hundred-percent sure I had gotten in over my head; I never would have been able to figure a tent out, let alone set it up on my own. I wasn't exactly known for my grace.

I was left to try to stay out of the way while this large, capable man, who most likely knew that I was a complete mess, rescued me from myself. I really did want to feel grateful for his help, because I was definitely stubborn enough that I would have struggled with the tent for hours before I gave up and slunk home defeated. But somehow, this felt more like a huge L than trying it on my own.

At least if I messed it up on my own, I could escape under cover of night, and nobody would be there to bear witness to my failure. This dude was going to remember me, and probably have a laugh at my expense with his friends, and I was fully prepared to preemptively hate him.

"I'm Ryan, by the way," he said when he'd finished. He extended a hand, sure and steady, and I figured I could put off loathing him long enough for a handshake. Dude had really big hands, but soft, like he had a big bottle of lotion in his backpack. I had expected them to feel like shaking hands with my mechanic.

"Matilda. Call me Mat." It was instinct to tell people my nickname, even if I didn't like them, because I loathed Matilda. I had the paperwork to change it at home, but I'd never had the heart. It was my grandmother's name.

"You got a camp chair?" Ryan asked.

"Oh, hell."

"No?"

"I have one. It's just at home," I said, just so embarrassed. More embarrassed than I ever thought I could be. I was just proving that I was a disaster every time I spoke, and he was just acting like everything was fine after he butted into my camping trip.

"Be right back!" Ryan said cheerfully. He jogged off, his pee-monster at his heels. I was still annoyed at him, but he brought back two camp chairs tucked under his arms and opened a couple of beers. IPA, which I wasn't a fan of, but in this case, it really was the thought that counted. Before I'd finished my beer, he had a fire going and was cooking red hots.

Okay, so maybe he wasn't so bad after all. I was willing to turn around on the dog, at least. Basil was clearly a puppy, prancing around the fire and sniffing everything, peeing on every tree and bush in the area. He wolfed down his dinner at top speed while we ate, and had to be distracted from begging for red hots with rope toys. It was a good thing, because even after the Pee Incident, it was really hard to resist those sad puppy dog eyes. I probably would have given him half my dinner if he hadn't been lured away.

After dinner, Ryan and Basil left for a walk, and I was relieved to be left alone for a while. That had been the whole point of this trip, and with some daylight left I could get caught up on reading. Though the leaves hadn't started to turn, the days were getting shorter. Fall was my favorite time of year, and I was looking forward to wearing comfy, worn-in boots and snuggly scarves and drinking hot cider.

Caught up in daydreams, I'd completely forgotten the book that lay open in my lap. Once I'd started reading, though, I couldn't stop thinking about real life lurking at the end of the weekend. The lists just formed in my head on their own. I needed to get into true weekend relaxation mode and stop dwelling on looming unemployment, but thinking about my current situation came with its own set of worries.

I glanced across the campsite at Ryan's stuff. It was clear that he was planning on staying there that night, which made sense since I was using half his gear. But it was also really weird to have some dude I barely knew sleeping ten feet away. I'd made peace with being murdered, but what if he snored? I'd die without getting a good night of weekend sleep first.

I was way more worried about my privacy and alone time, anyway, but when Ryan came back with Basil, he was carrying what looked like a smaller version of a hard guitar case. I resisted the urge to lean forward, instead watching him over the top of my book. I'd picked up ukulele a couple of years ago, and I couldn't not snoop. He pulled out a mandolin, and started noodling around on it, obviously meaning to leave me alone. I watched him for a while, his fingers moving over the frets and making shadows dance across the warm, red-orange wood.

Ryan had clearly been playing for years, teasing out beautiful sounds without even paying close attention. The thought made a fraction of my annoyance return; I wasn't consistent enough in my practice to ever be that good at ukulele. But the music was calming enough that I couldn't muster the full anger I'd felt earlier in the day. In fact, the thought was exhausting. I turned my eyes back to my book, finally breaking away from the paragraph I'd tried to read over and over and moving on to the next one.

IT TURNED OUT THAT NATURE WAS SUPER NOISY FIRST thing in the morning. It was like every bird on Earth had decided to scream at the same time, and with no apartment walls to insulate me, it sounded like they were all yelling right into my ears. I'd been having such a nice sleep, cozy in my sleeping bag, and now I had to pee.

After a quick, ice-cold shower (plus the walk to and from the bathrooms), I was pissed off, and all I wanted was a hot coffee. Instead, I pulled a cold one out of my cooler. At least I'd been smart enough to bring those. I settled into the chair Ryan had lent me to fortify myself with caffeine before I... did camping things? Hike? Something.

Ryan, I realized, was nowhere to be seen. Basil must have been with him, wherever he was. He'd apparently rolled up his sleeping bag and taken last night's beer bottles with him. He kept everything really neat, which led me to believe he was some kind of alien. Who had the energy?

For the first time since I'd shut off my GPS yesterday, I checked my email. I felt kind of guilty doing it, since I'd told myself I was doing a self-care weekend. Immediate regret. An email from work. I didn't open it, and locked my phone, dropping it into the mesh cup holder.

"Hey, Mat. You okay?" Of course, Ryan had chosen that moment to return, and of course he looked concerned.

I looked away. I had never in my life been able to fix my face, and I couldn't stand people acting all worried about me. It always made me completely fall apart. I just couldn't keep my mouth shut under the gentle pressure of someone caring what was happening inside my head. Ryan was turning out to be the kind of person who would care enough to shatter my shaky calm.

"I'm fine." When I glanced back up at him, I noticed he

hadn't shaved, a night's worth of dark beard stubble growing on his jaw. Oh no.

"I was gonna ask if you wanted coffee but hey, you remembered your own!" Ryan said. Any positive thoughts about his scruff fled, along with the wobbly feeling of being about to cry

"I'm forgetful, not a child," I snapped. It was actually a relief to be angry again.

"I didn't mean –"

"I don't care whether you meant it."

Ryan pulled out his own bottle of cold brew and sat down across the ashes of the fire from me. Basil jumped up in his lap, trampling Ryan and generally making himself a nuisance.

"Buddy, please, I'm trying to apologize. I'm sorry, Mat. I know you're new at this, but I'm not trying to be condescending. That was rude, and I'll do better."

I glanced up at him. His cheeks were pink, probably embarrassed at being such a jerk. I could have just told him to go to hell (it wasn't like I'd ever see him again), but I had never been camping in my entire life, and having someone around to help was actually really nice.

"It's okay," I said. "I am new at this."

"Basil and I are going on a hike today. Wanna come?" Ryan asked.

"How hard is it gonna be?" I asked. I worked in a cubicle and did spin classes on the weekend. I wasn't exactly prepared for a grueling trek through the woods.

"We can do one of the short trails. It'll be a nice walk, just enough to tire Basil out."

"Hmm." I looked at Basil. Border collies seemed to have infinite energy, and Basil was no exception.

"It'll be fun."

"Sure, why not." This dude was a pro at talking me into things. It was his earnest, hopeful smile that did it. The thought of wiping that smile – which I had to admit was cute as hell – off of his face was almost worse than bursting into tears in front of him. Almost. Cuteness could only get someone so far.

We had coffee and a quick breakfast before hitting the bug spray and filling up our water bottles and heading out. It was a gorgeous day, just past the turn from summer to fall. Warm enough that I didn't need a hoodie, but cool enough that I didn't feel like I was on death's sweaty doorstep after a few miles of walking.

The woods were overrun with cardinals, red wings flashing through the trees while they talked back and forth in the same sharp chirps that woke me up that morning. I hadn't realized how loud it would be out here, picturing more of a still and silent Rivendell situation minus the elves. Ryan was only mildly Aragorn-ish, though the stubble helped.

Eventually we came to a stream crossed by a little bridge, and Ryan put out a hand to stop me before I could cross. Basil let out a sharp yip, and Ryan hissed through his teeth. Basil quieted, but he shook with excitement at the end of his leash.

"Look," Ryan whispered. I followed his dark-eyed gaze and saw the mama deer and her two adolescent fawns. They were almost as big as she was, but their limbs were gangly and awkward. They watched us watch them for a few long seconds, so still that Ryan could have told me they were statues and I would've believed him. The stream burbled along its course, and Basil whined, the tension in the air thick as a down comforter.

The deer must have decided we weren't a threat, because they went back to grazing next to the stream, picking delicately at the plants that grew in the muddy place between water and land. They were close enough that I could see individual eyelashes and the movement of muscle under skin and fur. I barely breathed, afraid that any sound or movement would scare them away, though a bird in a nearby tree called so loud that I jumped. Ryan's hand rested on my arm, still as the thick tree trunks that stood all around us.

Basil barked, startling all of us, and the deer bounded away into the woods, barely making a sound. My heart pounding, I looked at Ryan, and for a few seconds, we just stood looking at each other. He let go of my arm, breaking the spell, and a nervous laugh bubbled up in my chest.

"I've never seen deer up that close," I said. "They're beautiful."

"Yeah. I guess I see them so often that I forgot how beautiful they are. I usually just keep walking," Ryan said.

"Why did you stop this time?" I asked. "I didn't even notice they were there."

"I thought you'd want to see them." Ryan said. I felt weirdly touched, like we'd shared something special. That was ridiculous, of course. Deer were everywhere. They were practically a plague. But I clearly wasn't in the habit of thinking like a normal human this weekend, so why stop being weird and dramatic now?

Ryan started walking again, Basil dancing along beside him like we'd stopped for hours. It kind of felt like we had. My arm was tingly where he'd touched it, and I rubbed it as I walked. He must have grabbed me harder than he meant to, harder than I'd realized when I was transfixed by the graceful doe and her wide-eyed teenagers.

It wasn't that I was surprised that Ryan was so strong. What was a shock was the way his strength made me feel, safe and sheltered. I had an urge to trot into step with him instead of trailing behind, in hopes that he might reach for me again. I shoved it down as hard as I could, annoyed with myself for even thinking it.

I watched the trees as we continued through the woods, hoping to get another glimpse of the deer. None came, though there were birds and chipmunks and squirrels everywhere.

The run-in with the deer left Basil even more energetic than before, still wiggling when we got back to camp and Ryan tried to check him for ticks. I helped out by distracting him with dog treats, keeping a hold on his harness. He nuzzled into my lap and licked my hands, being a generally sweet boy. I started to think that maybe I needed a pet to keep me company. A big old sleepy cat to snuggle when autumn and winter came along would be a great friend, but I really needed to get my life together before I could have an animal friend.

"Tick-free," Ryan said. "Thanks for the help."

"He seems like a real handful," I said.

"Yeah, but he's a good guy. Look at that face," Ryan said. He ruffled Basil's ears, smiling fondly.

"A very good, naughty, pee-monster."

"You can't hold that against him, he's a baby."

"I hold it against you," I said.

"Fair, fair." He seemed to know I was joking. He'd more than made up for the Pee Incident. "Lunch and beer?"

"Sure. I got cheese and tomato sandwiches. The tomatoes are from my mom's garden."

"Won't they be all soggy by now?"

"No, you never store tomatoes cold," I said. It astounded me that so few people knew that. I didn't even like gardening, I just liked food.

"What?" He sounded as baffled as I felt.

"It ruins the texture. They get all mealy. I haven't cut them yet." I brushed dog hairs off my jeans on the way to the tent, where I'd placed my tomatoes and paring knife in a corner to keep them safe and unsquished.

"Oh. All right. Sandwiches it is," Ryan said.

I held the glossy yellow tomatoes to my nose for a second, breathing in the bitter-green scent of the broken stems before I started cutting them onto a paper plate. They were so ripe that juice ran between my fingers and down my wrists, and Ryan handed me a paper towel to wipe it away.

We ate sitting opposite each other, sipping our beers and talking. I had been right about the 'never seeing each other again' part; we'd come from opposite parts of the state, me from the south and he from up north. It was actually too bad, since he had a way of making me feel calm when he wasn't annoying the hell out of me. Calm was exactly what I needed that weekend, and even though

I wasn't sure if I'd go camping again, I'd miss the careless feeling.

I don't know why I read that work email while Ryan was off walking Basil again. Maybe I was just alone and bored and needed something to do with my hands. Maybe I was hoping they'd emailed to say the place was falling apart without me and that they wanted to hire me back, but it was just an exit survey they wanted me to take. What did they expect me to say? They'd fired me because I kept forgetting things, and no matter how I complained to HR that I had a disorder and firing me was an act of discrimination, they didn't care.

Maybe I could have sued, but that would've taken time and money and, frankly, me actually giving a shit. I was back on the job market Monday morning at 8 am. I deleted the email and hoped my former boss got a papercut.

Right on the cuticle.

I slouched off to the tent and took a nap, because if I wasn't working, I might as well be well-rested.

IT WAS LATE BY THE TIME I BOTHERED TO GET UP AFTER rolling around and making an ill-fated attempt to read a little bit. Well, not super late, but dinner time, which was late enough to make me feel like I'd wasted half the day. It wasn't like I'd had a day to waste, but the thought still nagged at me as I emerged from the test to find Ryan cooking chicken skewers over the fire. Basil watched and licked his chops, too focused on the meat to notice when I scratched his head. I didn't know if it was because Ryan was making food and I was starving, or if the golden, failing light was hitting him just right, but he was looking pretty handsome that evening.

"I was about to wake you up," he said. I eyed the chicken.

"How long is chicken good in a cooler?" I asked. Cheese started off rotten, it could probably live in a cooler for days without giving me food poisoning. Chicken I wasn't so sure about.

"I dunno, I went into town. We drank all the beers so I was going anyway. I grabbed a salad, too."

"You're an angel," I said before I could stop myself. I hadn't thought about salad at all, and it sounded like the most delicious thing in the world. The last day hadn't been super full of fruits and veggies.

"That hike tired you out, huh?" Ryan asked. He was focused on the chicken, probably making a deliberate effort to ignore the rather weird thing I'd just said.

"No. I mean, it was a long walk, but real life intruded on my weekend."

"Exhausting."

"Yeah. Is that why people love camping so much? You can just peace out on all your problems for a minute?" I asked.

Ryan laughed. "It's definitely one reason." He adjusted the skewers. "I'm glad we ran into each other," he said, not looking up.

I could tell it wasn't an easy thing to say. I watched him for a minute, wanting to tell him the truth but a bit embarrassed by it. Besides, if I started being too truthful with this cute – okay fine, hot – dude, I might start opening up in other, even more ridiculous ways.

"Me too. I'd be lost without someone to help," I admitted. Ryan looked up at me, a tiny smile that I could mistake for smugness playing about his lips. Oh, boy. I hadn't noticed how pretty his dark eyes were. The silence turned awkward for a hot second, until his phone went off, playing a merry little tune.

"Chicken's ready!" His usual cheerfulness seemed a little forced, but things went back to their natural, comfortable state as I helped him dish out dinner, open beers, and feed Basil. Ryan told me some stories about his previous camping trips while we ate, clearly trying to make me laugh, and I found the good dark chocolate bars I'd put at the bottom of my backpack.

"Salted caramel or coconut almond?" I asked.

"I hate coconut," Ryan said. I flipped him the caramel one, and when I sat back down, I couldn't help but notice that he'd moved his camp chair to my side of the crackling fire.

My stomach did a hopeful little flip; he wanted to be closer to me, and I couldn't remember the last time someone had really wanted to get close. I'd gotten into a pattern of work-eat-sleep that hadn't left many chances for closeness. My instinct was to immediately talk myself out of hoping, especially since I was definitely too careful to let some stranger worm his way into my pants, let alone my heart.

Ryan had probably moved because it was easier to talk when you could actually see each other instead of squinting through darkness and flame. Camp felt much cozier this way, too. The fire danced, casting its warm, inconstant light in a glowing ring. Ryan's arm brushed my knee as he reached down to pet Basil, who sat across my feet with a loud doggy sigh, finally tired out.

"Choco-cheers," I said, trying to keep things light, and Ryan laughed. He tapped a corner of his chocolate against mine. "That was good dinner. Thanks."

"Thanks for being good company," Ryan said. "I usually spend these weekends alone."

"That's not very nice to Basil," I said. God, I hoped he didn't get all mushy on me. I was a sucker for mush.

"It's his first camping trip, remember? It gets lonely sometimes."

"I thought outdoorsy types liked being alone," I said. "Maybe that's why I've never been an outdoorsy type." I felt my shoulders stiffen as I realized I'd said too much and put a couple squares of chocolate into my mouth to shut myself up. I could barely taste it, really only aware of the texture of coconut and crunchy almonds.

"Sometimes it's nice to be alone. But I think this weekend I really needed the company." Oh jeez. He was being really open and sweet. "It's too bad there's not much of the weekend left."

"Yeah." I toyed with the ends of my braids, wishing I could say that my weekend was indefinite at this point. It might make me feel better to tell someone I'd gotten fired. It might make him happy to suggest we take another day. But I couldn't make myself admit it. I folded the wrapper back around my chocolate bar, no longer interested in it.

"Mat?"

"Yeah?"

"Can I kiss you?" Ryan asked.

I didn't answer. Instead, I leaned over and kissed him. It only took a moment for his hand to move to my jaw, his fingers brushing the exposed side of my neck. His lips tasted bittersweet and salty from chocolate, and the scent of him filled my head, sweat and something soapy, citrusy. I was dizzy, floating, clutching him to anchor myself as my whole body grew warm.

Excitement gave way to anxiety as I realized that getting close to him was a mistake. I was a mess and he was a complete stranger and I shouldn't have spent the money on this trip and all I wanted was to be at home under a blanket. I pulled away.

"What's wrong?" Ryan asked. I escaped to the tent before he could see me cry. "Mat?" He called after me. I thought I heard him sigh when I didn't answer. Part of me wanted him to come after me, care enough to check on me, but the rest just wanted to be alone. I was half-disappointed, half-relieved, when he spoke again. "Well. Let's get you in the truck before it starts raining, buddy," he said to Basil.

I bit my lip, guilt overwhelming all my other emotions, and dug my phone out of my pocket. It was a ninety percent chance of rain. Shit. I didn't want to let Ryan sleep in the rain or in his truck, but getting in close to him again was definitely dangerous. That kiss had messed me up. If we shared the tent, I'd end up naked before I knew what had happened.

The thought made my face go hot. I'd turned around on Ryan, sure, but now I was out here just blatantly having sexual thoughts? I was in more trouble than I thought, headed straight toward an unexpected heart-break tomorrow morning on top of everything else. That's how it would have to end unless I put a stop to any kind of fooling around right now.

My most immediate problem, though, was that I had to brush my teeth before I went to sleep, which meant making eye contact with Ryan at some point or another, unless I wanted to wait until he fell asleep. I had to be quick, grabbing my flashlight and toothbrush and rushing to the bathrooms while I brushed so I could get back before he did. It was anxiety hell, but I made it, grabbing my bag to protect it from the rain and tearing my bra and jeans off before I wriggled into my sleeping bag. If I had to get up in the night I'd need to find my pajama pants, but I didn't want to have to talk to Ryan, and the best way to avoid that was to pretend to be asleep.

I heard Ryan messing around outside when the first few patters of rain hit the tent. Overwhelmed by guilt but not willing to get up, I called his name.

"Yeah?"

"Are you gonna sleep in your truck?" I asked.

"Yeah."

"Come in here with me, okay? You'll be more comfort-able. You're too much boy for that cab."

Ryan unzipped the tent to poke his head inside. "Too much boy?" he asked. His face was all hopeful amusement, lit from beneath by his lantern.

"You're like eight feet tall. Get in here." There was plenty of room for both of us inside, Ryan's sleeping bag snugging in right next to mine with my backpack at my feet. The one that had the satin bonnet in it, but I wasn't about to put that on in front of a cute guy. My edges could survive one night. The way I was feeling, my emotions could not survive a possible explanation of Black Hair Stuff. "What about all your stuff?"

"I put it in the truck, too," he said. I hadn't even noticed on my dash back to the tent. He must have stopped to brush his teeth, too, because he smelled minty. I'd had all the time in the world, and I'd made myself nervous for nothing. "Are you okay?" Ryan asked again.

"I came out here to get less stressed, not more," I said.

"Am I stressing you out?"

"Thinking about what happens after this weekend is stressing me out." I couldn't look at him when I said it, afraid of what I'd see in his eyes. Afraid he'd know that I wasn't just talking about facing my real life, and that he'd think I was an absolute dipshit for wishing our time together wouldn't end. "I got fired on Tuesday and then spent a bunch of money to come camping this weekend because I wanted to escape so bad."

"Oh no," said Ryan.

"Yeah. Not my best move."

"Are you gonna be okay?" He asked. I bit my lip. I was currently not okay at all, but I'd already told him too much. "Mat?"

I looked up at him, found my eyes drawn to his. They were almost gold in the lantern light, and for the first time I noticed how large they were, how beautiful. There was a hint of sadness to his brow, his carefree attitude slowly melting away. Night was when we were too tired to pretend, and I was afraid to speak.

For a while, it seemed like Ryan was too. He propped himself up on his elbow.

"Money-wise, I mean. Will you be okay?" He asked again, breaking the tension.

"I have some savings. And I can always move back in with my mom. She's been wanting me to stay with her for like the last ten years. She says she misses cooking with me."

"That makes sense. You're fun."

"I'm the worst housekeeper on Earth," I said. "I don't know why I'm telling you this."

"It's cozy in here. Like a sleepover. That's when you tell secrets and stuff."

"Then you have to tell me a secret. That's just fair," I said. Ryan smiled the softest smile I'd ever seen.

"My secret is that I have a crush on you," he said.

"That doesn't count, I –"

Ryan's lips met mine, sending the last words spiraling out of my brain. Being so close made all the air leave my lungs, my fingers tingling as they found their way into his hair. His arms were strong and comforting, and I wondered how I hadn't noticed how solid he was until he pulled my warm sleeping bag open with the harsh sawing sound of a zipper being dragged open, his body blocking the cool air that rushed over my skin. I slid my hands into Ryan's shirt, brushing my fingers across his skin until goosebumps rose there. His dick pressed against my thigh, as his hands wandered from my waist to my hips to my ass, as if looking for something to hold onto, to find purchase.

I squeaked when he squeezed hard, warmth flooding

through me. Ryan's lips left mine, and he laughed, but it wasn't the clear, sudden laugh I had grown used to. It was a chuckle deep in the back of his throat, husky and surprisingly sensual, muffled as he pressed his lips against the sensitive skin of my throat.

Shivers scudded across my skin, and I writhed against him. I knew without a shadow of a doubt that Ryan was the kind of tease who would test my patience and break down all my walls.

The sky opened up, rain pounding on the fabric above us. The air had gotten chilly, making my nipples hard and sensitive to Ryan's touch when his hands found my breasts. His warm lips and fingers sent waves of pleasure from my breasts straight down between my legs. When I shifted my body against his, Ryan's hand slipped into my panties, gently caressing but never touching my clit or dipping inside. The anticipation was killing me, a wordless sound of desire escaping my lips before I could stop it. Still he teased, kissing his way down my belly but never going further until I whispered please.

Ryan pulled off my panties, gentle as a whisper. His tongue was slow and hot, and I had to take two handfuls of my sleeping bag to keep from grabbing him by the hair to show him what I wanted. What he wanted was to ruin my life, and I was ready to let him. Why shouldn't I? There was precious little of it left, anyway.

It felt like he ate me out all night, letting me get close and easing off a thousand times until I felt like I was about to die, until I told him how much I hated him. I expected him to laugh, but he moaned instead, his tongue moving faster. The sound was unbelievably hot, the sensation almost too much to handle. I came, a wave of lightning running through my veins and leaving me wrung out. My body wanted to give out, my hands shaking when I pushed him away to grab my backpack, but the thought of stopping to rest didn't even enter my mind. I dug in the front pocket of my bag, where I'd dumped my whole purse, and I had condoms in there.

"You came prepared," Ryan said. I kissed him to shut him up, tasting my own bitterness all over his lips and tongue. We both fumbled with his jeans – God, who went to bed in jeans – until he could slide them a little down his hips. He felt good in my hand, warm and hard. I felt completely carved out, starved for him.

I slid the condom onto the head of his dick, pushing it the rest of the way with my mouth. He gasped as my lips touched the base of his cock. The latex tasted horrible, but I sucked him for a few long strokes, listening to his moans grow more desperate. The sound completely bypassed my brain, burrowing inside me and making me squirm. Ryan used a handful of my braids to gently pull me away. In the pale light of the lantern, his face was flushed, his brown eyes smoky with desire. He looked as ready to come apart as I felt.

"That feels really good, but I want to fuck you. Lay back?" He asked. I did, spreading my legs open for him despite the chill in the air. "Jesus." He pulled off his shirt, his chest hot and fuzzy against mine as I wrapped my arms around his neck.

Ryan pushed inside me, the curve of his dick hitting just the right spot with a warm stretch. It was sweet relief to feel every inch of him, to hear his breath catch. He kissed my throat, slow strokes burning me up inside. I snaked my arms under his, grabbing two handfuls of his perfect ass, but I lost my grip when he pushed up on his hands, changing to a new angle that made me moan. He drove into me hard and fast, and I knew he was close by the way he bit his lip. I reached down to rub my clit, rushing myself to come so hard I saw spots. When I tightened against him, it made another orgasm crash over me, and he groaned, his body going rigid as he came.

He collapsed into me, both of us catching our breath in relative silence. The rain had slowed, playing a constant, gentle beat on the nylon above us, and after a while, Ryan pulled his sleeping bag open and over both of us. I kind of liked this part of camping, warm and comfortable in a cozy tent while it was horrible outside. I nuzzled into Ryan's neck, completely relaxed at last, and he held me tighter, letting out a long, contented sigh.

"You're like a big, cuddly teddy bear," I said. Ryan laughed and kissed my temple. It would be easy to get used to being loved on like this, and a little bit of regret blossomed in my mind. I missed him already, even thought I'd just met him. I had to shove those feelings out of my mind before they ruined my whole night.

"I'm glad you let me help you," he said.

"Me too, but you already said that."

"Well, I get the idea that you're not someone who likes to accept help, so I'm pretty grateful."

I was suddenly too hot, wrapped up in Ryan's arms, and our sleeping bags. I didn't answer, because if I did, I'd say something I regretted. It was like he was purposely trying to sound like my final work assessment just to remind me of my flaws. I pushed off the sleeping bag, found myself too cold, and put on my shirt. A drop of water somehow worked its way through the tent and spattered on the back of my neck, sending a shudder down my spine.

"I shouldn't have said that," Ryan said.

"Observant," I replied. Too sharply, judging by the way he widened the gap I'd put between us. I hated myself for being a mess who couldn't even keep my easiest job ever, putting numbers in spreadsheets for a paycheck that was big enough to feel like a mistake. I hated myself for being angry at Ryan, but I hated myself even more for letting myself care what he thought. For being sad that it had to be over so soon when I knew how it would end. For giving into desire in the first place. "I guess it doesn't matter. It's not like we'll ever see each other again."

"Yeah." Ryan's voice was strained, his expression hurt. There was a long, horrible silence in which I knew I'd said the wrong thing but couldn't admit it, or say sorry. Ryan was a better, more open person than I was, and that made me feel even worse. "I should go check on Basil."

He didn't come back.

MY ALARM WENT OFF AT SIX, SUNDAY MORNING. IT WAS A criminal hour for someone who was unemployed, and my eyes were puffy and itchy from crying myself to sleep. But I wanted to get the hell out of there before Ryan woke up and came back to our campsite. I felt bad about leaving his tent just sitting there, but not as bad as I'd feel if I had to talk to him. Or apologize. Or look at the campsite and make myself all sad about what had happened.

I went through a truncated version of my morning routine, not bothering to shower. I'd just do that when I got home. Maybe I'd even take a hot bath once I was in my apartment and felt like I could let my guard down. Obviously, I couldn't trust myself to do that around somebody else.

I packed everything up haphazardly and made a run for my car, but I felt my pace slow as I passed Ryan's truck. No signs of life, thank goodness, but I felt like I was catching secondhand regrets just by looking at a parked vehicle.

"Hey, Mat."

I stopped dead in my tracks. Caught in the act of escaping. Basil came up behind me and started licking my hand, so I had to turn around to give him some attention. I could ignore a human, but not a dog.

"You okay?" Ryan asked. He looked tired as hell and just as cute as ever. Damn him.

"Why are you always asking me that?" I asked. I wasn't trying to be mean; it was just something I'd noticed. Ryan shrugged.

"I'm always too open with my own feelings. I sometimes don't pay close enough attention to what other people are feeling, so I have to check in."

"That makes sense. I should start doing that so I stop being such a huge bummer." There I went again, saying things I shouldn't. I squatted down to give Basil some more pets. I didn't want to look Ryan in the eye. "I'm sorry. I just...got a little maudlin, I guess."

"I'm sorry, too. I didn't mean to hurt you. It was a good weekend, wasn't it?" he asked. I looked up at his wistful expression. It was like looking in an extremely handsome mirror, and it made my soft little heart ache.

"Yeah. Most of it." I made myself smile. His returning smile was tentative.

"You know, this doesn't have to be the last time we see each other. I'd really like to see you again," Ryan said. A gentle, hopeful warmth filled me. I wanted to see him again, every day, if I could. The sudden happiness faded. I stood, brushing Basil fur off my hands. This was about to get sad again, and I wanted to be able to flee as soon as possible. He watched me warily, like he knew I was thinking about making a run for it.

"It's a long way to see each other," I said instead. I tried to keep my voice steady, but it shook a little.

"Yeah, but this is halfway." His expression never fell. "Will you meet up with me again? Next weekend? I'll pay for your gas. Hell, I'll come pick you up."

"That doesn't make any sense," I said, but it felt good to be wanted. Maybe I didn't have a job, but at least one person thought I was worth spending time with. He stepped closer.

"Give me your phone so I can give you my number. We can make plans later. I just...don't want this to be how it ends," Ryan said. Looking into his dark eyes, standing this close, I didn't, either. I pulled my phone out of my pocket and unlocked it.

"Wait a sec, I've got a notification...oh." I froze.

"What?"

"I got an interview." I had never felt more relieved. I was anxious, sure, but relief was winning out for now.

"Already?" Ryan asked.

"Well, um. I felt like things were going bad at my job a while ago, so I started looking around, just in case."

"That was really good thinking. That's amazing." He was giving me a look that I thought might be pride. Like something serious enough had happened between us that he had an emotional stake in my life. I handed him my phone. "You'll text me and tell me how it goes, right?"

"Yeah." This felt good. So good that I had whiplash from how terrible my week had been. I tucked my phone back in my pocket and turned to go, then changed my mind. I couldn't leave without a goodbye kiss. I didn't mean for my arms to go around his neck, or to press so close, or to let a sigh slip out. I definitely didn't mean to murmur that I would miss him, but his returning smile and hug were worth it.

Back at my car, the pee-tent was still lying behind my rear right tire. It was completely soaked with rainwater and completely useless, so I chucked it in the closest trash barrel before I got in. Feeling like I'd relieved myself of more than one burden, I put the car in reverse, but sat with my foot on the brake for long enough to text Ryan.

We should go camping in a hotel next time, I said. A little way down the road, he texted back. I passed a few text stops on the highway back home, and thought about stopping to see what he'd said but chickened out. It wasn't like I thought Ryan would text me to tell me he'd changed his mind, but being at home would make me feel more grounded, more like this whole thing was real. Though waiting felt like the right decision for the first hour or so of the drive, it got harder and harder not to look at my phone.

By the time I got home, all I wanted was to talk to Ryan. I left most of my gear in the car, just grabbing my backpack since my wallet and toiletries were inside. When I finally sat down on the couch and curled up around my phone, the butterflies that had started my weekend returned, warmth spreading through my body as I read his short text.

I'll be happy as long as I get to see you again.

~

ABOUT THE AUTHOR

A.Z. LOUISE

A.Z. Louise is an engineer-turned-writer, whose conure keeps them company during the writing process. Their work runs the gamut from speculative fiction to contemporary romance, as long as there's a happy ending. When not writing, they can be found knitting, playing folk harp, or weaving.

Links to their work can be found at azlouise.com

ABOUT WHAT YOU NEED

Ness has one thing on her mind—advancing her career in real estate—but a snowstorm, one bed, and a passionate attraction to her co-worker threaten to bring joy back into her workaholic life.

WHAT YOU NEED

TORRANCE SENÉ

"You've got to be joking…" Ness sighed and stared at the chalet standing proudly in front of them. Like some defiant, mocking bastard. *Note to self: Add mountains to places I hate.*

The passenger-side car door closed, and soon, her colleague Bree chuckled beside her. "They call this a resort?" She snorted. "I mean, don't get me wrong. It's a gorgeous place, but this is *so* not a lodge. There's no one even here."

"Didn't need your commentary, thanks." Ness rolled her eyes and pulled the property's keys out of her coat pocket. The agency had stated it was an inn, and she'd expected multiple buildings with a spa or at least a few saunas—possibly a gym. Or even a ski shop with it being a terrain like this. A winter wonderland getaway tucked away in the Colorado Mountains. Appraising something like that would look amazing on her résumé.

It was the only reason she'd subcontracted Bree through work to come along for extra protection. She liked having someone with her in case of creepy men who had no idea what boundaries or human decency were.

The first few times that'd happened had been enough for her, especially after the last one. Another empty building, only that time with a squatter who was a little too happy to see her and had followed her around. She'd almost quit after that, but a friend mentioned hiring a bodyguard instead, since spending nights feeling unsafe was no way to get a job done. After meeting Bree, she knew it was the best way to keep her career moving forward.

But now, she'd be stuck with her. Alone in a house with no escape from the woman she'd been unable to stop thinking about since the day they met. The snow crunched beneath Ness's boots as she traipsed up the steps to the stone and wood chalet, duffel bag in hand. She just needed to get through this weekend and back to forgetting about her coworker and the sweet way the corner of her eyes crinkled when she laughed.

The two women didn't see each other often. Only when Ness needed a little extra protection on an away job. Ness enjoyed that, enjoyed the ability to push her out of her mind and focus on work. The last thing she needed was some stunning woman distracting her. She doubted she'd have much luck ignoring her this weekend, even if inviting Bree along had been her own idea. There wouldn't be anything to divide their attention away from one another. No guests or staff to talk to. And she'd forgotten the latest novel she'd been reading on the nightstand back in town.

Her skin bristled the more she thought about being

alone together. Bree threatened the tight rein Ness held over her life. And now she would have to deal with all this forced proximity.

"Didn't realize I needed your permission to speak." Bree's heavy footsteps followed her up the stairs. "That possible promotion is really going to your head, huh?"

Ness clenched her jaw. She decided it was better not to reply and keep her attention on unlocking the door. Bree got under her skin, always offering unprompted opinions whenever they worked together. She had one job—to be a bodyguard—but she was always so damn chatty. And her voice was like silk against Ness's skin.

Soft, smooth, … and distracting.

She should never have let the promotion slip, over after-work drinks one night. It felt like letting someone in a little more. And getting close to someone again, especially someone she worked with, didn't fall within the current version of Ness's five-year plan. Dating was a section of the pie chart she could live without.

The wind whipped around them both as Ness twisted the key, swinging the door open. The scent of cedar and pine greeted them and mingled with the musk of Bree's perfume. But the interior felt no warmer than outside. *Great.*

"They knew we were coming," Bree offered another unwarranted statement as she removed her scarf once they were inside and out of the wind. "The least they should've done was flip on the heat."

Ness sighed. "I'll call Mason and see what's up." She clicked her boss's contact in her phone and let it ring. The late afternoon sun filtering through the windows glinted off Bree's black hair and set off the dark blue highlights. She looked so gorgeous in that light.

What the hell? Ness shook her head. *Nope. Absolutely not. You work with her, for God's sake.* She turned around and focused on the wall, denying her attraction.

It would be unethical.

Wrong. Taboo. And feel so fucking good...

Heat rose to her cheeks, and she paced through the room, putting a little more distance between them. *Come on, Mason. Pick up the phone.*

Suddenly, the ringing cut off, and the connection made an annoying beep that could only mean one thing. *Fuck.* "The signal dropped. Stupid mountains." Ness pinched the bridge of her nose. Could things get any worse?

Bree bent over, admiring the antiques in a glass cabinet. Her ass looked amazing in those tight leggings. Tall boots accentuated her calf muscles beautifully. But then the rest of her gorgeous body disappeared under a puffy parka.

Yes, they definitely could get worse.

Ness swallowed. She'd hired Bree. Essentially, on paper at least, she was her boss. And as her boss, the last thing she needed to do was give in to this attraction. It was unprofessional. Not to mention it would put another woman at risk for a reprimand, and Ness didn't want that. She wanted Bree to succeed as much as she did herself. So, these thoughts needed to go away and leave her in peace. They were here to *do a job.* That's it. She needed her body to get on board with this fact and calm the hell down.

"Seriously?" Bree turned around and sighed. She shrugged her shoulders. "So, business continues as usual, then?"

"Yeah. We don't really have anything else to do." Ness chuckled wryly, crossing her arms over her chest and making her leather jacket squeak. "Might as well do my job and appraise the place. We'll get paid either way." Besides, she hated leaving anything unfinished. There was a reputation at work she needed to uphold. The cabin instead of an inn, the lack of heat and staff, these were just things she'd have to deal with, and adapt. They shouldn't keep her from doing what she came for.

Bree's eyes sparkled. "You say that, but this place must surely have something fun we can get up to." A smirk pulled at her lips. "Use your imagination, Ness."

Was that a flirt? Was she flirting?

Nah. Ness was simply imagining things. She had to be. It was merely a side effect of not getting laid in three years. Not since Anthony had broken her heart. She cleared her throat. She hated thinking of him. What kind of man dumps a woman just because he finds out she's bisexual? Who does shit like that? *Asshole*.

She stared at an imperfection in the wood paneling, pushing away the feelings of inadequacy that had plagued her since before she cracked the dam that held it all back. She wasn't good enough—whole enough—as she was. Not for anyone. Dating was no longer for her. She'd come to accept it. Besides, was Bree even into women?

She secretly hoped. Or … maybe she didn't. Maybe working with Bree would be a whole lot easier if she simply pretended the alluring woman was completely and utterly straight. Would that perhaps make the unwanted thoughts disappear? Ah, a possible solution. A sense of control washed back over her, tension dialing back to a manageable level.

"Yeah. Well, I need to do my job. But I guess do whatever the hell you want since the place is empty, and you spent all that time driving. Maybe there's playing cards or something in a drawer somewhere."

Bree removed her parka. "We both know I always pack a deck."

Ness slipped off her jacket as well and grabbed the clipboard and day planner from her bag. "Text me if anything … Never mind. No service." She disappeared around the corner and headed up the stairs. The cabin was gorgeous, and she had things to do. Her colleague was just a distraction. She needed distance if she wanted to keep her head straight and also shove all those disturbing feelings back down.

She definitely shouldn't think of how the car had smelled like Bree's perfume for the duration of the journey, and how that made Ness just want to nestle into her neck like a kitten. She cleared her throat. Okay, that was helpful and not helpful at the same time.

Consulting the papers, she ran through the checklist. *Focus.* Bree could entertain herself downstairs while Ness worked. It was the perfect arrangement. The first room upstairs wasn't what she expected. In fact, the upstairs seemed to have been remodeled into one giant room. So, this cabin was a getaway for couples—not families.

A bit of loneliness swirled in her belly. She stared at the massive bathtub, big enough for two. How amazing

would a secluded getaway like this be? How *romantic*…
She swallowed the lump in her throat and jotted some
notes as she made her way through the master suite.

Memories pricked at her mind. A trip to Napa Valley.
Sunshine, laughter, and wine at the height of a beautiful
summer. She and Anthony had the entire villa to themselves. Rows and rows of grapes stretched far outside
their window as he kissed along her shoulders and licked
up the column of her neck as her eyes fluttered shut. His
thick cock was buried deep inside her, leisurely thrusting
as he whispered sweet and filthy things between kisses.
She'd thought they'd be together forever. That he was the
one. But it had ended so coldly and with such prejudice.

Her eyes stung. It wasn't that she missed him. No. He'd
been a dick in the end and easy to get over. What she
missed was being with *someone*.

Being in love.

Being so certain of someone else and how they wanted
her, the assurance and stability in that. She blinked
quickly as she headed back downstairs, ending the tears
before they'd the chance to begun.

The stunning stone and marble kitchen featured a
breakfast nook, a gas fireplace, and a large workspace big
enough for an amateur chef to have a field day. She could
see the immense potential for opening this up for rentals
or even for buyers. Who wouldn't want their own private
oasis in the mountains? Think of all the candlelit dinners
with snow falling outside and cozying up together by the
fireplace in the living room.

Her chest ached. Her shoulders slumped. The
marketing side of her brain gave way to the personal. This

was the sort of place she wanted to share with someone. Though maybe on the beach in New England versus the mountains. But that meant opening herself up again, and she couldn't do that. The pain was still too real, too intense.

Anthony had made her question so much about herself. What she wanted. What she needed. It's the one thing she tried to cling to from that relationship.

Yes, it broke her, but it also gave her perspective. She wanted to be accepted, fully, by someone. Loved for who she was and not be expected to hide some of it or worse, deny it. But what if the next person did the same?

What if they also found her lacking by simply being who she was?

"Whatever," she said aloud to no one, before heading into the living area to survey it, and then outside. Work was all she needed. Anything else was too much of a risk. At least work could be somewhat predictable and controlled. Less emotion was involved. She found comfort in the lists, copywriting, and figures.

Snow was falling as Ness ventured to the terrace. The sound of burbling water caught her attention, however. She didn't recall the brief stating the home had any water features that would still be running in the dead of winter. She rounded one of the columns, and her breath hitched. Bree was in the hot tub.

And she appeared to be naked.

Her black hair was soaked through and slicked back against her scalp. Ness bit her lip. Suddenly, she was very aware of her own body, and all previous misgivings were momentarily forgotten. Warmth and an undeniable ache coursed through her veins. Her pulse rose in cadence. Her fingers itched to touch Bree's skin.

This was ridiculous.

Ness grimaced and briefly clenched her jaw. She needed to be a voice of responsibility. They had a job to do, dammit, and here her colleague was nude and dripping with water. Jesus Christ, she looked amazing... "What *exactly* are you doing? I thought you were playing solitaire or something."

Bree swiveled around in the water and smirked. "It's cold inside. I *was* trying to relax and have a good time. You should try it sometime." She drifted over, propping her forearms on the tub's edge. Water dripped down the sides. "That scowl you always seem to have might just dissolve." She flicked a little water at her.

Ness rolled her eyes, even if her stomach dropped at the teasing insult. She'd become a hard ass since the breakup with her ex; she knew it. "Or you could try not being so damn carefree for once. A foreign concept, I know."

"Oh, she has some bite." Bree motioned to one of the patio chairs, the look of amusement still on her pretty face.

Ness wanted to take her by the throat and kiss it off her.

"Could you hand me that towel?"

Bree's request snapped Ness back to reality. She grabbed the towel and flung it over to her coworker. Ness thanked every god in existence that Bree faced away when she stood. But that didn't stop the heat rising to Ness's cheeks as she watched the water slither its way down

Bree's spine and over her plump ass. Her own nipples hardened.

She looked down out of respect. *Yeah, respect. That's it.* It wasn't that she wanted Bree more than anyone or that she had turned down dates with others because she couldn't get Bree out of her mind. She downed the thickness in her throat. Her mind was the only place she'd get to be with her. She knew that. It was too messy otherwise.

Bree snickered. "Are you blushing?"

When Ness looked up, Bree was covered. Thank God. But the corner of her mouth was pulled up. "We should wrap things up here and then head back into town."

Bree stepped out of the tub. "I thought we were allowed to stay. It's why I took a dip."

"We are, but it turns out there's only one bedroom." Ness sighed, the wind picking up and blowing her hair across her face. Luckily, it blocked the view of Bree's muscular thighs. "The B&B back in town would be better. I left something there, anyway."

"Whatever you say." She shrugged. "Doesn't really matter to me where I sleep. I'm not fussy." She squeezed the water out of her hair. "Let me get dressed and warm back up some, and then we can head out. There's gotta be a hair dryer somewhere in there."

THE WIND WAS HOWLING WHEN THEY STEPPED BACK outside an hour later, bags over their shoulders. Ness just blinked. This had to be some sort of cosmic joke, right?

"Did you not even bother to check the weather?" Bree asked from beside her.

"You could have." She snapped her head to her. "I don't always have to think of everything."

Bree let out a laugh. "Well, there is no way in hell we'll get the car down the mountain in this. Visibility is only going to get shittier." She shrugged. "We're stuck for the night—if not longer."

Reality sank in for Ness. This cabin only had one bedroom, and that meant … only one bed. And by the sound of it, Bree didn't seem bothered at all with that scenario. Everything rolled off her with such ease. That had always made her so damn attractive and so irritating. Relaxed was not an emotional state Ness was good at. There was always a mix of envy and appreciation for Bree's personality prickling at her.

She looked away from her colleague, her fingers busying themselves on her necklace. Back and forth, she dragged the pendant. No no no no. This couldn't happen. She couldn't trust herself in such a romantic setting with Bree. What if she leaned in to kiss her without thinking? What if she accidentally rolled over in the middle of the night, and they woke up … spooning? That would be mortifying. *Ugh*.

Her head spun. Her heart raced. This was so *not ideal*. It was a nightmare. Her palms started to feel clammy despite the cold, dry air. Things were not supposed to turn out this way. She really didn't want to be placed in a situation that tested her. She wasn't even sure she had sound judgment in relationships anymore.

"But aren't you a survivalist or something, too?"

Desperate wasn't an apt enough word for how much she wanted to leave. "We'll be fine with you driving." My God, this woman was going to give her a panic attack.

"Are you honestly suggesting we risk our lives just to escape a perfectly cozy and free cabin?" Incredulity hung from Bree's every feature. "Rule one of survivalism: don't put yourself in unnecessary conditions."

Wind kicked up again, pushing Ness toward Bree. Even through the growing blizzard whipping around them like a snow globe, Ness caught something melt in Bree's cocky expression. Her pulse spiked again. What was it just now that Bree saw that made her soften? Was she looking too longingly at her? Oh God. *Did she know? Am I being that obvious?* Her thoughts weren't giving her a moment's rest, flying from one worry to the next.

"Let's get you back inside," Bree added. "I'll make a fire."

Moments later, Ness sat on a chaise lounge, watching as Bree stacked firewood and stoked the kindling so they'd be more comfy. Warmth unfurled in Ness's belly at that. When was the last time someone had taken care of her? After Anthony, the only way she'd been able to survive was to bury herself in her work. Achievement became her life's blood. It had also given her tunnel vision and no room for anything else.

But, she'd discovered, it all felt empty without someone to share it with. She wanted to come home to someone, to talk about their day, laugh, and make dinner together. To cuddle on the sofa and end up making out like teenagers who couldn't keep their hands off each other. If she ever let herself relax for long, the yearning for companionship gnawed at her. It's why she couldn't trust herself here with Bree. The skin hunger was overwhelming sometimes. Staying busy at least numbed the pain.

She glanced around the room to distract herself. The couch looked about as comfortable as an episode of *Mad Men*. Buyers and patrons ate up mid-century modern, but no one truly wanted to sleep on it. Ness thought about her plush sectional, loaded with pillows, back at home and groaned.

"I'm making the fire as fast as I can, woman," Bree retorted.

"No, sorry. That wasn't about you." She sighed. "Just thinking about things back home." Her racing thoughts had become much quieter inside, away from the growing storm. They were still there but without the urgent panic attached. She hoped Bree wouldn't think less of her for witnessing the façade crack a little.

Bree shoved some lit kindling under the logs and watched as the fire slowly began to spread before turning her attention to Ness. "Look, I'm sorry about teasing you earlier." Bree tilted her head to the side, looking every bit the adorable puppy. If adorable puppies were also devastatingly gorgeous and could kill a man with their thighs alone.

Ness shivered with arousal at the thought of Bree's thighs. *I bet they feel amazing.* She'd seen what Bree could do. The way she wrapped those legs around the neck of someone twice her size and twirled his body to the ground like a rag doll. She'd owned him, making him tap out. Ness had to slip between the sheets and handle herself after the first day they'd met at the ring. Bree's biceps had gleamed with sweat as she'd pushed some fallen hair off her equally drenched brow and beamed at Ness with the most gorgeous smile she'd ever seen.

The woman was a femme's wet dream come to life. Hiring her had probably been a mistake since Ness had been unable to think of anyone else since then. She longed to run her nails down those muscular legs, kissing her way back up before her face disappeared between them. Her mouth watered. Bree looked like a woman who should be worshipped, and Ness craved the honor.

"It just seems like cutting loose would be good for you, ya know," Bree continued, completely unaware of where Ness's mind was. "When was the last time you had fun? *Really* had fun."

Bree's tone was challenging, but soft. It wasn't a question meant to provoke her but guide her. And yet anxiety bubbled up, nonetheless.

Ness chewed her lip, her stomach twisting a little. "Why does it matter so much to you?" Was she a fixer? Or was she actually interested in Ness's well-being? Thoughts swirled as she tried to find some sort of stability among them. And did that mean as a friend or more? Dating women was always so confusing, and she loathed getting her hopes up. What if she made a move and looked like a fool because Bree wasn't interested? She'd been there before. Been ridiculed when she'd hit on a straight woman by accident and was met with laughter and derision. The woman had made her feel like some sort of creep simply because she'd asked her out.

Her fingers twitched for something to fidget with,

finding rest on her pendant once more. She rubbed the silver circle between her fingers. She bought this necklace to remind herself how strong she was. Touching it felt like the north star realigning her to what she wanted out of life.

"I hate seeing a beautiful woman waste away with workaholism and sadness. So, sue me." Bree chuckled, then grabbed a throw and placed it over Ness's lap. Her expression brightening as something caught her eye. "Ooh, is that a wet bar?"

Bree was already bounding over to it before Ness could truly raise any objections.

"We probably sho—"

"Hey," Bree cut her off. "I read the client brief. We're allowed back here. So, relax. Let's let loose a little, huh? There's a storm raging outside." Popping behind the bar, she observed the goods and grabbed a few bottles. "What's your poison, babe?"

Ness hated how much she enjoyed hearing that pet name from Bree's enticing lips. And being told what to do had a surprising effect on her body and soul. A weird sort of peace washed over her, almost as if she'd needed permission to exist outside of work, to let go every now and then. What real harm could it do? If one night of relaxation messed up her plans, then maybe they weren't so meaningful, anyway.

Her racing thoughts quelled some. And maybe it felt a little kinky to have a sexy woman order her around. Yeah. She definitely needed a drink now. Her body was buzzing.

"Um, a Sazerac sounds good."

"Aren't we fancy?" Bree winked then busied herself.

There was something wholly erotic about watching Bree mix cocktails. The way she commanded the bottles. Confidence oozed from every pore on that woman. Ness sighed softly, wondering what it would be like to be held down and made to come, over and over by her. She squeezed her thighs together and looked away.

Puppies. Kitten. Office supplies. Come on. Think of something else.

But her line of vision went straight back to Bree, pulled to her no matter what she tried to do.

"Here you go." Bree offered the drink and sat adjacent with her own. "Decided to have the same. Try a little class on for size."

"Thanks." Ness swirled her drink and then sniffed it, ignoring the fact that she was now highly aware of Bree's perfume, as well. Musk. Maybe now a touch of woodsmoke from the fire, too. It'd kept her throbbing the entire trip up. She sighed inaudibly into her glass.

Minutes of quiet fell between them as they nursed their cocktails. The snow churned outside the large windows. Nothing about time seemed real. It felt slower, as if they existed outside of it. Ness's skin grew warmer with every sip.

"So, what were you thinking about earlier?" asked Bree, breaking the silence.

"Oh God, nothing of importance." She chuckled and rubbed the pads of her fingertips against the glass. "Just about how uncomfy the sofa in here looked."

Bree raised a brow and smiled. "That's the sort of thing that runs through your mind? You must be real fun on a date."

"Shut up." She grabbed a cushion and whacked Bree with it, laughing. The teasing was growing on her. It felt a bit like foreplay. Or maybe she just wanted it to be foreplay. So much for putting her mind on something else. Maybe she could just blame the alcohol and her low tolerance?

"I like it when you're happy. You light up." Her hand slipped over Ness's knee. "You really are beautiful, Vanessa."

Their eyes met. The fire cast a suffused, heated glow on Bree's face. Rational thought left Ness's mind. Her body suddenly felt awake and buzzed. It felt like a million butterflies had just taken up residence in her chest. The air between them felt electric, charged.

She leaned in, closing the space between them and grazed her lips against Bree's. Mouths parted. Bree's soft, warm tongue slid against Ness's own, and her body shivered then relaxed. They yielded to one another like past lovers. Nothing in the world soothed Ness as much as kissing did. It was her favorite thing. Intimate, sexy, and connecting all in one. And Bree's kiss was as sexy as the woman herself.

But she needed to be closer. Needed Bree's scent all over her. Needed to feel the full warmth of her body. In that moment, she wanted nothing more than to belong to this woman. To be hers and hers alone.

Bree left her seat and ended up kneeling between Ness's thighs, her head raised for now but the delicious promise she could dip down at any moment implicit. Pillowy lips still devoured one another. Noses grazed. Fire rose in Ness's belly, and she moaned into the other woman. Objections to the fact they worked together were set aflame and destroyed. Bree's hands squeezed her thighs. Ness wanted them all over her body. Wanted to grind against them. Wanted to feel them inside her body. Goosebumps broke out over her skin. Her nipples beaded.

Suddenly, the kiss ended.

The world felt dizzy and jarring. Her pulse threaded in her ears.

"You coming to bed?" Bree asked as she stood and gazed down with hooded eyes. Her tongue trailed over her lips, taking in the taste of Ness left behind.

Ness swallowed, her body still humming. Had that really just happened? "I think… I'll sleep out here." She disliked how breathy she sounded now the spell was a little broken.

"You know it's much easier for me to keep one fire going all night than two. Especially, when they're on two different floors."

Ness chewed the inside of her cheek, not entirely sure that wasn't a euphemism. "There's only one bed, though."

"Are you serious?" She shook her head. "I don't bite, Ness."

No. Please don't. Now, I'm thinking of you biting me. Why are you like this? A whine almost escaped her lips. "I just want to make sure you're comfortable. I tend to hog the covers, and we're practically strangers."

"I want you to be comfortable, too. Now, get your ass in the bed."

Ness surprised by how that order made her cunt jolt. She wasn't entirely sure what Bree was unknowingly—knowingly?—doing to her, but she was beginning to like it. Her shame for wanting her colleague had blossomed into a full-blown and delicious arousal over the course of the evening. She let out a soft, shuddering sigh. *Stop being so afraid. Just go upstairs with her.*

"And you think after that kiss we're still strangers?" Bree held a hand to her own chest. "If I wasn't so confident, I'd be wounded." Amusement danced across her face, and she held out her hand. "Come on."

Ness slowly reached out, her fingers lacing with Bree's. She felt like safety. The other woman gently pulled her closer until their bodies were mere inches apart. Ness's heart thumped. Whoever would've imagined they'd be here?

"And yes." Bree stroked Ness's cheek. "Exactly, what you're thinking is going to happen." Her breath was hot against Ness's skin.

Ness looked into her eyes and swallowed, her position as boss all but forgotten. "But…"

"Shh. Let me take care of you, baby." Bree's pupils were blown wide. She looked needy, hungry, and animalistic. Without a doubt, she knew what she was doing. Everything about her body spoke of assurance and command.

There was a rasp to Bree's voice that made Ness ache even more. This was everything she wanted right now. She nodded her consent. Bree led her upstairs. She turned on a lamp, casting the room in a dim light, then sat on the bed and crossed her legs.

"Why don't you take your clothes off for me, sweetie?"

Ness gave a nervous scoff. Was this woman somehow dialed into how much Ness wanted her to take control? She rubbed her arm, loving and hating the attention.

"Come on. Don't be shy." Bree leaned back on her elbows, ready to watch like some reigning queen. "I want to see you."

Working up the courage to meet Bree's gaze, Ness slowly unbuttoned her blouse. She placed it on the bed. Bree brought it to her nose, inhaling Ness's scent.

"Keep going."

Socks followed boots, then the scraping sound of her zipper filled the silence between them. Jeans pooled at her feet. *This is happening. This is actually happening.*

"Look how beautiful you are." Bree marveled at her from the bed, then stood.

Her fingers drifted along Ness's arms and across her belly. The tender touch made Ness aware of everything. Chills broke out over her skin. Bree leaned in, gliding along her neck and trailing sweet kisses with occasional gentle nips.

"I said I wanted to see you. That meant all of you." She unsnapped her lover's bra and let it drape to the floor.

Ness shivered, the fabric of Bree's top scraping against her hardened nipples.

"Lay back for me." Bree looked her over like she was prey as soon as she laid down.

A lovely concoction of embarrassment and arousal washed over Ness. She loved being appraised, funnily enough. Loved being taken in, like something special and beautiful, something valuable. She couldn't recall the last time someone gazed at her that way. It melted any ounce of remaining resistance. She was in this now, fully. Once she was resting comfortably, Bree rolled Ness's leggings and panties off. They joined her bra on the floor.

"For a mouthy brat, I like how easily you obey." Bree smirked and kissed her way up her lover's legs.

A laugh escaped Ness's throat but quickly turned into a whimper when Bree nipped at her inner thigh. "You're driving me fucking crazy, you know that?"

"That's my entire MO, babe." Her face disappeared between Ness's legs, nuzzling against her mound before she trailed kisses up her hips and belly. "I want to make you ache. I want you to need me so much, it makes you mad. Think you can be a good girl for me?" She drew a line with her tongue between the valley of Ness's breasts before her mouth closed around one of her nipples. So hot and humid.

The softest moan slipped from Ness's lips. "Uh … Uh-huh." She couldn't believe the woman who'd spent so much time getting on her nerves was now making her feel this good. If only all of life held such sweet surprises. Bree worked her mouth over the bud, sucking and leaving wet kisses before repeating her motions on its twin. Ness was a mewling mess by the time Bree drew Ness's tongue into her mouth once more.

Bree's hand drifted downward and grazed over her lover's labia, teasing and tickling but never giving Ness what she craved. "Tell me you want me." The pad of her finger teased at her slit. "I want to hear it." Her touch ghosted Ness's sensitive clit. "Say it in that pretty voice of yours, baby."

"Please," begged Ness, daring to look at her tormentor. The gaze she saw made her stomach drop and her cunt even wetter. Oh fuck, she'd never wanted anything more than what was happening. "Please."

"Please, what?" Bree smirked like the wicked woman she was. Oh, she knew exactly how to work Ness into a frenzied wreck. "Come on, use all those words your smart brain knows."

More heat suffused Ness's cheeks. That slight edge of humiliation was really working for her. Somehow Bree knew just how she wanted to be treated. Made to beg. Made to admit her desires, to confront herself. She whined. How could someone read her so well?

"Please make me come."

"I thought you'd never ask." Bree's finger barely dipped into her lover's slick core before circling her swollen clit with all the mastery of a pro.

"Ah, fuck…" she whispered as her eyes squeezed closed.

"You've been thinking about this, haven't you?" Bree's breath was hot on her face as the woman hovered over her. Something in her gaze made Ness feel weightless.

Ness chewed her bottom lip, avoiding that unwavering gaze as she bit out "All day."

"Tell me," the line came out like a command.

It took a moment for Ness to speak, too wrapped up in the passion. "I was thinking about… I… I want your hand around my throat." Her cheeks burned with admitting that. Would it be too much? Would it bring an end to what's happening? Even that anxiety over asking did nothing but make her body feel more alive.

"Ahh," Bree chuckled. "I knew you had some kink in you."

The next thing Ness felt was the warmth of fingers gripping her neck. No pressure. Just the authority of ownership. It made her melt. It made her want to give Bree everything. Her hips bucked up toward Bree's touch, yearning for more as she was held down against the mattress. Lids fluttered, then closed. She wondered what it would feel like to have a slight squeeze added in, but she couldn't bring herself to speak.

Next time.

She moaned, writhing.

"You're so pretty like this, with your lips parted and your eyes shut tight," said Bree. "Do you want more, baby?"

Ness bit her lip, opening her eyes once again. "Yes. Please."

"Good." Her tongue darted out to wet her mouth, like a wolf licking its chops. "Because I'm dying to taste you."

Her brows furrowed when her throat was abandoned, but soon the skill of the other woman's tongue made all that loss fade away. Ness sighed. She gripped the comforter, trying to will herself to last. It was going too fast, ending too soon. Her hips canted against Bree's mouth, seeking out more sensation as her tongue slid between Ness's folds. Mewls turned to whimpers and whimpers to soft, sweet moans as her body was explored. Her lust multiplied, coating Bree's chin in her scent.

Quicker than Ness wanted, warmth unraveled at the base of her spine and exploded behind her eyes in climax. She wasn't much of a screamer, but the room filled with a guttural moan as she came. Her stomach tightened. Toes curled. Her legs shook.

Bree stroked and nuzzled her thighs, letting her come back down to earth with silent praise and touches. "I hope this means you'll let me take you out to dinner when we get back to normal human civilization?" Bree grinned as she crawled back atop her lover.

Ness chuckled and Bree nuzzled their foreheads together. "I'd say that's a yes."

Ness kissed her, feeling like their mouths somehow belonged together, then licked Bree's chin clean. "Now, let's make you feel good."

She deftly flipped her lover over, grinning as the tables turned. "I've been wanting to worship you for months." Her hand cupped a breast, kneading it through Bree's shirt. She liked the idea of being naked while her lover remained clothed. It added to the tease of embarrassment that'd been fueling her fire, but now it was time to fulfil the fantasy she'd been harboring for months. Her mouth watered at the prospect.

"By all means." Bree licked the corner of Ness's lips. "I won't stop you."

Her hands slid under Bree's tank top, pushing it up to just below her breasts. Soft kisses followed as Ness explored her lover's body. Those taut abs, that firm skin, and the thickness of an athlete. She'd been dreaming of tasting her skin. Her tongue dipped into her navel and journeyed back up as she pushed the remaining fabric off Bree's body.

Her clothes joined Ness's on the floor. She inhaled, letting the woodsy scent take every sense over. Her eyes never left Bree as she gazed up and nuzzled her cheek into her breasts. They were better than she'd imagined. So soft and full.

"Aren't you a sweet little kitten?" praised Bree as she

provided her with doting pets. "To think you've been hiding right in front of me this whole time."

Ness smiled. Oh, she was loving this.

Bree's fingers slid over the hardened nipples before giving them a squeeze. "These taste even better, would you like to try them?"

Ness nodded and moved toward the offered peaches.

"No, no. Not so fast," said Bree. "Open your mouth."

Ness blushed but did as she was told. She would do anything for this woman.

"Good girl." Two of Bree's fingers entered the balmy wetness, venturing along her silky tongue toward the void of her throat. In and out they moved, fucking her. Their gazes locked on one another. "You look so pretty." Bree purred; she pressed her fingers in a little more, testing Ness' limits.

She gagged ever so slightly. Bree smirked. Ness's cunt burned with need. This was so degrading, and it felt amazing. How could she ever go back to anything else after this? Pulling them from her mouth, Bree wiped the spit over the tips of her breasts.

"Now, you may enjoy them."

Ness wasted no time. Her tongue danced around each hardened peak, suckling at them like they were the sweetest of delicacies. A gasp slipped passed her lips when Bree pressed her thigh between Ness's legs.

"You're still so wet." She moved around, her voice breathy and low, tinged with a moan. "Feel how slick you are? Baby's been needing this for a long time, hasn't she?"

Wow, that condescension was shockingly sexy. This woman was certainly testing how aroused she could become. All Ness could do was nod as a nipple popped free from her mouth.

"Do you want more?"

Her brows furrowed. "But it's your turn…"

"Shh, we can both have fun." Bree gripped her wrist, slowly sliding her hand down her body until it brushed the hair of her mound. "Touch me. But don't you dare stop grinding against my thigh. Do you understand?"

Fuck. "Yes." She swallowed.

Bree gave her a stern look as if she'd forgotten something.

"Yes, ma'am…?" Her brows lifted. Hopefully, that was right. And to think she was the boss in their professional relationship.

That earned her a smile. A smile that made Ness's heart swell. Oh God, she could totally see herself falling for this woman. There would be no going back after tonight. No way of only being colleagues again.

Her touch trailed through Bree's slightly damp pubic hair as she inched closer to her slit. Their combined scents made the air heady and intoxicating. She stared at Bree as her fingers dipped between her folds to nudge her plump clit. Her lover was so sexy, her mouth barely parting as a sigh released. Time seemed to disappear as she worked her fingers. Every undulation of Bree's body brought her thigh up to Ness's core.

Ness pulled her touch away, bringing fingers to her mouth to lick clean. She smirked.

"Come here." Bree crooked a beckoning finger her way.

Their mouths met, opening for one another and

sharing the lust on Ness's tongue. Her touch found Bree's slit once more. This time, she teased her opening a bit before slipping a finger, then another, into her. She pressed harder against the leg between her own, rocking back and forth. Ness never wanted this moment to end.

She devoured each and every moan Bree gave her, letting them all pound into the dam surrounding her heart. Maybe she would try again. Maybe she would let Bree in. The woman seemed to have the key. She prayed it wasn't just the amazing sex talking.

Little whimpers escaped her throat now. Her slick cunt ground along Bree's muscular thigh. So wet. So powerful beneath her. Bree's pussy sucked at her fingers, greedy and hot. *Fuck*. It was becoming too much. She rode harder, faster.

"There you go." Bree smiled against her mouth. "Let it all out, sweetheart. You've been holding all this in so long, haven't you?"

Ness nodded, a soft whine following. She wanted to be talked to like this forever. It felt safe with Bree, safe to explore all of this. Whatever *this* was. Warmth rushed down her spine. She gripped Bree's hip and rode, letting each wave crash within her.

"You have absolutely no idea how gorgeous you are when you come." Bree stroked her cheek with the backs of her fingers.

She leaned into Bree's touch, panting as her eyes opened once more. "I want to watch you now."

Bree grinned, then moaned at Ness's re-entry.

Ness had come twice now. It was time to give back, to finally hear what she'd only imagined in her dreams each night. Her touch began slowly, teasingly, then once again she pressed two fingers deep, curling up to stroke Bree from within.

"Don't stop…" Bree's eyes clamped shut. "Oh God, don't stop."

Ness fucked her, the pace growing steadier, quicker. The heel of her hand ground against Bree's clit. Her body writhed beneath Ness. Ness wanted to lick her neck, to feel the tendons tense and release against her tongue, but that would mean missing the beautiful sight before her. She couldn't do that.

Bree bucked into Ness's hand. Her nipples were so taut. Her fingers gripped at the comforter. She moaned, her core pulsing and sucking at Ness's fingers.

"And you say I look pretty when I come…" Ness teased as she watched her lover.

Bree chuckled, her body giving a few more spasms as Ness moved slowly, trying to keep her climax going. Bree reached up and grabbed her neck. She pulled her closer, their mouths crashing into one another.

Ness's fingers disappeared into the softness of Bree's hair, trailing along her nape and back up. Her lover's hands roamed her body and pressed her closer. Their bodies fit so well together. She could get used to this. Used to how safe and happy she felt in Bree's arms, like maybe nothing could ever hurt her again. Like maybe she could give love another try.

She slumped against Bree once their lips parted. Ness sighed, feeling limp and spent. "I still never got to taste you."

Another chuckle. "We have all night and every day

after that. There's no rush." She pushed Ness's damp hair off her cheek.

"We do?" Ness gazed up at her. Did Bree want this as much as she did?

She nodded. "Only if you want."

"I do want that." Her fingertips traced circles along her skin.

Bree pressed a kiss to her lips and playfully slapped her backside. "Good. Now go to sleep, you little ass."

"Yes, ma'am." She snickered and nestled against Bree's chest. She couldn't wait to see what tomorrow brought.

ABOUT THE AUTHOR

TORRANCE SENÉ

Torrance Sené (www.torrancesene.com) resides in the southeast US and often dreams about the beach. When not writing, she can usually be found feeding her addictions to tea, planners, K-pop, and books, and also writing under the pen name Cassie Donoghue. You can find her work online through her website and in anthologies published by Cleis Press, HarperCollins UK, and more.

More Books by Torrance Sené

Burning Desire: A Stepbrother Romance (Forbidden Book 1)

Best Erotic Romance 2013

Paranormal Erotica

ABOUT HOLDING ON

An anxious woman and a man with a protective streak discover that sometimes taking a chance is the only thing you need to find someone to hold on to.

Author Note:
Please be aware that this story contains references to an off the page car crash, and has on page PTSD trauma. I hope I have treated these issues with the care that they and you deserve.

HOLDING ON

ALI WILLIAMS

She'd gotten lightheaded the first time that they'd kissed.

They'd been at her favourite bookshop in town and he'd been talking about listening to War of the Worlds on repeat, half singing little snippets of it to her, and all she could think about was the fact that she wanted him to kiss her. That for all their attraction to each other, for all his swagger and his ability to make her laugh, that it was this version of him that she wanted to kiss the most; sweet, a little self-deprecating, and ever so slightly geeky. And she'd found herself stepping up close, laughing at what he said, and then looking at him. There'd been a moment when his words died on his lips and he looked at her back, and that moment? That was the moment when she realised that this would be a Kiss.

And it was. He could kiss.

He could really kiss.

It had been gentle and sweet, and then as she deepened it, their lips scalding against each other's, he'd pulled her flush against his body and she found herself being thoroughly kissed in a manner that made her heart beat that little bit faster and her glasses fog up in a way they hadn't in years. If his hand hadn't snaked around her waist, anchoring her, she wasn't entirely sure that her knees wouldn't have given way. Then they'd come up for air, eyes averted, suddenly shy, with a slightly awkward laugh and a glance round to see if anyone else in the shop had seen them, when all she'd wanted to do was to grab the lapels of his shirt and pull him back towards her, to lean up against the bookshelves and kiss and kiss until they were dizzy with desire and she could feel him again, hard against her thigh.

Each time they'd met, it had been exactly like that. Spending lazy afternoons in pubs, singing their hearts out in karaoke bars, dancing at spontaneous gigs on the beach. They'd walk and talk for hours, eating up days and moments, as if time didn't exist. He'd tease her in a way that made her blush until he apologised in a half laughing voice that said that he wasn't all that sorry really, that he liked seeing her shy and laughing and flustered. And then eventually that look would creep back in. She'd catch his eye and there it was again. That need to be kissed.

She wasn't quite sure why it was that he affected her like this.

No. That was a lie.

There was the fact that he was funny, and a little more cool than she knew what to do with, and just the right amount of nerdy. And he was interested in what she had to say and her opinions; wanted to know her. Wanted her to take up space in his life. There was a comfort between the two of them that made her want to bare herself to him, to let her vulnerabilities and softness unfurl petal by petal until he held her delicate fragility in his hands. And when he kissed her there was laughter and desire intermingling in his eyes as he captured each gasp that she breathed out with his lips. Fingers dancing along the underside of her knee – the most innocuous of movements, but one that drove her wild – and then the feel of his breath along her neck as he bent to kiss along her jawline. They were the sweetest of moments. Ones that made her head spin with dreams of kisses pressed against her lips on Saturday afternoons on the couch in front of the tv.

And now she was here, at his flat. By his front door. The first date at his place.

She paused momentarily, not wanting to lift her hand to knock into the possibility of something going wrong. Up until here, up until now, anything could happen. But the moment that she stepped through that door, anything would. She'd end up spilling something on the carpet, or coughing at a really inopportune moment, or even embarrassing herself by shrieking at a particularly jumpy point in the film they'd planned to watch, and finish it off by falling off the sofa. None of those things appealed, and whilst she was outside the flat, none of them were actually happening.

It was, she decided, the Schrödinger's cat of romantic possibilities.

She'd probably have waited outside for far longer than

was entirely necessary if he hadn't opened the door, all ruffled blond hair and easy smiles. And then she felt all kinds of comfortable, all kinds of relaxed, reassured that he wouldn't laugh at her too much if she really did fall off the sofa.

Stepping into the apartment, he leant down to kiss her cheek, lips caressing her skin in a movement that made her sigh involuntarily, and then flush as his blue eyes met hers, amused. Delighted by that giveaway sound.

"Hey."

"Hey."

Words that would usually flow, unbidden, to her lips froze upon her tongue as she found herself grinning at him, unable to keep a smile from floating across her face. It felt like there was a warm glow inside her, one that heated her up from the inside out, and as his hand glanced against hers as she handed him her coat, she couldn't help but smile a more secret smile to herself.

It had never been like this.

Never.

The mere touch of his hand made her want more. Need more of the comfort between them that promised sweetness shot with fun and laughter. It made her think of afternoons sat on the beach, eating fish and chips and dodging aggressive seagulls. It made her think of running through summer storms for shelter, dripping wet and yet still laughing. And it made her think of being safe; of being able to just stop and cry in his arms.

She found herself slipping her hand into his, their fingers intertwining in a dance that ended when he tugged her towards him in one swift movement, bending his head to brush her lips with his.

His mouth was gentle but firm against hers. A sweet kiss. One that said how much he wanted to have her here, with him, in this moment of their making. And she kissed him gently back, her hand curling up to caress his cheek as she felt herself unwind. The remnants of tension, of the anxiety that had hounded her before she'd arrived, just melting away against the warmth of their touch.

Then one quick kiss dropped upon her forehead, where it sat, branding her skin with him, as she took her shoes off and they went into the living room.

It was a relief to realise that she wasn't going to have to explain her need to shuck cushions off couches before she could sit down, but she still stood, slightly awkward, until he raised an eyebrow in question. And then she sat next to him, bolt upright. All that nervousness edging its way back into the corners of her mind. She could sense him leaning back, finding that spot on his sofa that was his and she felt just so damn lost. Sat frozen like she didn't want to curl right up against him, to lie her hand against his chest and feel the thud of his heart beneath her fingertips.

It had been too long.

Too long since she'd sat with someone like this – shared space on a couch together – and she wasn't entirely certain that she knew how to do it. How did you go from sitting upright to that casual lean back, where thighs and arms kissed against each other? She didn't even realise that she was fidgeting, her fingers dancing a tarantella against her knees until his hands reached out to partner them in the dance.

Looking up, those blue blue eyes caught hers and she smiled shyly, loosing one hand to run it through her hair, the action allowing her to break eye contact for a moment and recentre herself. Allow a little equilibrium back into the moment.

She breathed in. Once. Twice. And then met his gaze head on this time. She watched as he stretched out one arm along the back of the sofa and she found herself curling inwards against him, the fragility of her trust fluttering against his like a butterfly's wings. His arm curved around her, and she raised her hand to rest against his chest, just like she'd wanted to do, and breathed out. This was okay. It was okay. They were okay.

With his free hand, he grabbed the remote and then they settled down to watch a film with less gore than she'd feared but a hell of a lot of jumpy moments. After one particularly startling scene, she buried her face in his shoulder, half-hiccupping with laughter that was not at all in any way covering the fact that she'd squealed far too loudly for her own liking and had almost thrown the glass of water that he'd brought her at the screen.

It was at that point, however, that he seemed to give up all pretence of watching the film. Moments of stolen glances put aside for a single finger under her chin, dancing eyes meeting her own embarrassed ones, and this time she was the one who kissed him. Who leaned up into his space and captured those laughing lips. And she'd captured his softness as well as his laughter. There'd been a split second where she felt as if she'd fall, Alice-style, into the kiss. Falling down down down until she landed in a space where her heart took up an echoey beat that reverberated around them both, where she became too big or too small to ever really fit back into the real world again. Fuck White Rabbits, this kiss was her pathway into Wonderland.

And then it had shifted, his hands cupping her face with an urgency that seared her skin. Branded her with fire. Her hands mirrored his until they ran through his hair.

One kiss. Two. Three.

It was seamless, the way that they deepened the kiss. Both of them caught up in the intensity of the closeness, of the emotion of it. They paused for a moment, taking shallow breathes that ghosted, the lips were mere millimetres apart and she realised that she was halfway across him in a weird up-on-her-knees and splayed-across-his-front way, without actually straddling him. She shifted awkwardly, almost toppling over until he caught and righted her.

"I'm a little clumsy," she explained, brushing her hair from her face and looking away.

He leaned in and kissed her gently. "You can be clumsy with me any day."

The gurgle of laughter that pealed from her made him smile, and he tugged her further onto his lap. "Wouldn't want you to fall again."

She grinned and shifted 'til she was comfortably astride him, trying not to let out a gasp of delight as she felt him hard against the seam of her jeans. "I wouldn't want to fall off this."

There was a momentary pause where they both seemed torn between more intense making out and just full on laughter and before she added, "God I'm bad at this."

"Not at all." He pulled her closer as she put her arms around his neck. "You. Are. Perfect." Each word punctuated with another kiss until she leaned in and stole all his sentences. There was a slight desperation in their kisses this time, a need to get as close to each other as possible, the freedom of having a private space emboldening them both. His hand skimmed the edge where her shirt met the top of her jeans, and she found herself hitching it up, before pausing and whispering in his ear so he didn't see her blush, "Can you...?"

"Can I what?" Each word buffeted against her neck and she gasped once, and then again as he traced the curve up to her jawline with his mouth. "Tell me, what do you want me to do?"

The words burst from her in a rush. "I need your hands against my skin. Please. If you don't mind–"

But before she could even finish her request his hands were cool against her skin, teasing, coaxing little gasps and moans from her as they ran up her side and back. A questioning glance as her top ensnared his hand, and then she reached down to hoist the shirt up and over her head, laughing as it got her glasses got on the way.

When she'd finally untangled herself enough to look back at him, her breath caught in her throat. The look in his eyes, darkened irises that drank in every single inch of her curves, made her blush and want to both cover up and take more off.

"What?" she asked, the questioning sounding almost defensive.

"You're just so..." That pause seemed like a lifetime. "So beautiful."

"Yeah yeah, flatterer." But she felt warm inside, even if she didn't know how to tell him how much those simple words meant. That he wanted her, all of her, with her big arse and her big tits and her clumsy attempts at stripping.

He laughed at – no, with – her, and she leant in to kiss his right cheek. He swallowed and she ran her hands down his front. "Your shirt. I mean, can I take it off?"

"Of course."

One swift motion and it was up and over his head, and as it floated down to the floor beside them, he sat up, shifting so that they were face-to-face, chest-to-chest, the sudden skin contact warm. Almost as warm as her core as she felt his cock rock up against her. She wondered whether her longing was painted in broad strokes across her face, whether he could tell that she just wanted to lose herself in the warmth of his touch until everything blurred together in the slick heat of their longing for one another.

His hand was tentative against her breast, a searching gaze looking for an acquiescence that he found in her eyes, before his fingers traced the edge of the bra cup, dipping in and grazing against her nipple in a way that made her cry out. Previously, she'd always felt incredibly self-conscious about how sensitive she was, the fact that she couldn't control or moderate her reactions, but this time was different. This time she found herself relishing being able to show him exactly how much she liked this. How much pleasure his fingers were bringing her. Because fuck if he didn't have magic fingers that coaxed all manner of sounds from her throat, his pupils darkening when she reacted.

And she savoured each moan and gasp he drew from her. Let that tight control over herself go until she was loose-limbed beneath his touch.

She slipped a hand down between them to feel the hard outline of his cock through his jeans and grinned at the curse he muttered against her neck. It was affecting them both then; this all-consuming passion had hit him just as hard as it had her. There was something very satisfying in that, in the knowledge that this wanting, this need, was mutual. That it wasn't just her losing her mind over something as simple as a make-out session on a couch.

Another kiss, more fumbling, and then, as they both came up gasping for air, a slowing down. Not an awkwardness as such, but more a wave of shyness that crashed over them both in a sudden about-turn.

They laughed softly, averting their gazes before sneaking looks at the other under lowered lashes.

"I had planned on feeding you before getting into your bra."

She snorted. "Well, it's never too late for food."

She wasn't sure quite whether this was a rejection, or just a postponement, but when they got up to move to the kitchen, he slipped his arms around her, hugging her close, before ushering them through to the other room.

This was intimacy of another kind, casual laughter together as they heated the food he'd prepared – tasting the sauce for the pasta, grating cheese and grabbing cutlery from drawers. It spoke of an easy comfort between them, and made her realise how much this meant to her. Cooking together, for each other, seemed such a key tenet of affection, proof of something more than people merely passing through each other's lives.

When they ate at the breakfast bar, she sat, legs curled up beneath her, and they talked as they ate, spooning warmth with every bite. The smear of sauce across his mouth would have been easy to wipe off, if it wasn't for the fact that he turned to press sauced lips against the inside of her wrist, infusing that simple action with a heat that took her breath away. Red to match the lipstick she'd left on his neck earlier. She'd muttered something about mess and thrown her paper napkin at him, but she'd been secretly delighted, had wanted to revel in the mess with him.

Even washing up together had been fun. She'd washed and he'd dried because, as she pointed out, she had absolutely no idea where anything went, but it had been an excuse to flick soap suds at him and then get chased around the kitchen in mock indignation before she let him catch her. Back to the door, arms braced either side of her until she smiled invitingly up at him and he moved in to kiss her again, his mouth stealing kisses she wanted to give him forever.

Dates like this didn't happen every day. She'd had enough experience to know that. To know that this comfort and ease with each other, as if they'd been together all their lives, wasn't the usual. To be able to flit from eating to kissing to laughing to comfortable silence in a space of moments.

When she'd gone to leave, each kiss of the afternoon a shadowy imprint on her skin, she'd almost told him how happy she was. How euphoric the afternoon had made her feel. But before she could, he'd pulled her in close and whispered how lovely she was against her lips, and how smart and funny and it was all she could do to not mount him right there by the shoe rack.

Instead, she'd kissed him again. Lingering this time. Slow and sweet and sensual and full of all the words that they'd left unspoken. Full of the promises that she wished she could make, the blossoming trust that she had in this new thing between them.

But when she closed the front door behind her, and looked out at the seafront, she realised with a crashing sense of foreboding that it was raining.

Normal rain wasn't a problem. A light shower, even a heavy shower, wouldn't be bad. She could drive in those just fine, but this? She swallowed once, twice, as the waves crashed against the shore, the sound of pebbles being dragged back over each other again and again echoing that sound and– She shook her head.

No. She'd worked so damn hard to move past this; the months of therapy, of developing coping strategies that were meant to help her in moments just like this one. She reached out for the coping statements that she'd worked on as a grounding tool with her counsellor and murmured them to herself over and over. "I can handle this. This will pass. The rain won't last forever."

But it wasn't until she was stood there, hand frozen on

her car door handle, hair plastered to her back as the rain lashed against her skin and every rumble of thunder made her shiver, that she realised that no. She couldn't. She really couldn't drive in this.

It seemed unbelievably unfair. It wasn't even as if she'd been the one driving the first time around. No physical scars. Everyone fully recovered. But that didn't prevent a wave of dizziness that overwhelmed her senses and threatened to cast her back into the unending loop of that night, her breathing falling back into that pattern of panic that she hated so. In and out so fast that she could feel her control unravelling.

Stop.

A long breath in. Held, then loosed in a barely contained rush.

She took a second, slower, jagged breath and realised that there was salt water mingling with the rain on her face. Tears betraying her.

A moment to make a decision. She could get in the car and sit and rock until the storm was done, to relive the sounds of that night until she became a sobbing mess; she could walk to a nearby pub, and to hole herself up in the bathroom until one of her friends could come get her; she could even give herself a ten-minute break in the corner shop across the road and then attempt the drive once more.

Or perhaps... No. The thought of him seeing her like this, broken and bedraggled, made her want to throw up almost as much as getting in that car did. But he was sweet and kind, and if she really wanted this relationship to go anywhere, then she had to be honest with him, had to show him this. Or at least she could dash the tears from her eyes and ask him if she could wait out the storm at his.

She shifted from one foot to another, and made a split decision.

This time, no Schrödinger's cat of romantic possibilities whilst waiting on his doorstep. Just fear and anxiety and more nervousness than she'd felt in aeons.

But he opened the door, took one look at her, and gathered her inside. No questions. No "what's happened?!" Just bundling her into the bathroom with huge fluffy towels and a hoodie that would dwarf even her curves, and a "what hot drink would you like?" question that she hiccupped out an answer to. Then the door closed behind him with a quiet shuck and she was left, just her and the bedraggled figure in the bathroom mirror, mascara painting their cheeks.

A step forward and she forced herself to meet her own gaze, her own reflection and then, slowly, she peeled back the damp clothes that clung to her, each layer a step further and further away from the feeling of pounding rain drenching her, drowning her in memories and pain and–

A knock at the door.

"Hey." Not quite a question, not quite a statement.

"I'm okay." Words gasped out as she felt panic threaten to engulf her. She looked down at clothes pooled around her feet, and a vague sense of bemusement at the starkness of her skin against improbably cheery underwear. Then jagged breaths as she grabbed the hoodie and pulled it up over her head, wet hair damp against the soft material, the hem falling to her knees.

But he didn't say anything, didn't reply, just waited until she pushed the door open and stood there, shivering in the onslaught of her emotions. It was one thing to be at the start of a new relationship, to be open with your feelings, to show that delicate vulnerability that caused a frisson of excitement. This was not that.

This was more than anxiety and catastrophising, this was drowning in memories and emotion and being a wreck of a person. This was not who she was. Not who she wanted to be. Not who she wanted him to see.

So she didn't look at him. Didn't look up into his face, didn't see the pity or the concern in his eyes, didn't even take a step out of the bathroom. She was stuck. Knee deep in quicksand that was rising fast. Opened her mouth and then closed it. Because how on earth could you explain being in this kind of state after a perfectly nice – a perfectly wonderful – date?

She almost jerked backwards as a hand brushed against her cheek, and it paused there for a moment. Waiting. Checking. And then it lowered the hood that covered her hair and replaced it with a fluffy towel.

There was something incredibly soothing about having her hair towel dried by him. She lent forwards unconsciously and found herself so close. His body heat warming her as slow movements, delicate deliberate movements, towel in hand against hair, helped ground her.

The quicksand subsided.

She took a shaky breath. And then another. And

another. Small jittery breaths until she was slowly but surely breathing again. A little jagged still, sure, but in a regular rhythm that didn't threaten to throw her off-kilter.

The towel moved away and he replaced the hood back up over her hair, and she found herself grateful for his understanding that, right now, the last thing she wanted to show him was her tear-stained face.

She pulled her hands up inside the sleeves, and used the corners to wipe her eyes, her cheeks, head still down, until they dropped, mascara-stained to her sides.

"I've got your hot drink in the living room, if you want to come sit down?"

A silent nod, and she followed him quietly, small little steps, shadowing his. Her hand reached out instinctively, and she felt him look behind to where she held onto the back of his shirt. Her sudden loosening of her hand and a step back placated with a smile and a nod of approval, before she held on again. And then they were in the living room, and he was curling around her. Arms enveloping, warming, protecting. The aforementioned drink in a mug so big that she cupped it in her hands like a bowl. Small sips. Small breaths. Her world slowly righting itself.

She'd never really found comfort in silence before. Bustling sounds and chatter kept her busy, kept her thoughts distracted, kept her from overthinking and reliving again and again, but this was comfortable. That comfortable silence that she'd read about in books. She put the mug carefully on the coffee table, leaned back, snuggling in, and sighed as his hand tentatively touched her hair. Gentle strokes that calmed her and made her want to lose herself in his quiet, in his gentle touch.

She didn't realise that she'd fallen asleep until she awoke suddenly, jerking upwards, disorientated and confused.

"What–? Where–?" and then as realisation hit, apologies tumbling over each other in a waterfall of sorries, the words barely able to keep up with her racing thoughts, a jumble of panicky self-recrimination. You idiot. He must think that you're pathetic, you're–

"It's okay." His hand beneath her chin, lifting it 'til she met blue depths. "It's fine." They weren't just words; he really didn't mind.

Then he grinned suddenly, adding teasingly, "You make cute little snuffly snores when you sleep."

She reddened, hiding her face in his shoulder in embarrassment, even whilst she was grateful for his lightening of the mood. "Oh hush up." He hugged her close and she found the courage to whisper, "Is it still raining?"

It was later than she'd hoped, but it was also still apparently storming, and the look on her face must have caused him some consternation because he said abruptly, "You can stay here tonight, if you like. I'm sure the storm will be gone by morning."

She looked at him sideways, and he shook his head, "You know I didn't mean it like that, but I'd rather you stayed than left if it's going to upset you."

A slow nod. "That would be...good. I'm sorry about all this, it's just..."

"You don't have to explain, no apologies. It's fine, I promise. Now, I'm thinking leftover pasta and Netflix.

There's an animated space series that I think you're going to love."

It was, she realised as he went to set everything up, his way of caring. Little tactile displays of affection that made him move with purpose. He wanted her to lean on him, to trust him.

"I was in an accident."

The bustle stopped and he came and sat down next to her, even as she couldn't look at him, couldn't do anything other than fiddle with the hem of the hoodie and blurt out words that made her want to curl up and hide. "There was a storm. An accident. And we're all fine now. No longer term. Injuries but still. I. I. I don't like driving in storms. Not that it was me who was driving in the first place and I guess that means that I should be fine with driving in storms now and I can't and I just couldn't sit in the car and wait it out because when it hits the windshield like that over and over and over I just–"

His arms again. Round her again. Comforting her again. "Shh. It's okay, petal. You don't have to talk about it; you're here with me, and I'll keep you safe."

For some reason, after that, she felt less awkward, a little more like herself again. Comfortable enough to snort with laughter when a sentient spaceship repeatedly denied a dorky character a chocolate chip cookie, and comfortable enough to flick pasta sauce at him when he tickled her to make her laugh some more. And she'd never been quite so grateful for streaming services' enabling of binge-watching; they worked their way through more than a few episodes, curled up on the sofa together, until her head kept dropping and she was fighting to keep her eyes open.

"Time for bed?"

She nodded, all of a sudden, feeling a little reticent, and he smiled gently at her concern, his hands cupping her face for a kiss. "I'll need to grab spare bedding so that I can bunk down on the sofa here, but after that, my bedroom's all yours. And I have a huge duvet that you can cocoon yourself in if you need to."

There was a pang of sadness as she realised that actually, she really wouldn't mind him curled up round her, under said duvet, but he was right. This was probably for the best.

So instead she followed him down the corridor to where a large king-sized bed waited for her. One so large that she thought she could get lost in its depths. She perched on the edge of the bed as he got the linen he needed for his own repose, as well as a spare towel for her, pointing out where she could charge her phone and where the switch for the lamp on the bedside table was. Some laughter. A long look that had her flushing, and then a gentle kiss that was as intense as it was tender. As he went to move away, she found her body following him, led by her lips back to his for another.

"Good night, petal." He whispered the words and she whispered "Good night" back, and sat there, teetering on the edge of calling him back as he left the room and closed the door quietly behind him.

Settling beneath the covers, the bed seemed unnaturally large. Too large to settle in the middle, with each side leagues away. Instead she set up on the starboard, glasses folded on the bedside table and light on for some reading before she slept. She might have been sleepy earlier, but now? Now she was far too awake to sleep. Every inch of her longed for his arms, for his touch, for his kisses, and the only way she was going to be able to distract herself, was to read a little before bed. Lose herself in a different world until she was too tired to focus on the words on her phone screen.

It might have helped if she hadn't been reading a paranormal romance, all turbulent shifters and hot sex, but even the world building wasn't enough to divert her attention from where she could still feel his lips on hers, the shadow of his touch on her breasts. She toyed with the idea of touching herself, of casting her ebook to one side and letting that tight control unfurl from her as she lost herself in thoughts of him. But she was in his bed, and that seemed a little unfair.

She could go to him.

She could ask him to come and sleep with her, even if actual sleep was all that they did.

Her face flushed at the idea of it. The idea of going and asking for what she wanted. What she needed. It seemed unlikely, she realised, that he'd find that abrasive. He'd liked it earlier when she'd asked him oh so politely if he could touch her. And even if he said no, she didn't think that it would be awkward.

Momentarily emboldened, she slipped out of bed and hurried to the door before she could lose her nerve and change her mind. But as she approached the door to the living room, she paused, suddenly shy.

One step. Two. And then she peeped round the doorframe.

He was sat on the sofa, blankets tossed casually on the coffee table, and he was watching a sitcom on the television.

"Ummm...?"

His head turned and she found herself dropping her head, and playing with the sleeves of the hoodie again. "You okay, petal?"

"I...I was wondering if you wanted to... I mean, it's a big bed and I..."

He stood and walked over to her, one finger under her chin, raising it 'til she could meet his eyes. "What is it that you need?"

"You." She blurted out the word and would have turned her head away sharply to hide if his eyes hadn't sparkled. Blue eyes, shot with a splash of gold, that were kind and happy and hungry. Oh, she realised, he wants me.

She'd technically known that already, especially if their make-out session earlier was anything to go by, but to realise it now, when her body was humming with need and he was close, oh so very close to her, well. It was certainly something.

He moved his finger so that his hand cupped her cheek, and then the nape of her neck. "Tell me again. What do you need? Who do you need?"

"You. Please." Her words were more resolute, more unwavering than she'd ever known them, and she felt a jolt of pleasure when his eyes darkened at that second word. At her pleading.

And then his mouth was on hers, hot and demanding, walking her backwards until she could feel the wall flush behind her, and at some point their hands brushed against each other, tugging fervently at the hoodie that slid over her head until she stood, clad in nothing but her underwear, his eyes caressing every inch of her.

"I want you too, petal. I want you writhing beneath my hands, my mouth, and I want you to come apart on my cock. Would you like that?"

She squeaked in reply, desire momentarily stealing her voice, and nodded eagerly, desperate to have him put his words into action.

He laughed then, delighted, this deep warm sound that felt like a stroke against her clit and she leaned towards him for another kiss. "Please?" In this moment, she thought that she'd do anything to feel him for real against the throbbing of her clit, his fingers replacing the caress of his voice, as she let go for him. Let it all go.

Then he was taking her hand and pulling her back into his bedroom, to that bed. Drawing her along, drawing her towards him, until he gestured to the bed, adding with warmth in his voice, "Sit down, I can't have you falling over."

Despite that, she almost fell over in her hurry to sit down anyway, her peal of laughter at the irony ringing out, echoed by him. And that was good. Laughter was sexy, even if tripping over her own feet wasn't.

"I'm sitting down."

"I want to make you feel so so good, but you need to trust me. Do you trust me?" As he spoke, he started to unbutton his shirt. She watched his hands' deft, swift movements, undoing button by button – as if there were any other way to unbutton a shirt.

She nodded, wide-eyed, as her lips parted and she leaned upwards for a kiss.

"Wait a moment."

She stopped. Waited for him.

"How will you tell me if it's too much?"

"Too much?" This was all too much already, too much waiting, too much tension, too much not enough-ness.

"Oh petal, I intend to make you come until you lose your mind, til you're begging me for a breather. So how will you tell me if it's too much? If you need a break, or you need me to stop? Because otherwise I'll just keep going and going."

She took a jagged breath, suddenly desperate for air. The thought of coming for him again and again had her pussy clenching and her clit throbbing. He chuckled at the look on her face. "Oh, you like the sound of that?" His belt was tugged through belt loops, then dropped to the floor, before his hands paused at the top button of his jeans. "Well then? How will you tell me?"

Her right hand tapped three times on the bed. Tapping out. Because she had a feeling that if he was going to make her come as much as he said he would, she might need a sign that didn't involve speaking.

"Oh I like that, petal, tapping out like the fiercely strong fighter that you are. Okay then. That's your sign. Now, move back for me."

His jeans were gone and she had a glimpse of a hard length straining against his boxers before she scrambled up the bed. He followed her and then, with confident hands that fumbled a little with the complexity of the clasp at her back, he undid her bra, sliding it down her arms and cursing softly as the fullness of her breasts came into view.

"They're not," she found herself stammering, "gravity defying," but he put aside her self-consciousness with a single kiss, reaching behind her to adjust the pillows, that small movement implying affection and tenderness far beyond the lust in his eyes.

"I don't need gravity defying. I need you," and then slowly, gently, he pushed her back until she was lying before him. Laid out for him, lace hiding soft curls, and breasts aching for his mouth. With tantalising slowness, he lowered his lips to one nipple and sucked, pinching the other with his fingers and she moaned out loud without meaning to. He looked up and met her eyes, lifting his head briefly so that each word he spoke teased the wet puckered peak he'd just had in his mouth. "I love it when you moan. I want to know each and every time I make you feel good, so you be as loud as you want for me."

She fought the urge to look away, to hide her shyness from him, but instead met his eyes and nodded slowly. And he kept her gaze as he lowered his mouth back down and made her moan again. Each lick and suck and gentle bite had a direct line to her clit, she realised. That he had her squirming beneath him just like he said he would, and when one hand danced along the lace gusset of her underwear, she realised she was wet for him too.

Well. Wet might be slightly underselling it. She was sodden, the material drenched through, and as he stroked her gently through it she closed her eyes and arched up against his fingers.

"Aren't we greedy?"

Her eyes flew open and she looked at him in such alarm that his hand moved swiftly to cup her cheek. "No no, petal, that's not a bad thing. I love how needy you are for me, how desperate."

"Oh okay, that's good." Her hammering heartbeat settled back into its echo of the throb between her legs. "I don't want you to think that I'm too much."

He kissed her slowly and deeply. "You are perfect. My good girl. And if I make you greedy for me, then I'm very lucky, aren't I?"

"Yes, yes you are." Her mischievous laugh was cut short by a gasp that he elicited with a stroke. Just. There. "Oh, please. Please."

Hands urged her hips up and soft fabric dragged down her legs and tossed aside. "Please? Please what?" Each word accompanied by a kiss on her inner thighs, getting closer and closer, and she moaned in frustration.

"Please, please kiss me."

"Here?" He partnered the single word with a kiss just above where she felt her need thrum through her clit.

"Noooooooo."

His chuckle had his breath dancing across her pussy and she arched up, trying desperately to reach his mouth. "Come on now, use your words. Where would you like me to kiss you?"

"Please please please kiss my pussy."

"Good girl," and with that his tongue licked all the way

up her pussy, ending with a swirl around the sensitive nub at the top.

The noise she made then was somewhere between a moan, a gasp and a sigh of relief, and it seemed to galvanise him further. Each lick against her clit had her breathing quicker and quicker, the intensity of his touch making her spiral higher and higher until she found herself teetering at the very edge of something, reaching out for a release before he pulled back, dropping a single kiss on her glistening pussy.

"Wha...what?"

"Not quite yet, sweetheart."

"But..." She was speechless, so utterly desperate to come and yet...

His hands skated across her skin, tracing patterns across her thighs, her stomach, her breasts, until they lay against her cheeks with his face close to hers. "If it's too much for you, that's okay, I promise I won't be disappointed. All you have to do is give me the sign."

She met his gaze, her body thrumming with need and the reassurance she saw there strengthened her resolve. "I think...I think I can take some more."

This time, his lips stayed against hers, teasing and demanding, as fingers danced against her clit, in a rhythmic pattern than made her feel like she were a bass guitar he was playing. An instrument beneath his fingers, ready to sing.

He stroked her once more to a peak, and once more pulled her back from it.

It was almost too much, to be so mindlessly brought to the point of release and then left there, left dripping and aching and yearning for that moment when he'd take her, waterfalling down into bliss. And yet, she felt so free. No catastrophising thoughts crowding her brain, no panic pushing out peace, but this almost serene neediness. Wanting. She was at her most vulnerable, completely open to him, and yet she felt the strongest she'd ever been. She was strength and power and desire all in one, and as he slipped his fingers inside her, the come-hither movement stroking against her g-spot, she thought she'd shatter.

"Are you ready for me, petal?"

"Please."

She followed his glance to the bedside table and nodded before he opened a drawer and grabbed a condom. And then his eyes were on hers as he entered her oh so very slowly.

She felt so full, so tight, so damn ready and as he began to thrust she found herself pleading again and again and again. The sweetness in his smile almost took her breath away and then his hand slipping between them to rub at her clit did exactly just that, stealing her breath and her words and pushing her higher and higher until "Come for me sweetheart."

And she did.

She rode each wave that swept over her, gasping and writhing and coming beneath him, around his cock, just as he said she would, and as the peak seemed like it was coming to an end, he pushed her into another crescendo.

"I think you've got some more for me."

He had her, a delicate, trembling thing, breaking in his arms over and over. Each wave taking her further and further away from anything other than this. This moment. She'd never before been so in the present, been so utterly in the here and now, with nothing else cutting in.

From somewhere far away, she heard him swear and then he was leaning in so close that she could have counted his eyelashes if she'd been so inclined. Not that she was in any fit state to do anything other than moan and plead in a never-ending cycle that had him kissing her and then coming with a murmur of affection that made her melt.

It took her some time to come down from the heady heights to which he'd taken her, and when she did, she found she was wrapped up in his arms, her trembling hands clinging to him as he kissed her cheek and stroked her hair.

"Oh. That was…" she trailed off uncertainly.

"It really was."

"Thank you."

He pulled her in tighter. "You are the sweetest thing; thank you indeed. Thank you."

"No." That wasn't it. The sex had been amazing, and she was fairly certain that she was still experiencing aftershocks, but she wasn't thanking him for that. "Thank you for looking after me, during whatever fireworks display that just was, to holding me after. And earlier. During the rain."

He looked serious as he met her eyes. "That's something you never need to thank me for, that's part of it. If you need me to, I'll hold you. Whether it's through tears or sighs or the most adorably cuddly aftercare. You trusted me with your vulnerability, with yourself, and I would never take that for granted."

She felt a smile roll across her face until she was grinning so uncontrollably that she hid her face against his chest and felt his rumble of laughter.

"And you holding on to me right now, petal? It does me the world of good. That's my aftercare right there."

She nodded, still curled up against him, untucking her head until she could meet those blue eyes with her own unwavering gaze, "Then I shan't let go."

"Exactly. Never let go, petal mine."

ABOUT THE AUTHOR

ALI WILLIAMS

Ali Williams' inner romance reader is never quite satisfied, which is why she oscillates between writing romance, editing romance and studying it as part of her PhD. She can be found at the foot of the South Downs in the UK, either nerding out over local mythologies or drinking cocktails on the beach. She believes with all of her bifurious heart that writing romance is an act of rebellion and that academia will be so much better when studying diverse HEAs is naturally part of the curriculum.

ABOUT VIOLET GAZE PRESS

Violet Gaze Press was born out of the desire to see Romancelandia flooded with diverse, sexy, romance. When readers ask "Help, where can I find characters like me?" the answer should always be "Where do I start?"

We are a small indie publisher, with a passion for romance novels and the community that has sprung up around it. Entrenched in it, we were dismayed to see readers struggling to find recommendations for romance that encompassed all the beautiful variations of relationships and the people who enter into them.

We want to bring books into the world that people have been yearning to read; books that foster a sense of being seen and that make people feel loved and lovable.

At Violet Gaze Press we believe that all love is valid, that all people deserve to see themselves represented in romance novels, and we strive to make that a reality

www.violetgazepress.com

twitter.com/violetgazepress
instagram.com/violetgazepress

CPSIA information can be obtained
at www.ICGtesting.com
Printed in the USA
LVHW031610170321
681768LV00002B/294

9 781916 125292